THE
ILLUMINATED

THE ILLUMINATED

ANINDITA GHOSE

HEAD
of ZEUS

An Apollo Book

First published in India in 2021 by Fourth Estate

First published in the UK in 2023 by Head of Zeus
This paperback edition first published in 2023 by Head of Zeus,
part of Bloomsbury Publishing Plc

9 7 5 3 1 2 4 6 8

A catalogue record for this book is available from
the British Library.

ISBN (PB): 9781803289793
ISBN (E): 9781803289755

Printed and bound in Great Britain by
CPI Group (UK) Ltd, Croydon CR0 4YY

Head of Zeus
5–8 Hardwick Street
London EC1R 4RG

WWW.HEADOFZEUS.COM

For my mothers and my grandmothers.

It is the moon that is drunk with its own light,
But the world that is confused.

— Bhasa, 3rd-4th century CE

When she talks, I hear the revolution
In her hips, there's revolution
When she walks, the revolution's coming
In her kiss, I taste the revolution.

— Bikini Kill, 'Rebel Girl', 1993

LAST
QUARTER

SHASHI MALLICK KNEW SHE WOULD HAVE TO DO THE cleaning herself.

That day, she wiped the kitchen counter using the new checked towel she had bought in a three-for-one pack at Patel's Cash and Carry. She had prepared breakfast and dinner almost every day since they had arrived in their son's apartment in New Jersey. And afterwards, she had wiped the counter clean, using those spray bottles of cleaning liquids, choosing between Tuscan Lavender and Pacific Breeze.

She always measured half a cup of basmati for each of them. The rest of the meal was decided by what the refrigerator held. She wasn't going to go to Patel's by herself, raising one foot after the other in the snow, pinching up the woollen slacks she only wore on their annual visits to meet their son. She planned elaborate feasts. She had time here. No one rang the doorbell in the morning. There were no servants to look over. No driver to raise petty errands for, just so he wouldn't get lazy. The vegetables arrived cleaned, and

3

sometimes chopped. The thought of her son eating frozen roti from a resealable plastic packet the rest of the year made her mouth sour. So she made dal in ghee, fish with mustard paste, minced mutton with potato and peas, brinjals shallow-fried in mustard oil. Afterwards, she aired the place with incense. Even in this open kitchen in her son's apartment, the smell of mustard lingered for days. But this week had been filled with different kinds of smells. She had not touched the stove, chopped or cooked anything, or even made herself a cup of tea.

When her husband had the stroke the week before, he had rested his hands on the kitchen counter before falling down. First, the whisky had spilled, cooling cubes pattering off the double-walled glass. He hadn't fallen straight and flat, like they did in Hindi movies. Something in his spine had suddenly lost its bearings and he had coiled down like a kathputli—the string puppets of her childhood—at the end of a show. They had all thought he was choking on a fish bone. She had thumped his back and tried to feed him a fistful of rice to push it down like her mother would when she was a child, when her fingers hadn't learnt how to manage fine fish bones. Their son, Surjo, had called 911. His wife, Laura, had jumped into the ambulance even though she had just had her embryo transfer and been advised rest by the fertility specialist. Shashi and Surjo had followed the ambulance by car. Ventricular fibrillation, the doctors at JFK Medical Centre had said. Robi Mallick was announced Dead on Arrival.

'You'll be all right, Ma?' Surjo asked from the front door.

He'd missed seven days at the bank. This made his voice shrill.

When she walked over to the door, he put his arms around her and rested his chin on her head.

Even with the little sleep she'd had in the last few days, Shashi noticed that his shoes, flattened out at the back, looked out of place with his clothes. But she didn't say anything. She wanted him to leave.

She'd had no time alone in the past week. She wanted to make herself tea and sit at the kitchen counter and sip it slowly. She wanted to see it all again and again till the memory became cold, till it cracked and fell on the floor. Her body felt heavy. She smelled of days-old sweat. Even this morning alone had been hard to earn. On learning that Surjo and Laura were going back to work that day, Robi's cousin Tutu had called and offered to keep her company. She said she would bring over food. There was no need, Shashi had told her. They would all be meeting soon for the ritual shradh meal on the thirteenth day.

After she closed the door behind Surjo, with the gaze a mother reserves for her firstborn, she wound her watch back—at home in Delhi, it was time to boil the rice for dinner. She didn't need to keep time here. But she wore the watch like an ornament every morning after her bath. A married woman's wrists should never be bare, her mother used to tell her. The small gold buckle of the watch would clink against her wedding bangle when she combed her hair. Until last week, she had never removed that wedding bangle, iron wrapped in gold. The only time she had removed it was to get it resized when it had begun to dig into her flesh. The goldsmith had to cut it off her. That was so many years ago. The children were still at home then.

Shashi sat on the sofa in Surjo and Laura's living room. Grey with no cushions. It had a chevron throw with a Made in India tag that made Robi laugh. A stackable centre table allowed everyone to have their own islands when they watched TV. The screen took up half the wall but didn't play any Hindi or Bengali TV serials or even any of the old BBC sitcoms she liked.

It wasn't ideal having to perform her husband's funeral here in New Jersey, away from their friends and family in India. But this place had everything, even the special kind of ghee needed for the funeral rites. Surjo, who was essential for the rites, was here. Being here also meant she didn't have to talk to the hordes of relatives and acquaintances she didn't want to see, the ones who'd show up and expect to be fed and taken care of through the day. Everyone insisted on being the last to eat, as if starving themselves proved their closeness to the deceased.

It had surprised her how many people had come. The Saturday after the cremation, the apartment was filled with fifty-four people; she'd counted. In America, even gods wait their turn for the weekend. What luck did an ordinary man have? Even if he had been a popular one.

Robi Mallick had not just been top of his class at Delhi School of Architecture. All these years later, he had also been the one with the most hair—a boyish mop of silver that fell in spikes across his forehead. The National Award had prompted him to be more sociable with his friends, in a charitable way. He was always the first to break into song at the reunion parties of the Class of 1974. He had kept up correspondence with his classmates, many of whom were scattered stateside. Those who had known him and lived on the east coast had turned up. Cousins twice and thrice removed had arrived. Laura's family had come. Surjo's colleagues too. But the person Robi loved the most in the world wasn't there. *The light of his eyes*, Nayantara, he called her. Their daughter, Tara. They hadn't been able to reach her in time.

Tutu, all bobbed hair and metallic sneakers, had managed to round up a Bengali priest. 'Don't wear trousers for the rituals,' she had told him on the phone. 'We want it to look authentic.' Both times the young man had come to perform the rites, he had arrived from his half-day shift at a travel ticketing office with his kurta-pyjama in a gym bag. Not what a priest would wear back home but it was too cold to go bare-chested here. On his first visit, he sat on Surjo's grey sofa and narrated the list of things that were needed for the funeral: banana leaves, sandalwood, coconuts, incense, five kinds of fruit, camphor, cow dung… He could bring it all for a fixed rate. Tutu had negotiated a package deal. Alongside the thirteen-day rituals dictated by the travel-agent priest, Laura had insisted on putting together an elaborate memorial service. 'Robi deserved the best,' she said, with the unsentimental clarity of her law school training. And so, flowers had arrived in the back of a truck early in the morning and an apron-clad florist had spent hours bunching up large-headed roses, lilies and spray chrysanthemums around the house, while struggling to instruct two assistants on stringing marigolds together for an Indian touch. Even though the bar was out of bounds on Shashi's request, it was a set-up she knew Robi would have approved of. If he were there, he would have floated around the rooms, speaking to everyone, banging a fist against the Georgian-style window frames to explain their constructional genius to a niece or two.

Shashi assigned her husband's nature to something in his blood. Robi was the only child of his parents—a rare thing in the India of their generation. First Class degrees, state-level swimming trophies, Diwali bonuses and double promotions, they cannot make a man's face glow like the privilege of being an only child can. To be named after the sun god. To be reminded every day that you are the centre around which every member of the household circles like an insignificant planet. To wake up as a young boy knowing that the shelf beside the dining table only stood to hold up photographs of him. Robi at age five or six as the God Krishna in a school play, peacock feather pinned to his hair. Robi shona again, with his first swimming trophy. A tall Robi in a wide-collared shirt and bell-bottoms, aviators hooked low on the nose, with friends at Digha beach. Five boys and one girl, Robi's fingers are looped with hers if you look closely.

Shashi was the one with a master's degree in Comparative Philosophy from Kolkata's esteemed Jadavpur University. She had written her thesis on Hegelian dialectics, read Hegel in the original. And yet, she would never dare to converse in German with Laura's Hamburg-born mother. Robi was better suited to rolling foreign syllables on his tongue. How beautiful his voice was, and how it spilled from his long neck when he sang, the Adam's apple rolling up and down like a batasha offered to the gods. He would call forth Tennyson and Shakespeare in a tongue trained to perfection by the Jesuit priests of his convent school. Nobody would correct him if he got a few things wrong. Tagore's verses, to suit the light and time of day, would come to him like known melodies. It wasn't a dinner party till he started complimenting the women's sarees, or teased them about the flowers in their hair. In his mid-sixties, he was handsome and uncommonly tall for a Bengali man. When Surjo had taken them to a French restaurant the day after they had arrived, a young waitress had coquettishly enquired if he was Amitabh Bachchan. 'Si vous voulez,' he'd shot back. The waitress had giggled with her hand on her chest.

During the memorial, one of Robi's aunts had wailed on Shashi's shoulder, her cranberry lipstick staining her cream-coloured blouse. She had peered into Shashi's eyes. They were too dry for a woman just widowed.

But Shashi had always been the practical kind. How much can you grieve when arrangements are to be made? Caterers have to be scolded because there isn't enough condensed milk in the patishapta. After some time, a funeral home becomes a teahouse. You have to serve tea or coffee to everyone who comes to visit. You have to remember to bring out the cream biscuits, not the glucose ones. And you have to remember which aunt has diabetes and which one wants her tea with a thumb of ginger.

WHEN SHE had woken up this morning, Shashi had realized that she hadn't had tea the way she liked all of last week. Surjo or Laura had handed her a cup with a tea bag every morning, as they coaxed her to have some breakfast, while rushing through their own. Laura only drank herbal tea—h silent. Surjo had cultivated a daily Starbucks habit because all his colleagues walked in for markets opening with a tall Americano. But tea bags, this idea of tea powder portioned in paper bags, upset Shashi as much as plastic flowers in a nice home. Shashi had never cared much for silk sarees or embroidered bed covers or Swarovski figurines—the things the women at their Delhi dinner parties discussed. When she travelled, she wouldn't carry any more jewellery than the wedding bangle

9

on her wrist and the pearl studs she always wore in her ears. But a small tin of loose leaf Darjeeling tea from Kolkata's Shyam Lal & Sons was always in her suitcase.

'Now you can keep busy with your hobbies,' Tutu had told her. She was being kind. Shashi knew Tutu had always wished her dear cousin, who she fondly called Robin Bird, had married someone more like her own self. 'No one knows where the time goes when they're around,' Tutu added. This part seemed true. Tutu herself had bloomed after her divorce. Her body had lost its apple-shape, her eyes shone when she spoke about her book club. What were Shashi's hobbies? Shashi used to graft, even make bonsais. But in the last twenty years, their garden had been overrun with ferns and frangipani. Time showed in their sprawl and girth, in how the delicate green stems were now rough brown trunks, marked with lines, like wrinkles. The frangipani that she had planted when Robi had bought their plot of land in Delhi, even before construction had begun, dropped its rubbery white blooms through most of the year on the grass. Robi liked this. He booked a professional service to maintain their front garden with its perfectly shorn lawn. He made it a practice to plant a 'Shashi tree' to mark the start of all his large residential commissions. People said he was devoted to his wife. He liked this too. Shashi grew jasmine, pinwheel and hibiscus behind the kitchen window for the gods on the altar that her mother-in-law had installed in their home on her first visit. Robi didn't want these bushes in the front garden. They were fragrant but wilful, too temperamental in their flowering patterns. Could she call tending to a handful of plants behind her kitchen window a hobby? Hobbies were for women who smoked and wore sleeveless blouses and had children in their thirties. Shashi did make time for the Sunday crossword—though not on Sunday, of course. There was a time she could have won any movie trivia quiz on the radio, but she was totally out of touch with news from the Hindi film world these days.

How thrilling it had been when she was a schoolgirl, the world of Hindi cinema, of Bombay, of Rajesh Khanna and his white car festooned with pink lipstick marks. Later, in college, she and the other girls would take turns to buy *Starglow* and read it aloud after the day's lectures. Most of the leading men were married, the women could never be. After affairs with their married co-stars, they married a film producer and promptly produced a child. They broke the mould on screen, playing political revolutionaries or hiding undercover with a love child, but the personal lives of the rich and glamorous had a set script. *Starglow* revelled in the details. Such filthy prose! It horrified even Professor Bagchi, who taught them modern literature. The Miss Misstry column painted colourful scenes of scandal. The way the pair met, how film producers were manipulated into shooting in outdoor locations, from Kashmir to the Keukenhof tulip gardens, to allow new lovers new rooms. How the lovers were caught by a make-up artist 'stuck like two grains of rice'.

Her father-in-law disapproved of Hindi cinema, and so she had stopped bringing the magazine home after she got married. Anyway, *Starglow* had stopped being what it used to be. Besides, is an encyclopedic knowledge of film trivia even a real hobby? Robi emblazoned the things he was passionate about in their homes and holidays, in the minds of their family and friends. There were so many things he was interested in: football leagues, smoked Japanese whisky, Jamini Roy, Brutalism, The Rolling Stones. When

11

Surjo made his trips back home from Yale, he would spend weeks deciding what to buy for Baba. Once he had got him a vintage leather-stamping tool set. He would always bring Shashi gift-packs of hand soap or perfume.

Perhaps tea could have been a hobby, or even a job, had tea tasting been a job appropriate for women. The love for tea had come to Shashi after her wedding. Her own mother had never allowed her to have more than one cup of tea in a day. It would make her dark, like too-hot bath water. Her mother never let her comb her hair back either. A young woman should have her hair parted in the centre in anticipation of getting married, she used to say. One day it would be marked in red by a husband.

IN THE months immediately following her wedding, back when they still lived in Kolkata, Shashi used to wake up from her afternoon sleep and ponder how she and Robi had come to be put together in this room with its tall almirahs on the first floor of the big house in North Kolkata. She had grown up in rented rooms around the city, a set of three rooms for their family of six. One room for her parents, one that she shared with her Didu and one for her two younger brothers. There were always relatives visiting from her father's village and they were welcome to stay for as long as their college degrees or doctor's appointments needed them to. Shashi was used to giving room, sleeping on a mattress that she rolled up in the morning, having fish only once a day, listening to the transistor radio leaning out of the window late in the night, studying while her brothers played. This luxury of a room to herself pleased her. But sometimes she felt terribly alone.

No grandmother's chest to press her face into when her stomach twisted into hot knots. No Manai or Shona to sing with when the city was plunged into darkness by frequent load-sheddings. She had stared at the ceiling of this new bedroom so much that she knew the contours of the shifting damp patches. She worried what would happen if the fan fell on Robi and her one night, crushing the newlyweds. Would they bother to put her back in the saree unspooled on the floor when they wheeled her body out?

Her marriage had been arranged with a boy from the Baidya caste, same as hers. But what else did they have in common? He didn't like Simon & Garfunkel. She liked movies with Uttam Kumar. He always wanted to watch the ones with Soumitro when they played on TV. What you got assigned in the draw of matches was fate. Handsome grooms wouldn't always have a beautiful bride. See what had happened to her own brother Shona? Being a tall girl was the worst. There were so few tall Bengali men that you would probably marry an old man or a balding man. Or worse, a businessman. At least they no longer married women off to infants to break the curse of dying unwed.

Not only was Shashi not tall, at twenty-two, she was just the right age for a bride. Robi was almost thirty. The right age for a Bengali groom. When her father's eldest sister, Bodo Pishi, had come home with the proposal, the family had at first suspected there was something wrong with the boy. 'Maybe an affair with an Anglo-Indian girl?' That old romantic blockbuster was still giving bad ideas to young Bengali men. The only son of the Mallicks, one of the oldest families of North Kolkata, why would they want a match with an art teacher's daughter? They both belonged to the small and proud community of Baidyas, but she had no property to her name and no chance of inheriting any. Her parents weren't members of any of the old clubs.

Bodo Pishi had seen their birth charts and approved. He was a lion and she was a fish. Their lives would be without conflict. She assessed Shashi as she brought over tea and Thin Arrowroot biscuits for her. A literature or philosophy degree was the mark of a girl from a good family. Study sociology and there is the danger of becoming the kind of activist who wears sarees without starch and her hair in an angry knot. Science streams almost always mean you're in the company of men who have their eyes set to go abroad. Those girls spend long hours in the library and get dropped home late in the evening by male classmates.

What really worked in Shashi's favour, Bodo Pishi believed, was her complexion. It was she who had named her niece Shashi, like the moon. Light skin was heavy currency in the marriage market. And then her beloved Shashi also had long hair that framed her moon face like dark brackets. When they heard of the proposal, other aunts said good luck had fallen on Shashi because she had been fasting every Monday, eating only after she poured milk at the temple in the evening. She was bound to get a husband like the God Shiva.

Bodo Pishi had asked her how they should describe her in response to the proposal. Shashi had thought about it all morning and come up with 'likes movies and books'. She believed she could be defined in efficient words. She did not think herself deserving of Homeric similes. She didn't have dimples like Sharmila Tagore. Some actresses of the time were known to get their molars pulled out to create the illusion of high cheekbones. But Shashi knew she would never have done that even if she

14

were an actress. What was more pleasurable in life than eating? When she wore a pale yellow saree and ate the season's first kuls with her Didu, the old woman would hold her face in her wrinkled palms and call her Saraswati, the serene goddess of books and music. Hers was a gentle beauty that didn't register in photographs. Not like Saraswati's sister Lakshmi, clad in red and gold, floating lithely on a lotus with a threat on her lips: please me or die poor. Shashi was beautiful to grandmothers and babies. Not to adolescent boys being ushered into manhood by the pointed breasts of Mumtaz on screen. A cousin had once tried to teach her to line her eyes with kohl. But she would make a crooked line always. Shashi didn't take notepads to the cinema to sketch the blouses that the actresses wore to show her tailor. Her only vanity was glass bangles. She had a pair in almost every colour. For their first wedding anniversary, Robi had made her a wooden bangle holder. She couldn't remember where it was now.

Shashi had wanted tuberoses for the memorial. The New Jersey florist had not been able to source them. She remembered the loud smell of tuberoses from her wedding night. Louder than the high and reedy shehnai music. Louder than the laughter and teasing. Tuberoses had been strung along the four posters of their bed. Strings of jasmine and tuberoses had been tied on her wrists and arms, around her neck and like a crown around her head.

SHASHI WAS still wiping the kitchen counter when she found a spot of dried-up dal. How Robi would leave kitchen counters like a battlefield! There was one dish that he loved to make. Tara had named it Baba's Mutton Delight. He put things in the pan after everything had been cleaned and chopped by their cook, and measured out by Shashi. When they had guests over and the pressure cooker whistled, he would excuse himself to 'check on the mutton'. Everybody praised Robi's mutton. They told Shashi how lucky she was that her husband helped in the kitchen. He used to glide along on those Sundays wearing the 'Master Chef' apron that Tara had gifted him.

Shashi washed and hung the towel she was using on a hook above the sink. She opened the cabinet where she kept her tea. She looked for the familiar rectangular tin but couldn't find it. She began to pull out the identical glass jars filled with cereal and dried berries and sea salt and spices, but her tin was nowhere to be seen. Laura had a habit of pushing it to the back as if the sight of it disturbed the orderly cabinet, the shiny metal a third-world embarrassment. Still, having an American daughter-in-law was better than having an Indian one. It was better than arguing over who gets what jewellery. It was true that Shashi had been taken aback seeing her wedding Benarasi saree crumpled in a corner of a suitcase filled with other Indian curiosities when Surjo had brought it down to look for silver utensils for the funeral rites. It was what she had worn for what her mother had said was the most important day of her life. And here it was, trying to battle a pair of wooden elephants, its golden threads caught around a tusk. She had given the saree to Laura because she'd said she fancied it. Shashi had learnt later it was a way of saying you didn't love something.

Shashi found the tin. It was behind a pack of low-sugar cereal bars. She let the air out of her lungs. At home in Delhi, she would boil tap water in a copper pan and wait for the first few bubbles to appear, nudging the heat back down to keep it from bubbling violently. Then she'd measure one spoon for each cup and a little more. She would let the tea leaves unfurl in the water. The copper radiated a gentle warmth when she gave the pan a shake. She'd watch the leaves dance in the water for another minute before straining the brew into cups. She liked watching the hot brew melt the sugar crystals as it was poured over. The milk, just a drop of it, went in last. Don't stir the whole thing too much because that would make the tea cold, she told Poornima, their cook in Delhi. She never used a timer. But everyone always said that her tea tasted the same every time. The few times in their married life that she'd travelled by herself to visit her mother, leaving Robi with the children, he'd asked her to instruct the servants how to make tea the way she did. But Shashi had always put off the instruction until it was too late. Over the phone, Robi would tell her what he'd eaten for lunch and dinner, whether her hibiscus had flowered, and how Tara was doing in school. When he told her that he missed her tea, a warmth would flood her stomach, like the embrace of a child who comes running and wraps his arms around you.

Her tea didn't taste the same in New Jersey. It was the water. When she was packing her tea before leaving home, she had considered carrying a plastic bottle filled with tap water. Water from the Ganges and Zam Zam had been making its way around the world on airlines, hadn't it? But there were too many things on Tutu's shopping list and too many winter clothes to carry.

She wished she had it now.

She was cold. A quilt that knew her body's secrets and scents, that she would sense being pulled away even in her sleep, had been wrenched from her while she was awake.

He was the only man she had really known. Her introduction

to intimacy had been from novels. Both the classic love stories and the Harlequin paperbacks they hid under their desks when the school principal did her rounds. The girls in the stories were always being pulled up by horsemen or cornered in barns. In the end, however, there was moaning and a flushing of the face. The principal called it patriarchal brainwashing but it's not like their fathers and brothers were encouraging them to read these, so it was confusing. Shashi had pictured herself with Rajesh Khanna in many of these scenes. But Rajesh Khanna wasn't hers alone.

When Bodo Pishi had come home with the photograph, she had seen Robi for the first time: a tall, lanky man clad in a safety jacket and helmet outside a construction site somewhere in Italy. A lock of hair escaped the helmet and fell over one brow. His face was tilted upwards to catch the light. He would be looking down on everyone who would see the photo afterwards. He had arrogant eyes but a boy's smile. She had liked him immediately. She'd never travelled abroad. She thought of how they might go to Florence and Rome for their honeymoon. How she'd wear a trench coat over her saree. Or how, maybe, her husband's family would let her wear the bell-bottoms and shirts she wore to college even after they were married. They would go to Tolly Club in the evenings. He would have a gin and tonic and she would have an ice-cream soda with a straw.

For almost a fortnight after their wedding, in the absence of any sort of courtship, she had invented her own ritual. She would sit in front of her dressing table and uncoil her hair. It would fall down her shoulders. Robi, usually reading in bed, would look up and look at her in the mirror. Then they would talk about their day.

They hadn't had a honeymoon. Surjo was born within a year

of the marriage. When she'd moved into Robi's family home, a sprawling three-storeyed affair in North Kolkata, it had seemed like she'd married a household instead of a man. The only time they had to themselves was somewhere between 10 p.m. and midnight. And the days Robi went swimming at the club, he fell asleep earlier. It was considered vulgar for the young couple to spend time with each other while the other members of the household were awake. Her father-in-law, whom she grew to love dearly, and who took great pride in the fact that his daughter-in-law studied at Jadavpur, raised an eyebrow if he saw them exchange more than the cursory in his presence. And so she had to pretend that the man she slept with every night was a stranger during the day.

THE MALLICK house stood off Beadon Street on a cross street between Shyam Lal & Sons tea house and Durga silk boutique. A grilled gate led from the street up a flight of stairs to a pair of Burma Teak doors. There was a world beyond those doors: a central courtyard with tall white Corinthian columns, a majestic thakur dalan—the ceremonial platform on one end of the courtyard—and rooms that wrapped around at three levels. There was a separate annex for the kitchen and bathrooms on either end, and a small shed for a cow that was milked every morning. There were red oxide floors and green shuttered windows and a soap nut tree that grew out of the courtyard and spread out its branches, sharing its fruit with the world. Inside the rooms, whitewashed walls glowed with the light from Belgian cut-glass chandeliers. It was a house so grand that the marble sculptures of Greek deities and oversized ceramic urns—gifts to Robi's grandfather from trading partners—didn't look out of place. Her father-in-law's sitting room had a Thomasson Chronometer grandfather clock imported from London in the early 1800s.

The newly-weds were given a room on the first floor, sheltered by the branches of the soap nut tree. Robi's parents were on the ground floor, in the largest room of the house. Even though Robi's father, Tapan Mallick, was the second of three brothers, he was now the patriarch of the Mallick house. His elder brother had died early, cradling in his arms his only son, when a hand-drawn rickshaw had toppled over with them and their bags of Pujo shopping. Father and son had been cremated in their new clothes while the ill-fated widow Lata took to white clothing. She was only twenty, slender and tenacious like the climbing creeper that she was named after. Had this been outside of Bengal, Lata might have been wedded to one of her husband's brothers—either Tapan or the youngest, Swapan. It was dangerous to have a fragile beauty in the house with unmarried men. But it was not the custom in North Kolkata. Lata was allowed to stay if she kept out of festivities. Some said it was her bad luck that had killed her husband, but this was not the kind of household that entertained such talk. She wasn't even asked to shave her head. Life doesn't stop for the wretchedness of young widows. Soon there was another wedding in the house. Tapan was wed to Kumudini. She was dusky but her family was very wealthy. Robi was born after three years to an exhausted Kumudini, and it was Lata Jethi who raised him while Kumudini recovered, and even later, as Kumudini ran the house.

Kumudini had an aquiline nose and a generous figure with no sharp angles—she and her siblings had grown up drinking a tall glass of milk with thick-set cream and chopped dry fruits every morning. Fearing a disruption in this childhood indulgence, her brothers sent large trays of dry fruits and boxes of milk sweets every month for a whole year after her wedding. Though she barely came up to Tapan's shoulder, Kumudini had an imposing presence. The gold adornments on her neck and wrists gleamed when she stood with her hands on her waist in the courtyard, surveying the servants at work. They called her notun bou, the endearing term for demure new brides, but they knew she was the kind who would check the bottoms of pans and the corners of steps. This is how she remained even when Shashi joined the household: feared by the servants, worshipped by her son and husband.

Swapan and his wife Sree, and their daughter Dolly, had rooms on the first floor. Lata Jethi had a small room on the second floor, besides the thakur ghor, the small room where the family deities were housed. Here, she spent most of her time in prayers. Though she sometimes cooked her bitter gourd and country rice in a corner of the kitchen, she also had her own stove on the terrace outside her room where she experimented with dried vegetable peels and new kinds of chutney. Even in the Mallick house, where women had BA degrees and wore blouses with French lace, widows were forbidden pink lentils and meat. That kind of food increased heat in the body, made women covetous. Tapan would have liked to do things differently. But what would people say?

The women of the Mallick house before Lata and Kumudini's generation had spent their entire lives around that courtyard, stepping out only for rare occasions like a family wedding or a pilgrimage. The saree and jewellery makers came to the house. The music and grammar teachers too. The servants brought in the fish and vegetables. The men and children brought news of the world.

Once a week, the barber's wife came home and polished their feet with pumice and outlined the feet of the married women with a red dye. Once a year, even the Goddess Durga visited. For more than a hundred and twenty years the Mallicks had hosted their own Pujo, like the other old houses of North Kolkata. The Goddess was sculpted from clay and painted and installed in their own thakur dalan in the courtyard. Why would the women of the Mallick house need to go out, when the world came to their doorstep? The festivities were open to all. The Mallick girls and women appeared when food was served to devotees. The courtyard could seat a hundred and fifty people at a time. All the big Kolkata babus, and in Robi's grandfather's time even British officers, would come and sit with the visitors from across the city. This single annual outing of the Mallick girls had a purpose: marriage proposals followed in the weeks after.

Even in Shashi's time in the Mallick house, for weeks leading upto Pujo, sculptors and artisans would live and work in a shed cordoned off from the courtyard. Once Shashi had peered in and seen this: a sinewy figure, the skin on his back glistening with sweat and mustard oil, lungi tied low on the waist. He stood on the balls of his feet, dipping his hands in a bowl of water and running his fingers softly along the thigh of the clay Goddess, her calves and hips, shaping the soft clay to obscene perfection even though nobody would see it. The devotees would only see her silk vestments and crown, her jewellery made with shola and tinsel. But every small muscle on the back of this man was stretching and releasing itself to perform the delicate action. She imagined his face, with his large, wet eyes dripping for his woman on his paddy fields. What would it feel like to be touched by a man like that?

Shashi couldn't imagine the life of the women before her. She looked forward to stepping out of the house. The car dropped her at the bus stop every morning and waited till she boarded her ride to the university, where she read Hegel, Kant and Adorno, even as her mind wandered. She thought about what she would eat at the university canteen that afternoon and the thick cream on top of the earthen pot of curd that she would scoop on their plates after dinner. The anonymity of traffic noises made her think of the specific domestic smells of Pears soap, mosquito coil smoke and tuberoses.

Shashi was grateful to be part of the Mallick household. Her new family was modern, they ate toast for breakfast. Unlike some of her Marwari classmates, she hadn't had to give up attending her classes after the wedding. She was still writing her thesis when she became a mother. But she didn't have to bother about Surjo's meals or baths. Everything ran like clockwork under the watchful eyes of Kumudini. Aside from spending a long hour every evening in the kitchen, as was expected of her, she didn't have any domestic duties. Before Pujo, she would draw Lakshmi's feet with a paste of ground rice outside every room in the house, which everyone praised. But otherwise, she was free to play Scrabble with herself, pore over her textbooks and her paperbacks through the afternoon, and listen to her Hindi music radio show with her evening tea.

It was around this period that teatime became a ritual. At 5 p.m., after her afternoon sleep, she would change for the evening. The kitchen was the women's social space, it was where she'd meet visiting aunts and neighbours. They gave her recipes to keep her hair black and her skin clear, information that she resolutely kept from lodging in her mind.

Shashi liked to make her tea before the kitchen fired up for dinner. Babloo da, the old kitchen hand, left the stove to her. He used that time to plate up fritters for his favourite new entrant into the family. She was still too quiet and too preoccupied with her books to bicker with him like the other women of the household. She used a small copper pan to make her tea because Babloo da said the cast-iron kettle was too heavy to bother to wash for a single cup. She carried the tea back to her bedroom. This was the happiest part of her day. This time, and its tastes and thrills, were all her own.

When Shashi finally told Professor Mitra that she wouldn't be continuing after her master's degree, her teacher had barely spoken a few full sentences. But she had reached behind her to a shelf and given Shashi a book of poems by Kamini Roy. Shashi had been hurt by Professor Mitra's reticence and opened the book only much later to learn why the poet had stopped writing. 'My children are my living poems,' Roy had written in the book's foreword.

When Robi's job took them to Delhi some years later, the contours of her day changed. She was thrown into managing the domestic terrain. Some years later, Tara was born. As Robi established his own practice and began to take more commissions abroad, she saw less of him. The children, who she had raised most devotedly, forgoing a life in academia, went their own ways. Shashi began to fill her afternoons teaching at an observation home for juvenile delinquents.

Robi always had a lot going on. He was the sort of man all the women would fawn over at the South Delhi Bengali Culture Club. Bengali women of her generation, the ones who called themselves mod, had the peculiar habit of wearing sleeveless blouses that barely concealed the undersides of their breasts. And they held on to the arms of men they called brothers in high-pitched voices. When you live with that sort of thing from when you're twenty-two, it is easy to accept it like one would a mild, seasonal allergy.

SHASHI WAS interrupted by a loud trilling noise. She had just put the kettle on boil. It was Laura calling to check if she should order lunch for her through her app. 'No, no, there are too many leftovers,' said Shashi. But she was moved by the gesture. She appreciated Laura's outward courtesies. Her Surjo would be lost without his wife. Surjo and Laura were the type of couple that frequently quarrelled about insignificant things, and went to couples' counselling the minute things took a turn towards the rancid, beyond who was supposed to renew the internet plan and who had thrown out the milk carton. But even after they screamed and shouted, and said terrible things to each other, Shashi would see them reach for a quick kiss at breakfast. Or make an elaborate dinner reservation, which seemed code for we'll be home late and we'll make some noise shuffling around when we are back.

Modern love was different. Surjo had broken off a three-year relationship in his senior year at Yale, the week he had met Laura. Tara had so many boyfriends that Shashi couldn't distinguish one wild-haired boy from the other.

Shashi was struck by the thought that she had never known love. Not like her own children had. Not like Robi had with the girl he looped fingers with in that photo taken at Digha beach. Not like the faceless man in the shed.

The water began to bubble. She took the kettle off the heat and spooned the tea leaves in. She opened the refrigerator to fetch the milk. The carton was unopened and the kitchen scissors weren't where they were supposed to be. She remembered she had a pair in her room. She walked to the guest room and found them in her grey toiletries pouch. But under the pair of scissors, her eyes fell on Robi's nail cutter. Surjo had taken great care in packing away his father's things after the cremation. But this had remained hidden, amongst Shashi's creams and lipsticks. She zipped up the pouch and returned to the kitchen with the scissors.

When Robi cut his toenails after his shower on Sunday mornings, he used to sit on the edge of the bed with a towel wrapped around his waist and another around his neck to catch the water from his hair. Nail clippings would gather on a newspaper on the floor. He always left a wet patch on the bed.

During the holy bath before the cremation, when the body is washed with milk, ghee and honey, her eyes had lingered on Robi's toes—it was easier that way. As she saw his big toes, drained of colour, being tied together with a thread, she remembered the time she had painted one of them red. The chemical smell of nail polish filled her nostrils.

Robi had returned home early one afternoon and come straight up to their room. Her Hindi music radio show was on. She had been so startled seeing him that she'd knocked over the bottle of red nail polish that she had open. She should have been sad. It was a bottle of Chambor that a cousin from London had sent. But Robi, who knew what had come over him, had carried her straight off the chair to their bed, like a Mills & Boon hero. She had remembered this flourish for months, aided by the bright red stain on the floor.

Later that night, under the mosquito netting, Robi had held her palms in his hands—eight fingernails red and the other two still unpolished—and asked her why she liked painting her nails. 'To make myself more beautiful,' she had said, staring at her own hands to see what he was seeing.

'Make me beautiful, Shashi,' he had joked, switching on the bedside lamp. She had shyly put a fleck of red polish on one toenail. They had let it stay there till Robi had had to remove it with a cotton ball dipped in acetone a few days later, after a disapproving look from Kumudini.

Shashi held the pair of scissors in her hand. She cut the carton of milk. She opened the cabinet to fetch the jar of sugar. It was empty. The priest had used it up for the rites.

Her lips started to tremble.

Shashi strained the tea into a cup. She carried it to the kitchen counter. She sat down and ran her fingers along the cup's rim. She took a sip, and placed it back on the saucer, pushing it away. It was not how it was supposed to taste. Some tea spilt on the counter and Shashi wiped it up with the edge of her saree. Her upper lip turned salty. She brought the damp saree to her face and began to weep.

WANING
CRESCENT

THE MORNING THEY HAD BEEN UNABLE TO REACH HER, SHE was in the café. Tara Mallick was sitting on a wooden bench in the balcony with her back to the room. She had a view of the tops of the deodar and peepal trees, their conical leaves stiff with the first few weeks of winter. There were green roofs, yellow walls and strings of prayer flags criss-crossing the narrow streets like veins. There should have been faint birdsong but she heard a distant drilling sound instead. There was the thup-thup of cement being slapped on. Construction workers singing lustily of summer heat that reminded them of villages far away. New buildings were coming up everywhere like unseasonal green shoots in an ancient, forgotten field.

It was good to feel melancholic once a week; to scratch an old wound till it felt raw. She looked at her bare wrist. It had been over a month of living in this small town of Dharamsala but she often forgot she was without her usual things. A smartwatch cut time into smaller units. Her days here were divided instead into generous slices of breakfast, study, lunch, study, run, steamed chicken momos with watery Schezwan sauce, masturbate, sleep. It was cold in the Himalayan foothills. The hours seemed to hang longer because the air was foggy. There were also fewer things to do. She didn't apply eyeliner or have to shampoo every day.

She looked at the corner of her laptop screen. It was eleven-thirty. At least an hour until she could order lunch. The gongs from the temple at the Tsuglagkhang Complex would ring in some time. When she had first arrived, she'd been to the Dalai Lama temple every afternoon. She had turned the prayer wheels and tried to feel moved by the pilgrims who slid along on wooden boards because they couldn't walk. She had joined the small groups of people who practised a kind of walking meditation on the edge of a hill. It didn't make her feel at peace. But she visited because it was wrong to stay in a temple town and not visit the temple. She had shopped at the stalls selling beaded jewellery and incense holders to support the local economy of the Tibetan refugees. But the smell of faith clung to everything like a sickness, even to the lazy dogs who lay about all day. This perch at the café, away from the temple and market, was quieter. It was too much of a walk for the two-day tourists.

Tara turned her glass between her palms, thinking back to a work of video art she'd seen in a gallery in South Delhi. A man in a suit was in the sea with a glass in his hand. He was trying to empty the sea, and kept going back and forth from the shore. It was titled *Togliendo tempesta al mare*: Removing storm at sea. The Italian artists who had made it, two men in their forties, had asked her for restaurant suggestions and then invited her to join them for dinner. She had let one of them give her a foot massage in the car.

Translating was easier than writing. The ingredients were at hand. All you had to do was cook them. Here, she blamed the view—the storyteller trees, the snow-capped Dhauladhar, and the beautiful Buddhist monks in their maroon robes—for the lack of progress with the paper she was writing. Were the monks really celibate?

Can dreams become novels? Her dreams would make better movies. There was always a lot of scenography. That morning, she had woken up from a dream in which she was desperately hungry. Amitabh had walked over and broken apart a pomegranate and fed her each seed, one by one. They were sitting in a bower. They hadn't seen each other for months, and they were talking in seeds. Seeds as phonemes, seeds as morphemes, seeds as syllables, seeds as words. Seeds as lies—how pathetic that the ability to prevaricate is one of the distinguishing features of human communication. Charles Hockett said that. She was wearing the white cotton dress she'd bought from a stall in the market. The juice from the fruit was running down her chin and falling in large, lazy drops on her dress. Then, after he was done feeding her, he had torn into the skin of the pomegranate. That part had seemed violent.

On her laptop, Tara could select an option to clear data 'from the beginning of time'. But tabula rasa was a difficult concept to grasp. How can one swim upstream in the flow of memory? How can skin that has been scorched become new again? How could she forget how he had called her to him: a gaze, a raising of the chin, a barely detectable movement born from the confluence of many synapses?

It was the events of the past year that had brought Tara to

Dharamsala to take a semester off. She'd told everyone, including Ma and Baba, that it was to study the Prakrit languages, that she needed it for her research work. She did do lessons in Prakrit twice a week. She and a group of students were instructed by a monk named Jigme. Those daily prostrations had given him beautiful shoulders! They met at a long table at a café in one of the lanes off the market road.

The reason she was in Dharamsala was that being unable to reach the man she so desperately wanted to reach, she had decided to become hard to reach herself. The stay had started with a ten-day silent meditation retreat. Then she had gone on to rent a flat that had no connectivity, deactivated her mobile phone, and cut herself off from the internet. To reach her, the world outside Dharamsala had to call the reception desk of the Tibetan Culture and Language Centre. When she stopped by a few times a week to transfer reading material marked out by Jigme, she checked for messages, and the old woman with the leathery face at the reception desk always offered her a kind smile, sometimes even a cup of butter tea. It was like living in the Dark Ages, her brother Surjo had laughed.

In spite of all this, she was waiting for a call. She was hopeful every time she asked the old woman if anyone had left a message. It wasn't her mother's calls asking if she had received the money they'd transferred or if she was wearing a thick-enough sweater that interested her. Nor was it other students from the campus in Mysore informing her of some sudden, terrible development at the institute that needed her to be back immediately.

She was waiting for a call from Amitabh Dhar. She wanted him to make the effort to reach her.

•

SHE HAD met him just six months ago in Mysore but now the first few months at campus were a foggy diorama. Her short time at the campus was cut in two: before AD and after AD. Though she had done fairly well in her coursework, it was a wonder to her that she had studied at all. It helped that at the time she was working on Bilhana's *Chaurapanchasika* and had much sympathy with the titular hero of the eleventh century Sanskrit epic poem, 'the love thief'.

Now Amitabh was back in Chicago. He had asked her not to call him. She could mail, like the other students. Maybe he would be back when campus reopened. It was uncertain. Tara was uncertain, and not just about Amitabh's whereabouts. Had enrolling in Mysore been a mistake? Was taking a semester off a wise decision? What if they took her off the translation project? Should she have accompanied her parents to New Jersey? Would the blue sweater take her through the month? Should she really be boiling drinking water with a silver coin in it like the Tibetan healer asked her to?

Worrying was new to her. Tara hadn't been worried about her academic prospects when she had arrived at the Indian Institute of Languages and Literature (IILL) in Mysore. She had a distinction in her Sanskrit master's degree from Delhi University, relevant research experience, excellent recommendations from her professors and a line of enquiry for her doctoral thesis already charted out. She was among a handful of students who had received the dean's scholarship for a fully-funded doctoral programme. But that was more a badge of honour than financial relief. Her father spent more on her airfare.

She had arrived on campus a week before classes began, to wrangle a decent hostel room. But she had soon realized that the fact that she didn't speak Kannada, didn't oil her hair, wore ripped jeans, and was from Delhi, didn't work in her favour. Her meeting with the head of campus administration did not go well. He was a man whose belly made an unapologetic protrusion in his bluish-white shirt (too much Robin Liquid Blue). She was told that rooms were allotted based on a random lottery. But when she was assigned a room next to the bathroom shared by the twenty-three girls on her floor, it didn't seem that way. The clack-clack of aluminium buckets and the sound of running water woke her up by 7 a.m. every day. And there was the high-pitched chatter of the girls screaming at each other to turn the water heater on. Or pass the Colgate.

Not one to be beaten, she started to wake up at six when the bath stalls were unoccupied. She would pack in a quick morning run, shower, change, and then do her best reading for the day sitting on a bench in the hostel compound till the first bell rang for breakfast.

- Avoid sleeveless clothes.
- Avoid shorts.
- Avoid skirts or dresses above the knee.
- Avoid skin-tight jeans and other tight clothes.
- Brassieres are compulsory at all times.
- Clothing must come up to collar bone.
- Avoid see-through tops.
- Avoid low-waisted pants.
- Avoid red clothing.
- Avoid piercings other than on ear or nose.
- Avoid visible tattoo on body except for religious tattoo.
- Hair must be tied at all times.
- Avoid fringe in hairstyles.
- Avoid colour in hair.
- Avoid tying sweater or jacket around waist.
- Avoid tie-up or backless blouses with sarees.
- Sarees must be worn with full petticoat.
- Avoid glitter makeup.
- Avoid chemical perfume sprays.
- Avoid platform sneakers.
- Avoid clothes with slogans or messages of any kind.

This was the first time that Tara had lived away from home. But in place of her mother's tiresome instructions about eating more rice and combing her hair, there were the 'recommendations' of the Mahalaxmi Seva Sangh, a volunteer organization set up to serve the interests of women. Tara had seen them on the internet but not in the flesh. They never visited the neighbourhood in South Delhi where she had been brought up.

Always impeccably dressed in their starched white kurtas, the women from the Mahalaxmi Seva Sangh made regular checks on the girls' hostel. They checked the rooms when the girls were in lectures. Tara and a few of the other girls had been shocked when they learnt of this in their first week, but were told that they had agreed to it in the hostel admittance form. The sevaks—'the ones who serve'—as they called themselves, were occasionally useful. They offered to buy stationery and other essentials from the market if the girls shared a list and exact change beforehand. If you had fever, they brought rice and dal to your room and listened to you complain about your misery. But sometimes they did peculiar things. Once, they had taken away her electric toothbrush and left a note in its place: 'Call your local Mahalaxmi Seva Sangh (MSS) chapter for support group and guidance.' There was a phone number and an email address in the note, which Tara had promptly tossed away.

Growing up, Tara had spent summers in the big house in Kolkata and in vacation homes around the world. They rarely stayed in tourist hotels. Her father said it was middle class. Her favourite childhood memory was from the month-long cruise around the Côte d'Azur when she and Surjo had eaten beurre noisette ice cream twice a day, every day. And there she was, in a small town named after a slain demon king. Friends, neighbours, their cook Poornima, they had all asked her to bring back Mysore paak when she came home for the break. But she detested even the town's eponymous sweet—a too-sweet buttery blob that stuck to the roof of her mouth and rendered everything tasteless for the next half-hour.

After some weeks of hostel living, on a morning the girls had been greeted with a notice that said the bathroom's water heater wire had burned, Tara had taken a pair of scissors, bent over the sink and cut off her hair. Her long, stiff curls had fallen like Maggi noodles in the sink. She didn't do a very good job of it but she was certain the beauty parlours in Mysore wouldn't have done much better. The girls who happened to be in the bathroom had watched on in horror. This had delighted her.

Every part of the hostel building was painted in punishing shades of grey, as if a wash of colour here or there might make the women go errant. Drinking was banned in the hostel. Smoking was banned in the hostel. There were strict instructions from the warden to label every article of clothing with a black marker pen, even Tara's pastel lace underwear. The rooms had regulation furniture: a metal cot, a desk and chair and a metal cupboard. Staying outside the campus was not allowed. Bringing in outside furniture was not allowed. One day, Tara found her copy of *The O Word* missing. After that she started keeping her clothes in suitcases under the cot and her books in the cupboard, under lock. As a PhD student, at least she had a room of her own. The others were two to a room. Tara decorated her room with a pair of purple curtains, a black and white poster of Anaïs Nin, a round rug and tiny papier mâché bowls from Delhi Haat. But the smell of Mysore Sandal Soap and coconut oil seeped in from under the door, marking everything with a dull similitude.

'Had I known my Nayantara would study at IILL some day, I would have built the girls' hostel too,' her father had said, when he'd dropped her off.

The campus reminded her of him every day. He'd won his National Award for building a series of government institutions, including this one. Architecture is the precise manifestation of what it means to be human, he used to tell her. It was a beautiful campus, built in the trademark style of Mallick Architects—a marriage of modernism with the vernacular. He had been horrified to see the garish glass facades and the hostel buildings that had been hastily added to house the expanding student population.

There was a model of the campus in her father's study in their home in Delhi. But Tara hadn't come here for sentimental reasons. She had chosen the Indian Institute of Languages and Literature because it had the best Sanskrit department in the country. Many of her classmates from Delhi had gone abroad but returned halfway through their academic year because their residency status had been revoked. She thought it best to finish her doctorate in India, devoting to it the time and focus it demanded, before setting out to become the foremost Sanskrit scholar in the world.

Noting the interest in Sanskrit overseas, IILL had set up exchanges with the University of Chicago and the University of Heidelberg. There were opportunities for research scholars to travel abroad. The idea of a handful of male university professors jealously guarding an ancient language seemed wrong to Tara. She was keen to go beyond Panini's grammar. Beyond the poet Kalidasa's widely accepted genius. Unlike the religious texts, Sanskrit poetical literature seemed to have been badly served by translators. Classical Sanskrit literature boasted an exquisite canon of poetry devoted to love, particularly erotic love. And because of the compactness of which Sanskrit was capable, a single four-line stanza could cover as much ground as a European sonnet. It was precisely the difficulty of translating the telegraphic poems of Bhartrihari, Amaru and Bilhana that ignited her. She wanted to convey the sensuality and rich imagery of their work to a larger audience.

It had started with a visit to the National Museum with her father when she was eleven. He used to take her to museums and artists' studios on weekends. His friends would accompany them sometimes. There were Zeenat, Daya, Khosla, Cyrus. She called his friends by their names and they called her Miss Mallick. An artist who painted circles within circles and circles within squares had asked her for her views on a new painting. On her request, he'd included an isosceles triangle in his next one. On one visit, Baba had taken her to the National Museum to see a rare suite of miniature paintings of the Ashta-Nayikas that had just arrived from London. The paintings were small and kept in glass vitrines instead of being hung on the walls. They were very fragile renditions of the eight types of heroines by Bharata. Tara would read Bharata's Sanskrit treatise on performing arts, the *Natya Shastra*, only a decade later. But at the time, the paintings were at her eye level, and the women were dressed in what looked like her kathak dance costumes. Her father had explained each of them to her.

Bharata's eight nayikas or heroines represented different states in relationship to the hero. One woman buried her head in her arms, while a maid stood waiting with a tray of food. In another, she was flinging a necklace of jewels at a man, her eyes burning. The one that remained in her memory was the Abhisarika nayika—the one who braves the night. It showed the heroine walking through a forest full of snakes. It is dark but she walks without fear, her skin is the source of light. She lifts her long ghagra to step over a puddle, barely glancing at the golden anklet that she has lost in the forest path.

Over the years, Tara had sought out the Abhisarika in poetry and paintings. She learnt that the Abhisarika was usually on a mission to meet a lover. Tagore made her a tragic figure. Tara had found a version in a book in which rain had been added to the list of obstacles the Abhisarika must conquer. But to the woman determined to meet her lover, the rain is merely a curtain of pearls that she parts with a painted hand. While it had perplexed Tara that the Ashta-Nayikas existed only in relation to a lover who was late, absent or deceitful, she was stirred by the Abhisarika. She was the heroine of her own story.

There were few heroines in Sanskrit departments across India, especially among the teaching staff. Her department in Delhi had been restricted not just by gender but also by caste. The professors and assistant professors were all Brahmins, and she often heard them joking with each other about who was a superior Brahmin. They asked her if Baidyas were really Brahmins. She said she wasn't sure. They laughed nervously while ribbing each other: be careful, there's no quota for us upper-caste men in this country. When they called her Miss Mallick, they narrowed their eyes and dragged their sibilants like they couldn't remember her name. She never helped them finish. She knew that staring back at men usually made them say what she wanted to hear.

At IILL, when the other students learnt that her father had designed the campus, they nodded like everything was now clear to them. Her father must have pulled strings to get her in. Tara stopped engaging in conversations about the campus architecture but never failed to admire it herself every chance she had.

The central building had three circular windows where sunlight entered at a slant at different points of the day. The faculty offices were here as well as the main hall and the lecture rooms, arranged around a courtyard that was open to the sky. It had a shallow water body in the middle, and the rippling water scattered sunshine like a flirt. The student hostels, five buildings for boys and two for girls, were on one side. And on the other side, divided by a great green swathe of banyan and neem, was a suite of bungalows for professors. These were arranged around a garden that had swings and slides. The younger professors' wives and children were sometimes seen here. Beyond the professors' housing, touching the campus walls, were the service quarters: a row of squat buildings to house the institute's peons as well as the cleaners, gardeners, maids and cooks who kept the institution and the professors' homes running. Their children played wild games outside the boundary wall. Sunday cricket was an exception. It was when students and children from both sides of the wall banded together for raucous afternoons in the garden. A few of the assistant professors sometimes joined in. Through those hours in Mysore's sweltering sun, all the boys and men were rendered sweaty, mud-stained and capable of the same filthy abuses in English, Hindi and Kannada.

The library building was the plat de résistance—it was around here that Tara spent most of her time. Vertical wooden slats in lieu of windows did the same dance with light and air here that she had been used to in her home in Delhi growing up. Her mother always complained of the dust this invited. Not practical for a polluted Indian metropolis, she said, as she instructed the maid to clean between the slats with a long-handled broom.

Tara liked to read cross-legged on a bench outside the library building. The watchman never failed to be censorious when he saw her there. 'Why outside AC?' he would almost scold, as if it was the lure of air conditioning that had drawn people to this institution of higher learning.

The first few months had passed in a tedious ordeal of stating her research goals again and again to various professors. Classes had begun but she had not yet been assigned an adviser. The professors liked to call on new doctoral students when they were bored, as if to audition them for a low-budget movie. But more often than not, they would be sipping milky coffee out of a steel tumbler and staring absent-mindedly out of the window when she spoke. Or ask short questions that led to long answers to pretend they were listening while their eyes roved her body, her clothes, the silver bangles on her wrists. Then they asked her to type up everything she had said and leave it with their office assistant.

It was from this sludge and grime that Amitabh Dhar had lifted her, like a lotus from a mud pond.

A month before his arrival, the Sanskrit department students had been asked to assemble in the main hall at 9.30 a.m. It was the largest auditorium on campus, only used for events or announcements of significance. She had been there for the orientation at the start of the semester and for lectures by guest speakers. There had also been that embarrassing Bihu dance by the Assamese department. Dean Patnaik valued cultural diversity as much as linguistic diversity and went about it by setting uncharacteristically low standards for anyone who proposed a reading, performance or film screening that promised to help the institute project a diverse image. Hindi movies were never screened.

The dean had an important announcement that day. Lecture rooms had been punctuated with this rumour for a while now. Professor Amitabh Dhar, the Sanskrit and Indian Textual Traditions chair from the University of Chicago, was to come to IILL for a special collaborative project—the first of many potential exchanges between the two institutions. They were to build a Sanskrit verb form generator that would make Sanskrit conjugations digitally accessible for scholars and researchers. The project involved extensive data mining, transcribing, translation and computation. The funds from the project would enable IILL to set up its own computational linguistics laboratory, the first in the country. Two volunteers were needed to lead the charge. At the end of his stay, Professor Dhar would be part of a committee that would pick one or two fellows to relay the project back to Chicago. He would also conduct a special lecture series in his time here. Interested students were advised to register immediately. But first, who was interested in volunteering?

Amitabh Dhar's work on Sanskrit storytelling traditions had been part of Tara's Delhi University curriculum, though some of her teachers didn't appreciate his proclivity for controversy. He had made a name for himself as a young Sanskritist at the University of Kashmir in Srinagar. Then, while his family and neighbours had been forced to flee haphazardly to cities and small towns during the violent 1990 exodus of Kashmiri Pandits, he had escaped to the safe confines of Columbia University in New York. Chicago had happened soon after and the story of his quick tenure sparked envy in academic circles. In less than fifteen years, he'd established himself as the foremost authority on Sanskrit in North America, and hence, the world. He had acquired the kind of professional fame that allowed him to wear creased linen shirts to meetings and reply to emails in lowercase.

Amitabh Dhar had gained notoriety after the publication of his book, *What You Should Know about Hindus*. He was the target of a lawsuit filed under Section 295A of the Indian Penal Code, accused of seeking to maliciously hurt the religious sentiments of Hindus. His remarks on the erotic dimensions of sacred Hindu texts had made international headlines. Fanatics in India had threatened violence if he stepped foot in the country. The BBC had done a documentary on him. He was erudite, articulate, a brown man with a Kashmiri shawl thrown around his shoulders. He was also under threat in his home country—excellent TV material.

Not everyone agreed. 'Easy for him to sit in Chicago and rewrite history.' 'A Kashmiri Pandit that too, a Brahmin! He should know better!' 'Being a Brahmin does not give him the impunity to mock the faith of our ancestors,' they said. Senior sevaks from the MSS routinely condemned him in the press. Originally set up to serve women, the MSS was increasingly gaining political cache. The sevaks were increasingly invested in all matters of Indian culture, because they believed it was the corruption of Indian culture, a departure from Hindu tradition, that was corrupting Indian women.

In a shrewd PR move, the Indian government had promised Professor Dhar protection for this visit. State-sanctioned bodyguards would patrol the IILL campus if needed. Tara could read the excitement on Dean Patnaik's face as he explained all of

46

this. There was a press conference scheduled right after the student assembly. She knew they would all be toadying over him when he arrived from Chicago. The plastic tables would be covered in white cloth.

Who was interested in volunteering? Tara raised her hand as did Ajay Iyer, another first-year PhD student. Yes, she was interested in volunteering for the role of the poorly paid project lead. Yes, she understood that this was a volunteer role for the moment and no concessions would be made for coursework or other deadlines. To start with, one of the volunteers was meant to receive Professor Dhar at the airport and set up his meetings for the first week, while the other was to set a screening test for the transcribing team.

Four weeks later, a little too early in the morning, Tara was predictably the one sent off with a driver in the dean's powder blue car to the closest international airport in Bangalore, four hours away.

She was looking forward to meeting Amitabh Dhar, and the headstart she would have with him on the long car ride back. She had highlighted some passages in his latest book to query him. She was meant to meet him at the airport and drop him at his hotel, one of the best five-star hotels in town, and then pick him up again in the evening for a reception at the dean's house.

At the airport, she was expecting a weathered man to emerge. When she had looked him up online, she had learned he was fifty-two but there were only images of him as a younger man. There were the usual photographs of lectures, seminars, award ceremonies. A profile in the *Chicago Tribune*. There was one of him flanked by eager students. One at an art opening, his arms around the waist of an athletic woman with copper-coloured curls.

When he walked out with his suitcase, a brown leather duffel bag swung on one shoulder, she recognized him as a smudged version of those two-dimensional photographs. His nose and body had lost their sharpness, the hair was tempered from fierce black but still falling urgently across his forehead. The same kind of horn spectacles framing blackest-black eyes.

Tara was waiting with Rajkumar, the dean's driver, who held up the placard he'd made for the American sahib. 'Mr Amydav/IILL', it said. Tara had seen it too late and there had been no time to correct it.

He saw them almost immediately and, after cursory introductions, scanned the signboards and proceeded speedily towards the parking lot across the road. They followed him.

He sat in the back when Rajkumar opened the door, squinted at some sheets of paper for a few minutes, excused himself and dozed through the rest of the car ride. He'd been on three flights to get there. Tara had slipped in beside the driver. She glanced unhappily at the placard resting on the dashboard for the entire ride.

When the car jerked to a halt at the Mysore Palace Hotel, he woke up, got out and proceeded to pull his luggage out before Rajkumar or the hotel staff could, unleashing a wave of panic. Tara was grateful for the hours he had slept in the car. Because when he was awake, it was hard to keep up. Papers were shuffled, pens were wanted, bags opened and closed, cigarettes got lit, cigarettes got stubbed, lozenge wrappers came undone, dustbins were needed.

'We'll be back at six to pick you up,' said Tara. She tried to relax the muscles of her face, hoping to ease the awkwardness of the past few hours.

'What would that be for?' he said, swinging the duffel bag between his hands.

'There's a reception for you at the dean's house.'

'Ah, yes, yes. How far is the campus?'

'It's walking distance…'

He put his duffel bag down and looked at her encouragingly. It was the look you give a stuttering child, waiting for them to say the right thing.

'Well, oh, well less than half a kilometre,' said Tara. 'But the car will come for you. There are autorickshaws too. Don't pay more than twenty rupees though. Do you have Indian money?'

After hours in the air-conditioned car, the sun seemed to have suddenly gathered a menacing power. She could feel her ears turning red. Had she just offered him money? Her ears were probably a deep red now, the colour of ripe apples.

'I'll just walk over,' he said.

The proposition disturbed Rajkumar, who had dressed in the white uniform he only ironed for special occasions. He also feared the reaction of the dean. But they left with the understanding that Amitabh would call for the car if he changed his mind.

Once back on campus, Tara went to her room to change. She had worn jeans and a pink shirt to the airport, its sleeves arranged in a precise master roll. She chose a deep violet silk saree for the evening. The teaching staff, their spouses and the PhD students had been invited. As Tara walked around in a petticoat and blouse in her room waiting for her mascara to behave, she could picture Patnaik coming around and saying, 'Looking very grand, Tara.' He was in the habit of feeling sarees between his thumb and forefinger and naming its weave and origin. Chanderi, Kota, Maheshwari.

He usually got it in the first or second try. If he didn't, Tara had been advised by the girls to feign an urgent need for water. In the girls' hostel, he was called Patting Naik. The girls had giggled about someday inventing a fabric that sent mild shockwaves. Not enough to maim a man but, well, to shock him. The dean went about his routine in such a polished, avuncular way, the girls had nothing specific to complain about.

Dhumaketu Patnaik was the kind of man who impressed journalists. Sleepy-eyed newspapermen from the regional bureaus of national newspapers waited outside his office often. Photographers made portraits of him, always in his bandhgala waistcoat. Sometimes, there were also large TV vans when they needed quotes from him. Women with bonded hair and bandage dresses held microphones in front of his face as he spoke about the problematic hegemony of Hindi.

Patnaik was singularly responsible for convincing the Education Ministry to grant the funds to set up the neurolinguistic lab in IILL. He saw the future in digitization and collaborations with other elite institutions in the country like the Indian Institute of Technology, apart from foreign universities. He fancied himself as progressive, never failing to mention in interviews how many women he had hired as part of faculty, or the special scholarships he had instituted for Dalit and Adivasi students. The central building was wheelchair enabled. He cared about optics. Even though his residence was less than a five-minute walk from his office, he was always ferried around in his powder blue car. Until the announcement of Professor Dhar's arrival, his big campaign had been to harness solar power for certain areas of the campus.

Patnaik had planned his academic career to be stoppered with retirement in bucolic bliss in his native state of Odisha. He would sit on a planter's chair with a view of the rice fields his grandfather had owned, while his wife served him fermented rice and sukhua for lunch. A side of deep-fried pumpkin flower on good days. His son would visit from California with his wife and two children. He would teach his grandchildren to fish using the simple line hooks he had played with as a child. But before all of this, he would establish the Indian Institute of Languages and Literature on the global map as an elite Indian institution. That would be his legacy. He wished his father was still alive to see all of this happen. To see the fruits of the sacrifice he had made by moving to the big city and living like a clerk so his son could have an English schooling. When he was growing up, his family had had status but not wealth. Now he had both. And he always bought his wife the finest sarees on Diwali to ensure it showed.

TARA WAS late for the reception. She didn't like taking her makeup pouch to the girls' bathroom when the others were there. Somebody always wanted to borrow something and they pressed too hard and broke the tips of her twist-up eye pencils. Tara hadn't taken a liking to any of the hostel girls. It wasn't just her. Each side had decided, without the empiricism expected at an institution of higher learning, to dislike the other from the start. The girls disapproved of her clothes, and stared at her wrinkle-free jumpsuits and shirts while they ironed their block-printed kurtas on the ironing table in the corridor. They didn't invite her to the dance parties on Fridays, when they shuttered the windows and wore everything red they owned. They offered her sweets when they returned from the temple on Mondays in a shuttle organized by the MSS. But that they offered almost everyone. Tara was careful about what she shared with the girls. Some of them were close to the MSS sevaks. Many of them even attended MSS workshops on weekends.

Here she was today, dressed in a Muga silk saree that had taken her fifteen minutes to drape. There were safety pins in several places, including the all-important one that brought the saree and her blouse together on her left shoulder. She checked it from time to time as she walked. Still there. Still there. Still there.

She moved swiftly on the gravel path towards the dean's gate. She could see the top of the powder blue car parked just inside. Rajkumar, who was reading a newspaper outside the gate, gave her the look. It was a look she was used to receiving: a look that said his meagre salary, the low prospects of his unborn children and the heat he was grappling with at the moment were all, somehow, her fault. Clearly, no word had been sent from the hotel for the car.

The sight of the car made her miss home. It was one of the few cars on campus. Where would she go even if she had a car? There was not much to do or see in Mysore for those who lived there. For visitors there was the Palace, the zoo, Sri Chamundeshwari Temple, the sandalwood oil factory, the musical fountains of Brindavan Gardens. But they had a one-time appeal. On weekends, some members of the teaching staff might be seen with their families at the bus stop on their way to the city centre. They looked away or pretended not to notice if a student happened to be taking the same bus. Being spotted without their armour outside campus would diminish their invincibility. On the bus they were ordinary husbands and wives with two children, carrying tote bags with water bottles and apples and banana wafers for a day at the zoo.

By the time she neared the gate, there was a thin film of sweat on her thighs under all the layers of woven silk. The sun was promising to set. Tiny lights glowed like frozen fireflies on strings along the shrubbery. A maid bent low, moving like a crab, lighting mosquito coils in the garden. Tara let out a laugh. Man has been to the moon but can't figure out mosquitoes.

She saw him when she was close to the gate. The poets called it godhuli, cow-dust hour, when cows return home from pasture, kicking up dust with their hooves. In colloquial Bengali, her Dadu, her father's father, would call it kone dekha aalo—the ideal light to see a bride in. She would always return to this moment as when she really saw AD for the first time. Ribbons of gold hit his hair, his white shirt, the highs of his cheeks. That was what 'Amitabh' meant—boundless splendour, the one who shone with the splendour of a hundred suns. The hours of rest seemed to have made him new. His features had rearranged themselves. He walked languorously. A sheaf of papers in one hand and a cigarette in the other. Smoking was banned on campus, even for professors. But who would tell him?

She watched as he transferred the papers to his right hand, the cigarette to his lips, opened the gate, and went inside, leaving the gate swinging. Others came up from behind her and she got swept in. The dean welcomed them as they entered.

Amitabh Dhar greeted the dean warmly, and then the professors who were introduced to him. The dean poured him a glass of single malt and held on to the bottle—it wasn't for everyone. A server holding kebabs on a tray fixed himself beside him.

Dean Patnaik introduced him to the bright young men from

the department of computational linguistics. The department drew students from engineering, statistics, mathematics, computer science—they were the dean's favourites. It was the department he had himself graduated from many years ago. The only one that had corporate career prospects. The one he had protected from reservations of any kind.

The dean went on to introduce the Sanskrit, Tamil, Kannada, Telugu, Malayalam and Odia language department heads. He ignored the sociolinguists. There was no knowing what one of them might say. They had been averse to this collaboration with its focus on a classical language when languages from North-East India and the Adivasi belt needed attention. He had little patience for their unwashed faces. They were delusional, some of them still believed in Esperanto! It was his goal to project IILL as a progressive institution. He'd taken a renewed interest in promoting the Sanskrit department because it had been dubbed the most computer-friendly language in the world, and become the hotbed for grants from international universities and foundations. It was also getting a lot of attention from the Indian government lately, though for different reasons.

Patnaik coaxed the students to help themselves to drinks. The women didn't want to be seen drinking by their professors and were gathered around a table that held soft drinks. As Tara sipped on her ginger soda, she looked across the room. Amitabh wasn't actually taller than the other men. He only looked taller because of the way he stood.

She spent some time talking to Thulasi, a post-doctoral fellow driving the new neurolinguistic lab. Even those who had never spoken to Thulasi were familiar with her voice—it was in digital posters and emails and text message broadcasts around campus, mostly call-to-action group meetings. Tara hadn't attended a single one of these meetings because she assumed they wouldn't want her there anyway. Seniors from her department had told her that Thulasi and 'her tribe of angry women' had been trying to have the Sanskrit department shut down for years.

The few times they had met in the past, whether in the canteen or the library or the fruit stall just outside campus, Thulasi had always told her she was looking for something: more assistants, more computers, more lemon in her poha. She spoke like she was making a speech, picking her words with precision and filling her lungs with air before pumping out her sentences. To Tara, she never indicated any problem with the existence of the Sanskrit department but instead conveyed her campaign points swiftly. Her Dalit grandparents had lived their entire lives as untouchables. Her parents were tailors in rural Tamil Nadu who had been wise to invest in her education. She was a beneficiary of the reservation system in India and then a Harvard scholarship. She wanted transparency in the way reservations were applied at IILL across all departments. It had started to get difficult for her to run the neurolinguistic lab when she started petitioning for a transparent upward appraisal system for faculty. 'If they speak about meritocracy, let's see where the merit lies,' she told Tara the first time they met while waiting for tea in the canteen. When Tara nodded, she told her, 'Come for our meetings.'

Tara was in awe of Thulasi. She was in awe of her work in the lab, the way she picked her words, the way she wore her navy blue blazer resolutely in Mysore's inhospitable heat, how she had shaved her head clean to stand up to the MSS sevaks' prescribed codes of appearance. Tara was even in awe of Thulasi's boyfriend Adrian, a classmate from her time at Harvard, who visited the campus every few months. She imagined them having sex, two pairs of taut limbs entwined like branches in the wild. She thought she wanted an Adrian too, but she preferred dark men, she liked hair on men's chests.

After Tara had cut off her hair in the hostel bathroom, Thulasi had given her an approving smile across the food warmers in the canteen. Tara hadn't had the heart to tell her it was more humidity, less idealism.

TARA WAS talking to Professor Goyal, a mild-mannered man who was the head of the Sanskrit department, when she saw that Amitabh had an audience around him.

'There's a lot of other stuff that I write about, but it's Kama and the erotic dimension that people are interested in. It's because you folks here have not been paying enough attention to Kama,' his voice boomed. 'I alone have the task of explaining to the firangis that life in ancient India was not spent in a haze of theosophical speculation.' Everybody laughed.

'Yes, some of us need to do the boring stuff panditji,' said Professor Goyal, as he walked over. Amitabh thumped him on the back. The two had been classmates as undergraduates in Srinagar. They talked to each other for the better part of the evening. Tara had never seen Professor Goyal so animated. Once or twice, she even saw him look to his side and smile into his glass.

Mrs Patnaik announced dinner and guests started to move towards the buffet table. Ajay Iyer joined her as she picked a plate from a stack on one end. Flimsy paper napkins were folded on each plate because the caterer was trying to copy how they did it in hotels. Most people just brushed them away, and they settled like leaf litter in front of the table.

'Is he friendly?' asked Ajay.

'He slept most of the way,' said Tara.

They looked at Professor Dhar together. A curious specimen that had just arrived under a bell jar. He was forking spoonfuls of mutton pulao into his mouth and now speaking in conspiratorial whispers to Goyal and Patnaik. He held his head and shoulders straight and brought the fork to his mouth, not bending over his plate like the others around him.

'What do you think they're talking about?' said Ajay.

'Who knows, and who knows when they'll stop,' she said. She looked around the room, saw Thulasi nursing a beer by the window and went and got one herself.

The three men didn't leave each other's company the rest of the evening. The guests started departing in batches. Tara went over to Mrs Patnaik to thank her for dinner. They were still talking when the guest of honour joined them.

'How lovely to be assaulted with mutton pulao on my first evening. You'll have to promise to keep this up,' he said.

Mrs Patnaik blushed. She didn't wear any makeup except the thick lines of kohl around her eyes and a large red bindi on her forehead. She looked radiant; the type of woman who had surely oiled her hair everyday as a young girl. In Madras, where her husband was stationed before this, she was a drama teacher in a school. Now, with her husband's elevated post, it did not behoove her to be an ordinary schoolteacher. So she directed her energies into maintaining the too-large home with the impractically large windows that let the dust in.

Seeing that being a gracious hostess was a full-time job now, she played it well. She saw that Professor Dhar's plate was almost empty. 'Ice cream?' she asked.

'Ice cream would be highly inappropriate after this gorgeous Indian meal. And I've already been accused of blasphemy by the righteous in India.'

Mrs Patnaik laughed with her lips pursed. 'Let me get you some chenna poda from the fridge. I made it at home last night,' she said. 'I'll get some for you too, Tara. You girls have made a villain of sugar these days, but taste it. You could do with some fat on your bones.'

Mrs Patnaik walked towards the kitchen, the edge of her saree swaying, the jasmine strings in her hair leaving a scent trail in the still air. Tara admired her draped posterior.

Shronibharat alasagamana stoknamra stanabhyam.

The one who walks slowly because of her heavy hips, bending forward slightly with the weight of her breasts. That was what Kalidasa's picture of Indian beauty was all about. Women walking slowly because of heavy hips and heavy breasts and other imagined impediments. Tara was always told she walked too fast, like a man.

'It *was* walking distance,' said Amitabh, turning to face her. 'Though it's a risky unit of measure, isn't it? It depends entirely on how much one can walk.'

Tara touched the safety pin on her shoulder. She could feel the tops of her ears turning red. Soon her face would be flushed. It wasn't what this man said but something about his manner. She shifted her weight from one foot to the other.

She was rescued from the prospect of an awkward reply because Dean Patnaik remembered that he should introduce Professor Dhar to the project volunteers. 'So you've already met… Tara is most stylish, you should ask her where to shop in Mysore,' Patnaik announced. 'And this is Ajay Iyer. He's doing brilliant work comparing case in Latin and Sanskrit.'

'I'm a first-year PhD student in Sanskrit poetics,' Tara said, holding out her hand. She drew her shoulders back, and imagined a rope pulling the centre of her head to the sky. Her kathak Guruji used to ask her to do that at the start of every dance class.

'Looking very grand, Tara Mallick,' said Patnaik. 'What is that, Muga?' he said, walking towards her. Tara already had a beer in her hand. She couldn't say she was thirsty. She said, instead, that she had to leave. She had a submission deadline. It was decided that they would all meet at the dean's office the next morning at 10 a.m.

The next morning, Tara arrived ten minutes early for the meeting in the dean's office. She picked a chair that had fewer cracks on its rexine upholstery than the others, and sat facing the secretary's table. She had on her lap a folder with her master's dissertation and a photocopy of a recently published paper in a journal of contemporary investigations in Sanskrit literature. Dean Patnaik's secretary was just settling in for the day, opening and closing drawers, fiddling with her water bottle. She stared at Tara with suspicion. Tara didn't look like someone who should have the morning's first appointment with her boss.

At 10 o'clock, Ajay appeared. He strolled towards her chair in his slippers, carrying tea in a small paper cup. The secretary asked him if he had an appointment. Before he could answer, the dean and Amitabh appeared at the end of the corridor. Had they had a meeting before the meeting? It was hard to understand the ways of grown men. Professor Goyal and some others joined soon after.

It was only the second time Tara had been in the dean's room. It was a large office on the ground floor of the central building. Dean Patnaik had picked furniture that was slightly undersized, which made the room look even larger. It was something her father had told her people did. In this country, space was a bigger luxury than a plush sofa. The dean's windows opened onto the gardens in the front, a large tamarind tree provided shade and birdsong, but also gave him a view, through its branches. He knew who was coming and leaving the building at all times.

This project now seemed more serious than Tara had imagined it to be. She was glad she had volunteered. Here she was in the room with just the professors and the inconvenience of Ajay Iyer. The professors seated around the dean's table introduced themselves once again to Professor Dhar as the projector was being set up. He didn't need to introduce himself to them, but he still did, in the way important men do to be charming. Tara was distracted by the patches of talcum powder on Professor Goyal's neck. She began to imagine animal shapes in them. Then the room plunged to darkness and the talc-animals began to dissolve.

Amitabh Dhar took the assembled group through a presentation outlining the project. Yes, they were to build a Sanskrit verb form generator. The University of Chicago would fund the laboratory set-up entirely. He suggested the data collection be done by graduate students. It would need to be supervised and refined by the two research assistants he'd requisitioned. They would be in charge of liaising with the data and computing teams and the software engineers. His last slide was on the long-term benefits of this project. Building this generator in Sanskrit—the root of several Indian languages—would help minimize cost and effort while building technology for other languages.

At the end of the meeting, which was very quick and American, Tara Mallick and Ajay Iyer were handed over to Amitabh Dhar like small islands being traded in a geopolitical agreement. The other professors departed for their engagements, each making a mention of their day's meetings and how busy they were to the dean.

Amitabh wanted to put Tara and Ajay to work right away but they had classes to attend. He suggested they meet late afternoon somewhere they might get 'terrific chai'. The canteen on campus did serve chai, but it was boiled with so much milk and cardamom that it tasted like hot sharbat. Tara picked a café close to campus for them to meet, but by the time they had seated themselves, Amitabh had changed his mind and ordered a beer. Local beer, he specified. Did they please have Kingfisher Strong? How he'd missed it.

A waiter brought a couple of beer bottles in an ice bucket, which made Tara laugh. An ice bucket? Tara never knew a place like this even owned an ice bucket. But something about Amitabh had made the waiter bring one.

Amitabh turned to Ajay. 'This one tempted me last night,' he told Ajay.

Being spoken about in the third person was one of Tara's Top Ten Hates. Did he mean he saw her having a beer last night? Did that mean he was paying her attention? He'd slept through the car ride, extolled the virtues of mutton pulao to Mrs Patnaik instead of having a conversation with her, and now here he was talking about her in the third person to Ajay Iyer.

At times like this, Tara usually started talking about what she was reading currently.

What were Professor Dhar's thoughts on the variant versions of *Shakuntala*? What compelled Kalidasa to reduce her to a weak, whimpering child-woman? What did he think of the fact that Goethe and Tagore thought her to be an embodiment of Nature? And why did Sanskrit poets insert their own names in their compositions?

Ajay shuffled through the two-page menu, suddenly confused. Tara knew that in the days to come he would be more patient than her at correcting tatpurusha and sandhi, the determinative compounds and complex morphophonology of Sanskrit. The graduate students would go to him for their queries because he was—that thing people seemed to appreciate—approachable. Tara had crossed the long rivers of Sanskrit grammar to arrive at the sea: the promising world of narrative poetry. But now here she was again, going upstream. She would need a few quick, powerful strokes to change direction.

At first, Amitabh was taken aback. He had just pried open the beer bottle on the edge of the table like he did back in his college days in Srinagar. He had scraped a bit of the laminate from the side of the table while doing so. But he knew no one here would make a fuss over that. He had thought he would be the one asking questions this evening. Keeping up the gregarious foreign academic act had been inescapable during the day. It was tiring. Now, he could finally send his mind for a little wander. Mysore was no Srinagar but it was closer to home than Chicago. He was looking forward to having rice at every meal. And eating with his hands. But this girl was bent on making him think.

It wasn't that he didn't feel welcome abroad. Amitabh Dhar had students fawning over him at all times on the campus in Chicago. Some men are born with privilege and some know how to acquire it. The American faculty was very complimentary about him. They had to be supportive of a brown man with tenure. It made them look good. They mentioned him in interviews, hosted Diwali parties for him. But he would always be an outsider. He had no capital outside academic circles. At the barbershop or while waiting with a date at the bar of a restaurant, they did not rush to seat him. He carried the watermarks of his origin on his face, in his knitted eyebrows, in the hair on his knuckles, in his accent, in how his kitchen smelled of asafoetida the days he cooked a meal for one. These would never go. In Chicago, when he came home and shed his black wool pea coat, he would be the man from Srinagar who had, by sweat and Sanskrit, found himself minor notoriety at the University of Chicago.

It wasn't easy to be back in India after all these years. For him it was the site of many sorrows. The pain was buried here. He had travelled light. He had moved with his parents and his sister to the outskirts of Delhi after the exodus from Kashmir. He had lived with them for a month, barely helped them settle in, when it was time to leave for New York. His father had died two years later, and his mother had pleaded with him over a scratchy long-distance line. 'Please do not return. Do not compromise your visa status. You thrive so we can live, lal,' she had said. When his sister was to get married and move to Australia, he had had the means to come, but the Hindu fanatics were after him then. He was advised by the university, and again his mother, not to come. He had sent them money for the wedding reception at Delhi's Pamposh Club but he wouldn't be able to see his little sister in her wedding dejhoor. And then, barely a year had passed when his sister called to tell him their mother had died. She had coughed up blood and collapsed one afternoon at home in Delhi, alone. His sister was unable to travel for a reason he never seemed to be able to remember. Some relatives were managing things but how early could he fly? Amitabh had sent money to his mother's brother, and authorized him to sell the house. He hadn't come. He had done what his mother would have wanted him to do. He knew now, as he knew then, that had he come back, he would never have wanted to leave again.

India then and now was not without its difficulties. The everyday difficulties seemed more pronounced after the decades abroad. There were still beggars knocking on car windows, paying for things in the hotel was still not contactless. The air conditioning was turned on using battery-operated remote controls, and the batteries were always down. In the name of modern fusion, the food was unpredictable—fish in a magical sour mango gravy one day and ghastly, gluey okra the next. Public toilets were a joke. The idea of power failure, or load-shedding, as it was gently called, was part of a routine. But there was failure everywhere in the world. At least in India, the failures were familiar. And he had the privilege to overcome them.

It had taken Amitabh Dhar a full day to come to ease with the humidity. To learn again the smells that lurked in every corner. Here in Mysore it was incense, burnt oil, filter coffee, sweat, jasmine. Would India be India without her smells? It was an additional sensory load for the brain. Now he had, for the first time since he'd arrived, rested his back on a chair without anyone to greet enthusiastically. But this girl was posing questions, forcing out long, measured answers. He found himself making an effort, drawing comparisons to Greek and Celtic myths, throwing in lines of poetry here and there, making contemporary pop culture references because it made her eyes dance. She didn't behave like the ingratiating undergraduates in Chicago, claiming they loved his books. She hadn't even mentioned the most important of them so far.

'That… I write about that in *What You Should Know about Hindus*,' he said tentatively, taking a sip of his beer.

'Yes, I know. It was in my syllabus at Delhi University,' Tara said. 'I think it's one of the reasons I continued to study Sanskrit. I read out parts of that book to my grandfather too.'

Amitabh felt the beer in his throat, the pleasant acidic wash cooled the insides of his mouth. He leaned back in his chair.

'Do you make the unfortunate man read all your coursework?' he said. He resisted the urge to smile.

Tara sucked her cheeks. She was not going to giggle.

'Just the good stuff,' she said.

Ajay ordered a coffee. He asked for extra sugar and took a long time to stir it in.

Tara had now crossed her legs. Her sandals had slipped off her feet. Her hands moved up and down, the silver bangles jangled on her wrists. Her face was flushed. From time to time, she took a sip of her ginger soda, taking care not to leave lipstick on the rim. She hated when that happened.

Amitabh ordered another beer. He was enjoying the attention of the young girl. It's not a real drink until it makes you think of fucking someone. Even if you will never fuck that someone.

His eyes fell upon the girl's feet under his side of the table. They were long, arched. Her toenails were painted the colour of brinjals. So strange, this girl. There was a ring on the second toe.

'Do you dance?' he asked.

'Fourteen years of kathak. Started at six.'

'And then what happened?'

'Paninian grammar.'

He had to laugh.

The more that Amitabh softened—now he was asking her about her grandfather's reading preferences, the reason for her ambivalence about Kalidasa—the more Tara shone. Now she was the one doing most of the talking. If Ajay or even Amitabh interrupted, she cut them off, spoke more loudly and assertively, called for the waiter to bring them this or that. More peanuts. Not the salted ones, the masala peanuts. Tissues. When she finished her ginger soda, she ordered a beer. *Try third person with me again.*

Amitabh's cell phone rang. Everyone in the small café turned towards the source of the noise, and not in annoyance. Amitabh fished out his phone and tried speaking into it, but the signal was weak. He'd been out of the country for so long he had forgotten his countrymen's love for benign staring. He stepped out of the restaurant to finish his call.

Tara pushed back into her chair, avoiding Ajay's eyes. She looked at AD through the glass front of the café. He had the body language of a Non Resident Indian, or NRIs as they were called. It wasn't that his clothes were better. In his time here, he wore half-sleeved linen shirts creased around the corners like a dictionary that had seen some use. He wore loafers without socks. It was an anomaly in these parts where, despite the oppressive heat, men of a certain stature wore light shirts tucked into dark trousers held up with a belt, socks and lace-up leather shoes. At least women could feel the breeze on their navel in their sarees, even as sweat pooled under their armpits, marking its arrival in dark patches on their blouses.

The waiter had picked up on these markings. He didn't need a textbook on semiotics. These were signs that he would get a fat tip. By the time they left the café, Tara's head was spinning lightly. But a few things were established that day. Amitabh Dhar understood he had trouble on his hands. Ajay Iyer realized he would have to work very hard.

IN BETWEEN the dry logistics of setting up the lab, Tara's incessant querying turned serious. She began with a major question in the morning and continued in shorter bursts through the day. At first, she had just wanted to make conversation, to exhibit her own erudition. But this had evolved into genuine admiration. She admired how Amitabh leavened his scholarship with playful turns of phrase. He had already widened her frames of reference. Eros was Kama. Dionysus was Shiva. Poseidon was Varuna. The iraicchi of Tamil akam poetry mirrored the nature metaphors of Sanskrit poetry. She wanted to take notes all the time, but feared she would come across as gawky. Ajay also asked questions. He asked specific questions about how the Sanskrit verb form generator would deal with exceptions, which Amitabh dealt with patiently. Tara marvelled at Amitabh's ability to switch from poetry to pragmatism. He contained the river and the sea. He'd been a grammarian in his early days but had since moved on to textual studies. He was doing this project, he told them, in order to give back to the language that had given him so much. To draw more students in to Sanskrit with the trappings of a computer-generated something.

There was a lot of waiting involved in the following weeks. Waiting for systems to arrive, waiting for software engineers to write code, waiting for a call back from the team in Chicago. While they waited for calls or meetings, Amitabh often retreated to read. He was researching his next book. The dean had arranged for loans of several rare books from a library in Benaras for him. It was well known that Professor Amitabh Dhar only referenced original source material in printed form.

The rumours of Amitabh Dhar arriving on campus had been accompanied with entertaining footnotes. He could recite all of Kalidasa's *Meghaduta*. He only slept three hours a night. He played the sarod. He had dated Salma Hayek. He had been married thrice. Undercover bodyguards accompanied him at all times. Only two of these were true.

There was a sense of virtuoso about the man and also a sense of mystery. No matter how busy the days were, he wrapped up at 6 p.m. There was really nothing to do in Mysore in the evenings. Even the zoo and the Palace and the other tourist attractions closed early. Where did he go? What did he do? From whom did he receive all those phone calls?

Amitabh had been given a large office on the top floor of the central building, which was even decked with a mini refrigerator. His name had been printed on a piece of acrylic and stuck on the door. They were to work here till the lab was set up, which would take a few more weeks. It was here that Ajay and Tara studied different models of linguistic generators, like the one developed for Hebrew at the University of Haifa.

Tara was inclined to brand him as difficult. But just as she would arrange her thoughts to freeze, just as that film would start to form, AD would say something to make her crack. Two words from him and she would dissolve to 'I'll transcribe pages and pages for you,' 'I'll skip my lunch to sit here with you,' 'I'll miss my morning run just to hear you say "Well done".'

The students could buy coffee at the canteen. For the professors, a peon came around to the rooms at 10 a.m. and then at 4 p.m. with trays of coffee and biscuits. The coffee was sweet and frothy, and usually spilled over the edges of the steel tumblers, drying in thin brown streams. Since Tara and Ajay kept exalted company these days, the peon grudgingly brought them coffees twice a day too. One day, after the calm of the morning coffee, Ajay announced that he had devised a questionnaire to screen the graduate students who would do the data collection work and was ready to conduct the first screening.

Did Professor Dhar want to look it over?

'No.'

Did he want to meet the students who would be taking the test in the lab a floor below?

'No.'

Should he take Tara with him?

'No, let her be here,' he said.

Tara was both pleased and made nervous by the suggestion. What if he complained about the air conditioner remote again? Everytime he had done it so far, Ajay had leaped to his feet, slapped the remote a few times, adjusted its batteries and handed it to him. Worse, what if he posed a technical query that she knew the answer to but wouldn't be able to answer in the moment?

As she sat there, Tara slowly built up a stomach acid. She needn't have. Amitabh barely registered her presence. He sat on the three-seater sofa near the window at one end of the room, his legs raised on a centre table, smoking, reading, making notes in the margins once in a while with his tiny silver mechanical pencil. Tara sat at a seminar table at the other end of the room, writing ticks against a long list of declensions. She held off going to the loo, thinking it might just be the moment he looked up to ask her something.

Tara and Ajay sat every day at that long seminar table. Amitabh started the day with them at the table, made a schedule for the day, answered their queries. When he left the table to sit on the sofa to read or write, it was as if he wasn't there any more, except for the cigarette smoke that lingered in the air. And the soft rhythmic tap-tap of pencil on paper. Or the tak-tak of shoe on tile. She believed he was kinder and more talkative the days he didn't receive a phone call in the morning.

He hadn't received a call so far today but still seemed reserved. Her hypothesis had been proved wrong. He sat on the sofa the entire time Ajay was away.

She did not regret that she had volunteered for the project. It would be good for her resume. It had certainly pleased the dean and Amitabh would have to give her a recommendation letter at the end of it. But how would she impress him if he didn't ever take an interest in speaking with her, in getting to know her? How would she get selected for Chicago? When would the trials end and life begin?

Tara was startled by a loud ring. It was Amitabh's cell phone. She studied him as he paced around the room. He wasn't looking at her, so she could watch him more closely. It seemed like the man was spilling out of himself. Though he carried a brown leather satchel with him at all times, there were always books or stray papers in his hands. As if it was impossible to contain him. As if he always had more important things to do than stuff papers into a bag or do up the top button of his shirt. He carried several small notebooks. One was on the sofa right now. On it he scrawled in his neat but tiny handwriting with that beloved silver pencil. How Tara wished she could steal a glance at the notebook. What was it about him that made people hold open doors, that made ice buckets and single malts appear? What was it about him that compelled even the most somnambulant watchmen into salutation?

And what was it about him that was making Tara desperate for his approval? At times she thought it was the worst misery she had ever experienced. To wake up and not know how she would feel at the end of the day, and all of it hinged on some lines uttered by this man. 'Very well done, Tara' or 'Ah, that was a quick one.' To think of what to say to make him hurriedly take off his glasses and squint in her direction. (He only did that when he was really interested in something she was saying.) She wanted to be told that her area of study was daring. She knew it was. Studying Panini or Chomsky was the more expected thing to do. She wanted to be told her Sanskrit pronunciation was impressive. Everyone told her that, even Dadu. She wanted to be told that she looked beautiful in the violet saree that day at the dean's dinner party.

As a girl growing up in Delhi, Tara was used to feeling eyes on her, even when she walked to her gate from the school bus stop in her PT clothes: an inconceivably unattractive uniform of white t-shirt with the school emblem, white divided skirt, white socks and white canvas shoes. Hair tied in two braids fastened with white elastic bands. A nervous woman with a teenage daughter had surely thought up this uniform. Even before her mother had bought her her first trainer bra, she had become aware of the eyes on her. At thirteen, she remembered how Surjo's friends acted loud and brash when she came into his room to borrow a pencil sharpener she didn't need. Later in her teens, an uncle had suggested she enter the Miss India contest, staring at her in a peculiar way he had never done before. All her life, she had been coveted foolishly by foolish young boys. Confused creatures who subsisted on sci-fi theories and cricket updates and too much Paco Rabanne. They said they wanted her but when they were alone in a room together all they wanted to do after a quick fuck and wipe down was to smoke pot, eat pizzas and watch subtitled movies.

For the rest of that afternoon in the office, until Ajay returned, Amitabh didn't speak a word to her.

So far, it had been enough for Tara to be in his circle of light. The work itself was mechanical and not stimulating. In the stillness of the days that passed, she felt she had regressed to the nights under a lampshade studying Sanskrit in her room in Delhi while her school friends went for rooftop parties and live music nights at clubs.

Tara began to slow down. She thrived on praise and there was little to be had. She and Ajay would be assigned ten pages each and Tara would do only eight overnight; Ajay would help her finish in the morning. One morning, Amitabh took Ajay with him for a meeting, leaving Tara by herself in the office. When they returned after several hours, laughing, they had the satisfied look of men who had lunched. Tara was hungry. She shot a look at the two of them as they entered the room and got up from her chair, kicking it back.

'I have my own studying to do. This is basic transcribing. Surely you can find someone else to do this,' she said, before Amitabh had even put his satchel down.

Ajay looked troubled. This Delhi girl was going to ruin everything. She was going to make them all look bad. He was sure she didn't even need to be at IILL. Her father could send her anywhere she wanted. He had been working so hard to keep Professor Dhar in good spirits. He had even invited him for Sunday cricket, where the professor had turned out to be surprisingly good. He told them he had a Kashmiri willow bat back at home in Chicago. It was one of the things he'd carried with him from Srinagar.

'If you have classes, I'll finish that up,' said Ajay, in his most patient voice, the voice he used to cut through long queues saying someone in the family was ill.

'That is not in the spirit of volunteering. If Mallick thinks the work is beneath her, she can… we're trying to achieve something here, goddammit,' said Amitabh. He lit a cigarette and looked out of the window, not granting her the privilege of his anger.

In her head, Tara had stormed out of the room, slammed the door, never looked back, become a major professional rival of Professor Amitabh Dhar and shown him up in an international conference. Her book sales had exceeded his. Her books had replaced his in bookstores. He had regretted his ways and written her a long email to apologize and she had not bothered replying.

Instead, she sat sullenly and finished the work. Ajay sat nervously across from her, opening and closing books, leafing through papers pointlessly. Amitabh went to his perch on the sofa and pretended he was alone. He made phone calls, smoked, folded and unfolded a newspaper many times, wrote in his notebook. At 6 p.m., he left the room.

THERE WAS a dance drama that evening in the open-air amphitheatre on campus. Tara had been waiting for it for weeks and she wasn't going to let the afternoon bring her down. Tagore's *Chitrangada* was a story from the Mahabharata that her Dadu had told her many times. Chitrangada, the Manipuri warrior princess, falls in love with Arjuna, but fears he will reject her. She is Kurupa, the ugly one. She asks Kama, the god of love, to make her more womanly. She becomes Surupa, the beautiful one. Arjuna is charmed by her beauty and they are married. But when Manipur is attacked, people cry out for their warrior princess. Arjuna too longs to meet this extraordinary woman. Chitrangada begs Kama to restore her to her original form. When Arjuna learns of her betrayal he is surprised, but he loves her even more. To hear the story is one thing. On seeing it dramatized, Tara found herself overwhelmed.

When some graduate students walked up to her and asked her how she had liked the dance drama, she was tempted to say it was disappointing. Tara Mallick was not supposed to like things easily. But the dancers had spoken to her with their feet, fingers, eyes. The bare chest of the dancer who played Arjuna had swollen when he had to project anger. It had quivered to emote desire. She told them that it was true to Tagore but that the costumes were garish. The lighting could have been more expressive.

She joined a small group that was headed out for biryani and beer. Picking a place to go was always a tedious drama on campus. The vegetarians refused to go to a place that didn't have a separate veg kitchen. The group split. She went to Habib's with five others. They ordered Special Mutton Biryani and a dozen bottles of beer. Over dinner, they discussed the dance drama and the India–Sri Lanka cricket match the next day. Where would they gather to watch it? Who was betting what? As they were walking out, a poster for the new Rajinikanth movie waylaid the group. Even PhD students could be spontaneous on Saturday evenings. But Tara hadn't prepared herself to watch a movie that evening. She didn't like surprises. They dropped her back to the campus en route to the movie theatre.

The hostel wings were quiet when she returned. So quiet that she could hear what the TV was playing in the hostel warden's room on the ground floor. A lot of the students who lived close by went home for the weekend. Even the dull inhabitants of the grey-washed hostel were altered on Saturday evenings. They became real people with glossy lipstick and movie tickets.

As she was walking up to her room, she saw a girl knock on a door. She was carefully holding up a brown paper bag. Must be food for someone on a submission deadline, she thought. Girls could be so nice to each other when they wanted to. It was a choice. Tara liked to assign behaviour to a person's zodiac sign but she had come to believe that most things were a choice.

She went to her room. The alcohol was warm in her stomach. Excellent time for a shower, she thought. The bathroom would be quiet. The bath stalls would all be empty. She undressed. And then she did something quite unexpected.

Over the next year, she would come back to that moment over and over again. What makes milk turn to curd? When do flowers start rotting on the forest floor?

She pulled out her suitcases from under the bed and picked out her clothes. She put on a silver anklet with tiny yellow beads. She wiped off her makeup and applied it carefully again. She rubbed perfumed oil on her wrists, and behind her ears and knees. She was the gold-tinted king's daughter from *Chaurapanchasika*. Bilhana described her as *'balmed with the exhalation of a flattering musk'*.

Then she walked out of the campus, taking the longer route through the staff gate, and hailed an autorickshaw. It had just begun to rain.

'Mysore Palace Hotel,' she told the driver. 'I'll pay only twenty rupees.'

- Girls must enter and exit campus in pairs.

- No walking or running in campus between 10 p.m. and 7 a.m.

- No walking or running in body-fitting gym clothes or shorts.

- No wearing white t-shirt when walking or running in campus.

- If cycling in skirts or dress, girls must wear tights.

- ~~No walking with male student.~~

- No sitting on garden bench with male student.

- No texting on phone while walking.

- Must carry Identity Card in duplicate at all times.

NEW
MOON

THERE WAS A LIGHT DRIZZLE THE DAY SHASHI RETURNED home. As the plane prepared to land in Delhi airport, the cloudy waters of the Yamuna came into view, and mothers combed their children's hair, buttoning them up in sweaters knitted by the grandmothers they were about to meet. For many of the young families around her, this was the annual visit back home.

'Say jai jai when you meet dadi,' the woman next to her told a bespectacled boy, who was trying to finish a video game before the screens went off. A teenage girl was sulking because she had been asked to change into full pants that covered her legs.

A well-bred child is better than a Louis Vuitton bag. Just because their children spoke in foreign accents didn't mean they had forgotten their Indian manners. These children would bring their mothers pride. Nobody would be able to say, 'Look how she raised her child.' They were going to have it all. The Spelling Bee and the arangetram. The summa cum laude and the Big Indian

81

Wedding, preferably to another one like them. It would be a destination wedding, perhaps in a beach resort in Maldives or Bali. That way they wouldn't have to invite all the awkward relatives, the ones who sprayed perfume on their clothes.

After straightening their children, the women fixed their lipstick. Men pulled down cabin baggage that looked artificially plumped like fruits in supermarket aisles. The suitcases held gifts for everyone: the newly-weds in the family, parents, cousins, neighbours, the old family servants.

The air hostesses had exhausted their quota of smiles during the dinner service. No, there was no extra yogurt. Yes, the chicken was halal. They were now asking everyone to remain seated till the captain's announcement. The same people who behaved timidly overseas, forming queues even when none were needed, were now transformed. Just before landing, they became ruder, louder, more possessive of their belongings. They crowded the aisle with their suitcases, fingers clutching Duty Free shopping bags.

Someone tossed a magazine out of the way. Someone stepped on a headphone cable. 'Excuse me! Don't step on this,' the teenage girl, now resignedly in full pants, shrieked.

It was early in the morning. The aircraft smelled of toothpaste and coffee. There was a full day that lay ahead but everybody was in a great hurry. Even the old man in the grey safari suit scolding the others not to rush was in a hurry. They had family waiting for them. Mothers who would cup their chins and say they'd grown thin. Friends waiting to see photographs of their new four-bedroom house with a pool. There was the promise of hot meals and no dishwasher to load after.

Shashi was returning with one suitcase. It had been checked

in. She had travelled so much, vacations twice a year, almost every year, with Robi. Sometimes a site visit by Robi that a client was paying for would extend into a holiday. Business Class for the whole family. She had boarded a plane for the first time only after her wedding. This was her first long-distance flight on her own. Surjo had told her that it would be difficult for her to manage two suitcases by herself. He had wanted to come with her. He had figured it all out. He would work out of India for a month. He would sleep during the day and log in to American market hours in the evening and work through the night.

'We'll have luchi-aloo for breakfast every day, Ma,' he had said.

What a cherubic face he had. She had stroked his hair, which was hard with some kind of hair gel that made her fingers smell like lemon sharbat. But seeing how nervous the suggestion had made Laura, Shashi had made him change his mind. She was not a mother-in-law competing for her son's affection, from one of those sentimental TV serials. She told Surjo his stay would inconvenience her. She told him that relatives from Kolkata would be visiting. And that she would want to resume work at the juvenile home as early as possible. Surjo had looked at her, eyes liquid with disbelief. But in the end, he had believed her. It was so much easier to raise boys. They believed their mothers.

Shashi's hand luggage was in the compartment above. It had remained there since the transfer at Heathrow. When the others started to deplane and Shashi remained seated, a young girl—must have been a little older than Tara—asked if she could help. Shashi said she didn't need any help. She was only waiting for the others to get off. It was a light bag: it had a book, some magazines, the funny puffed jacket she only wore abroad, a shawl, various kinds of antacids, her toiletries, and the round tin with Robi's remains. But the girl stayed around as Shashi tried to pull it down, and gave her a hand.

'Have a great day, Aunty!' she said, rolling off with her trolley bag and highlighted hair, eyes on her phone.

Their driver, Jose, was supposed to be waiting outside. Her friend Sunita, a colleague from the juvenile home, had insisted on being there as well.

'Just tell me the flight number, no arguing,' Sunita had said over the phone.

Shashi was herded out of the plane with the others. Her left foot had gone numb from the hours of travel. There was a metallic taste in her mouth. But more than that, a peculiar lethargy had set in. It wasn't lack of sleep. She had slept through the flight. It was her body making its resistance known for things she didn't want to do, like meet their family physician, Doctor Joshi. He had insisted on seeing her that afternoon. He wanted to explain to her exactly what had happened. He'd spoken with the doctors at JFK Medical Centre when they had phoned him to discuss Robi Mallick's medical history. But what was to come of it now? She'd meet him next week. Or next month.

As she walked towards the baggage area, she saw her name on a placard. She wouldn't have noticed it but the man in khaki who was holding up her name in bold capital letters was staring at all the women walking his way. MRS SHASHI MALLICK it said, the printed black letters in a single line, leaving so much of the white board unoccupied. She was used to MR AND MRS MALLICK. When she waved at the man carrying the placard, he looked at her with mild surprise. He was used to receiving VIPs. Men in white kurtas. Men in suits carrying slim briefcases. Husbands with wives who wore sunglasses and heels and perfume that you could smell before you saw them.

'Surinderji sent me, Ma'am,' he said. 'My name Jaggi.'

Surinder Singh was Sunita's husband. He was high up enough in the Delhi Police to assign someone to receive his wife's friend at the airport with a vague remark like 'special circumstances'. Jaggi hailed an airport buggy for Shashi. He insisted on carrying her shoulder bag and walking alongside the buggy. His uniform cut through queues at immigration and customs. She was out sooner than she had wanted to be. The noise of the car horns weighed on her ears. Even the slanting morning light felt oppressive.

Outside, Jose stood beside Sunita and her driver, who held a large umbrella over his Madam's head even though the rain was just a trickle, just enough to leave muddy footprints on the airport floor. The home smells caught her nose. Rubber tyres on rain-dampened concrete, fuel smoke, phenyl, the artificial floral fragrances to mask the smell of phenyl, the smell of cardamom chai being dispensed from coin-operated machines.

Jose had tears pasted on his face. Shashi nodded softly at him. She'd reassure him tomorrow that he still had his job. She had never learnt how to drive. 'Why would you ever have the need?' Robi would tell her. 'No Mallick woman should have to drive in a city where these bloody villagers never learnt how to dip their headlights.'

Sunita came forward and held her by the shoulders.

'Kaisi hai tu? Ride in my car. Jose can follow.'

Tu. The informal pronoun. Sunita was the only one who used that for her now. It made her feel like she was in college, reading

Starglow after classes with her friends. Shashi was grateful for women like Sunita. Women who always packed enough paranthas for picnics. Who always had the extra-large custard bowl you could borrow for parties. Who carried loose change and safety pins, and always knew immediately when they were on the wrong road.

In the car, the classical radio station was playing Raag Megh Malhar to mark the unseasonal rain. The singer pronounced that her heart was a rose that would wither and fall if it wasn't plucked immediately. Sunita shouted at her driver to turn it off.

Sunita opened a steel tiffin box packed with aloo parantha and pickle. The paranthas were moist and fluffy, coriander speckling the mashed potato. She placed the tiffin box on Shashi's lap. Then she took Shashi's hand and pressed it in hers.

'Flight food is getting worse these days, no,' she said.

From the back pocket of the driver's seat, Sunita pulled out a stash of newspapers. It was the crossword from the last three Sundays, their Monday routine at the Yuva Vikas Juvenile Home.

Shashi had barely cried since the day she'd come across Robi's nail cutter. She didn't want to cry in front of Surjo. How would he feel if he saw Ma crying all the time? But she could cry now.

Shashi wasn't hungry but she ate small bites of a parantha. This wasn't food, it was sustenance. Shashi knew Sunita would have woken up with an alarm that morning. She would have removed the potatoes boiled the night before from the fridge and mashed them with her hands, adding spices and coriander as she did so. She would probably have asked her maid to knead the dough but she would have stuffed the dough with the potato herself and patted it on the tava, while the maid looked on, confused. She would have smeared them with more ghee than usual before packing them in the steel tiffin box. She would have cried while packing them so she wouldn't cry at the airport.

Shashi looked for familiar shapes on the road. The car ahead made grey emissions that remained suspended in the polluted air. A cow was disrupting traffic. A man in the car next to them had rolled down his window to pray to the cow. He poured something into his mouth from a sachet and continued to pray. There were hoardings for gold bridal jewellery. These days they had started featuring dusky models but not much else had changed. The models still looked vacuous with false eyelashes and a silly exhilaration on their faces. The gold lettering always said something on the lines of, 'What will you give her on the luckiest day of her life?'

The car turned into the gated colony in South Delhi where Robi had built their home. He had designed a few of the other houses in the colony as well, and its collective real estate value had gone up after he had won the National Award. This didn't matter because no one sold their houses in this area. Shashi had understood a few years into their move to Delhi that people like the ones who lived in their colony didn't need money in their bank accounts. They wore their money instead, in the way they refused to dress up to go to restaurants. They carried it in their voice as they supported anti-infrastructure protests and made calls to place their children in internships with the city's top law firms and media houses. These houses were built for their children to live in, and then grandchildren—they went to the same schools in Delhi and the same colleges in England and New England. They married each other and multiplied their privilege. They could study obscure subjects, become artists and entrepreneurs and public intellectuals who said blasphemous things on TV because they would always have these homes to come back to. They could live out of backpacks in hostels abroad, have sex with strangers in dingy hotels in Europe, but they were never too far from the comfort of their childhood home.

What would happen to the house, Shashi wondered. Surjo had gone too far to return. And even though Tara had left only earlier that year, Shashi knew she would take a while to return, if she ever did. She had seen it in her feet the day she had left. Shashi shook her head. How she wished she could hold her daughter close. Tara's voice filled her head. The anger and the distrust that had made her daughter's voice soggy over the phone the last time they had spoken.

A son is his mother's from the day he is born. She sends him out into the world as her emissary. He looks for her in the women he enters, hoping to find something he has lost in his adolescence. The nakedness to say, 'Don't leave me.' Or 'Tell me you'll be here when I wake up.' He might be saying it to other women, but he is always speaking to his mother. What is it about a daughter that makes a mother terrified to send her out of the door? Why does she cease to be hers?

The houses in their colony were lined up on either side of a broad road. They had cleaner lines and quieter colours compared to the nouveau riche developments around, which a contemporary of Robi's had famously named 'Punjabi Baroque'. Theirs were all old wood and old money. There were lawyers, doctors, architects, a newspaper editor who had made the right friends in the government at the right time. None of the inhabitants was ever seen on the road. A few young people went for runs in revealing sportswear, lycra stretched over muscles manufactured at the gym.

Servants walked the dogs. Nannies rolled along infants in prams on the pavement, showing off to each other about the price of the imported organic milk substitute they used. Visitors who didn't know better made the mistake of walking on the pavements. But otherwise, the colony roads were for servants and delivery persons only.

When they reached the Mallicks' gate, the watchman Ramcharan was praying at the altar he had made for himself in his cabin. He forgot his gods when the car arrived, and scrambled to open the gate, still holding an incense stick in one hand. Sunita left, promising to return soon. Like Jose, Ramcharan wept inconsolably. He told Shashi he had been praying twice a day for the safe passage of Robi sahib's soul. He would offer prayers in the village temple where his uncle was a priest when he went home for Holi. Their cook, Poornima, stood by the door.

'Have you eaten, Didi?' Poornima said. Without waiting for an answer, she went into the kitchen to make tea.

Shashi studied the front garden. It smelled of wet earth and wet grass. The leaves were freshly washed in the morning's drizzle. The white frangipani flowers formed their carpet as usual. Water droplets stayed captive on the terracotta bodies of the two Bankura horse sculptures, waiting for more rain to slip to the ground. Everything looked like it should.

At this time of the morning, Robi would walk barefoot on the grass in his thin white cotton panjabi. It was a habit from the days when he used to smoke. He had given up smoking sixteen years ago on the urging of Doctor Joshi for better cardio-vascular health. Why him then, Shashi thought. 'Why me?' she almost said aloud as she let the air out of her lungs.

She'd not given in to self-pity so far but she was in Robi's world now. She felt like an interloper being there without him. She walked around the house to the back garden where her jasmine shivered in the breeze. The pinwheel liked the rain, its virginal white blossoms were unkindly cheerful. One hibiscus flower had bloomed. Shashi plucked it. She threw it on the ground and crushed it slowly with her feet. It lay there pathetically, staining the concrete with red juice.

'Didi, your tea is ready,' Poornima said, suddenly appearing at the kitchen window.

If Poornima had seen Shashi's casual act of cruelty, she didn't show it on her face. That's what servants are paid for. Shashi finished her circle and entered the house, where Poornima was waiting with a tray of tea and nimki.

'How are you, Didi,' she said. 'Robi da was so young, so healthy. In our Sundarbans they say Bonbibi takes the chosen ones early. How else can you explain the little children who are taken by the tiger? And my drunken, rogue father is still alive!' Poornima made brave attempts to fight back tears but a slow trickle formed on her plump cheeks.

Shashi wanted desperately to hold her hand. She sat on the sofa, locked her fingers around her cup and sipped her tea. The house did not know yet that Robi Mallick was never going to come back. From where she was sitting, she could see the cup rack in the kitchen with Robi's Top Dad coffee mug. On the centre table lay the architecture and design magazines that arrived once a month in thick envelopes with their many postage stamps. In brass frames on the side table beside her, there was a constellation of family photos. In one of them, Robi was laughing with his teeth showing, head thrown back. There was one with Surjo and Tara on a swing set. Then there was a photo of Mishti, their dog who had died as a puppy. Something in the garden had bitten her. In Shashi's memory she was frozen in a jump, the hair on her golden ears flying. She'd never had the courage to bring home another dog after that. This was a bad omen. Mixing the living and the dead. She hurriedly removed the picture of Surjo and Tara from the tableau of photo frames and put it face down on her lap. On a high shelf in front of her were their trophies. They were Robi's trophies. After so many years of being married you think in collective nouns. The laughter of your spouse in photos feels like your joy. Their victories and resentments become your own.

'I've made shukto the way you like,' Poornima shouted from the kitchen. 'Your clothes are on the bed, Didi. You change and come have lunch and take some sleep after that. Don't put on the computer-shomputer now.' Poornima now stood by the kitchen door. She waved a ladle at Shashi.

Shashi smiled at Poornima. Robi used to call her the chief architect of the house. She had arrived in a train from Kolkata to help Shashi soon after they had moved to Delhi. She was Babloo da's niece. She had landed up from his village in the Sundarbans, and since there was nothing for her to do in the big house in Kolkata, Kumudini had sent her off to Delhi to help look after Surjo and do the cooking. She was seventeen then. All Babloo da had told them was that she had given birth to a child and her brothers had chased her with a katari. They would kill her if she went back to her village. Her newborn had been given to a married sister and they had fixed her so she could never have children again.

Shashi and Poornima had together discovered the markets in the neighbourhood, what the laundry rate per shirt was, that sitaphal was another name for pumpkin and not custard apple, like it was in Kolkata. Poornima was younger than her but after a few months of settling in she commandeered Shashi like an older sister.

Poornima was short but of a strong build. She could lift sofas and suitcases with Ramcharan and move heavy plant pots around in the garden by herself. When Tara had got locked inside a room as an infant and Ramcharan had been scared to climb the slippery water pipe, Poornima had tucked in her saree and climbed up the pipe to open the window from the outside. She never waited for anybody to praise her. She would supply the words herself. 'Have you seen my strong ankles, not like you weak city folk,' she would say. 'These ankles have walked over all the boys in my village.' A few times, she had told Shashi that she had left her village because her father had slapped her. Shashi didn't believe her but it was no good challenging her story. She was made of stories. Stories about the time she thought she was being chased by a swarm of honeybees when actually they were leading her to their honeycomb. The story of the time she saw Bonbibi, the forest goddess, swinging on the roots of the Sundari tree. There were many versions of stories about seeing a pair of glowing eyes in the dark—the eyes of a tiger. When they were small, Surjo and Tara did not finish their food or get into bed without Poornima di's stories.

Poornima had refused Shashi's old sarees early on. They were too pale, too sober for her tastes. Before Pujo every year, she asked Shashi to give her money instead so she could buy new clothes for herself. She liked bright colours: orange, leaf green, peacock blue, magenta. She never sent any money home. She saved diligently and spent the rest on indulgences like trips to the beauty parlour where she had the nails of her left hand shaped oval and painted a dark, glossy pink. 'I have to take care of myself, Didi,' she would say. She bought gifts for her friends, for Jose and Ramcharan too—spicy samosas or sliced guava with rock salt—from her visits to the market. It never failed to surprise Ramcharan, who counted every rupee towards his money transfers back to the village. Poornima had filled the walls of her room with posters of the actress Sridevi: in her golden headdress as Miss Hawa Hawai, legs angled out in a triangle from *Himmatwala*, in two ponytails and a silly Beatle hat from *Chaalbaaz*. Her room branched off from the kitchen and had its own entrance from the back garden. 'I come and go as I like,' she would gloat to the other maids in the neighbourhood. On Monday evenings, she went out to eat golgappas—crispy, full-moon-shaped delights filled with tangy tamarind water, sweet chutney, potato and chickpeas, fashioned to burst in your mouth. None of the other maids had an evening off and so she had made the golgappa vendor her friend. She would sit with him and they would trade lies about their pasts. Sometimes, young men conned Ramcharan at the gate and came around to the kitchen window to talk to Poornima. She offered them the choicest abuses. 'If I see you around here again you will have your cock in your mouth,' was a favourite one. Just as the men would walk away hurriedly, she would laugh and say, 'What! Got scared so easily?' in her affected Hindi.

In the early days after she had arrived, Shashi had tried asking after her son. Would she like to go see him, or perhaps bring him to Delhi? He could live with them and go to school. But any talk of that made Poornima's face become dark and hard. Robi told Shashi that it was none of their business. But Shashi knew it was.

It was hard for anyone living under the same roof to escape the crests and troughs of Poornima's moods. You would know them from how much salt there was in the dal.

The Mallicks had taken her along on a holiday to Kashmir once. But she had not enjoyed it at all. It was too cold and all they did was walk around apple orchards and pay money to row their own boat. She loved when the family went away on vacation so she could watch TV all day. 'This is my real holiday,' she would say. The audacious runaway children, the one with the daredevil female cops, the girl who dreamt of becoming a pilot, these stories excited her. She had no patience for those twisted family dramas where the heroines went to bed in full makeup.

Surjo had taught Poornima to balance her chequebook and she did that with great dedication once a month, announcing her savings to one and all. Surjo used to joke that he might need a loan from her if he didn't get a job. 'I'm going to start my own business,' she would say. If Tara left food on her plate she knew what Poornima would say. 'Now you think Poornima is a chicken in your backyard. In a few years, I will start my own business, my restaurant, and you will pay hundreds of rupees to eat my food.' When she was at her sarcastic best, she would gesture with her hands like she was turning an imaginary ball. A few years had become more than thirty years. Surjo and Tara had left home, one after the other. Poornima still spoke about her business plans to amuse them when they visited but they felt it would be cruel to laugh about it now.

SHASHI HAD taken a six-week leave from the juvenile home before leaving for New Jersey. It would be hard to return to work. Some would ask, 'How was your holiday?' They would expect the large packs of chocolates she always bought at the airport. When she would tell them how the weeks had passed, they would stare at their palms awkwardly. Most of the administration and teaching staff suffered from what Sunita called compassion fatigue.

At the Yuva Vikas Juvenile Home, they never made a fuss about long leaves or absences. They were grateful to have any qualified teachers at all. When she had first joined, just after Tara had graduated to secondary school, they had asked if she expected to be paid. Shashi had said yes, she would like a salary, but she was okay with what their budgets would allow. She and Sunita were among the longest surviving teachers there; the others had moved on to better paying jobs. Shashi taught English and effective communication skills and Sunita did group counselling and therapy. The administrators were lax about schedules and class timings. Often, the room she was meant to teach in would be locked and Shashi and the students would have to wait till someone arrived with a key.

The juvenile home was on a road near the Delhi University campus. It was a run-down, expansive complex with pale yellow walls, which had served as a warehouse for arms and ammunition during the British rule. The complex housed three of the six correctional facilities in the city for those aged between fourteen and eighteen. There were usually around seventy children in the complex. It was in a part of town that Shashi didn't otherwise visit, all the way in the northern end. She could usually finish the crossword on the hour-long drive there on Mondays. Between classes, or at lunch, she and Sunita would compare notes on their success.

The watchman gave them a small-sized fire extinguisher every time they entered the complex. Teachers were expected to keep one near them at all times. Some of the children were there for more serious offences like burning down a car or sodomy but they stayed in a separate unit and were not allowed to attend group classes. The reasons most of the children were there had surprised Shashi. It wasn't just petty thievery. There was a girl of fourteen who had been detained for making hoax calls to the police. She had called the police saying that there was a bomb blast at India Gate to scare her younger sister. There was a boy who wore salwar-kameez and makeup to college; his own family had conspired to turn him in. There were girls who had been rescued from sex trafficking. They were brought to the juvenile home because their families wouldn't take them back.

The days she went there, Shashi wore a cotton saree. She never carried her Italian leather handbags. It was something her mother had always told her, not to lead the lost to temptation.

When she had started, she had been given a loosely defined syllabus that had clearly been put together by someone who'd never set foot on the campus. She had modified it over the years, paying close attention to what she included in their reading lists. Shashi believed that an introduction to the right stories could help alter some part of their minds. The children had what Sunita defined as a 'psychophysical' intelligence. They had survived abusive and alcoholic parents, sadistic policemen, adults who promised to put them on a bus back home and then raped them. For some, schooling had been interrupted and many had had no schooling at all. They read Tara's books from when she was eight or nine at age fourteen and fifteen. But dancing bears and enchanted forests did not interest them. They liked it when Shashi read out from

David Copperfield, *The Adventures of Tom Sawyer*, *Anne of Green Gables*. All of them had seen the *Slumdog Millionaire* movie. They wanted stories like that.

But there were also days like the one when a boy walked into the classroom and started vomiting on his desk because he had tried to drink floor cleaner. The guards came and took him away, an arm under each armpit. They held him away from their bodies like he was infected. Shashi went back home smelling of phenyl on most days; a thin layer of dust formed a film on her face and neck and arms, the parts of her body that were exposed.

Jose was never pleased about the three days in the week he drove Shashi there. There was no decent place nearby to have his afternoon chai and samosa. The children would throw pieces of wet soap at the car from the windows or spit at it and he would have to wash it before picking up Robi sir in the evening. With Robi sir, he only went to good places. And if they went for site visits to the outskirts of the city, there were foreigners in the car who would tip him at the end of the day.

In the early days, it had been especially hard for Shashi. She would go back home and be in tears in the evenings or stare in silence at Tara's old toys, which made Poornima worry even more. When he found her like that, Robi would ask why she wouldn't let him do something about it. If she had to teach, Robi would much rather his wife taught at St Stephen's or Lady Shri Ram College. Unable to get her to relent, he had offered to call someone to shift her to a better facility at least, but Shashi had made him promise he wouldn't intervene further. Eventually, he changed tack to boast to people at parties: 'I make beautiful buildings. My wife does our duty to the state.'

Shashi had found her way to the Yuva Vikas Juvenile Home after reading a newspaper article about a girl from there who had been accepted to an elite engineering college. The article quoted the head administrator saying they were looking at hiring patient, qualified teachers to repeat this success. Robi had called a client who knew someone in the Ministry of Women & Child Development. When Shashi had arrived at the juvenile home, they had gladly accepted her, even though she didn't have the government-mandated training to teach children. She had lasted almost fifteen years.

As a result of Shashi and Sunita's persistent campaigning, Yuva Vikas had, over the years, expanded its definition of vocational training beyond making the children cook and maintain a kitchen garden for the campus. An old, bearded tailor in a lungi came in and taught a handful of them to draw patterns and use a sewing machine. There was even a music class, but no teacher, or guitar string, had survived this.

There were days when Shashi felt the job had trained her how to feel. To feel sorrow, disappointment, anger, disgust, empathy, love. The children routinely cried during letter writing class. Even the rowdiest of them, the ones the administrator had warned her about, would cry when writing imaginary letters to their mothers. It was emotionally draining work. And it was difficult to form any real bonds with the children since there was no knowing how long they'd be around.

After a few months at Yuva Vikas, the children were either released on bail or moved to more specialized shelters. Some were held back because their cases were stuck or because they had nowhere to go. These were Shashi's best students. Shashi had once asked where one of the girls had been moved; she wanted to send her a book. But the administrator said he didn't know. Interaction beyond the classroom was strictly forbidden between teachers and children because of that incident with Shankar Sir, but some of her students would write to her years later. They sent emails like she had taught them to, with subject lines, salutations and a proper sign-off. Many of the girls sent wedding cards to the office for her and Sunita. The weddings were always somewhere far away. They had never attended any but they always sent a gift cheque to the address on the card.

THE WORLD caught up with Shashi over the next week. Relatives, friends, neighbours and colleagues stopped by with fruits and flowers—white flowers, often in hand-tied bouquets. Poornima had to run around looking for a vase when yet another one of these arrived. Nobody thinks about practical matters when comforting mourners. Shashi made a note: she would send flowers in set arrangements when she needed to. There were phone calls, baskets delivered by drivers, communication from the bank and insurance companies. There was also a lot of paperwork to be processed. Surjo had set some of these rolling.

Obituaries in the papers mourned the loss of a great genius. People cried over the phone to her about losing a person as wonderful as Robi. Some asked her how she was feeling. What do you feel when you lose an eye? The world itself is changed. You are changed. The question of feelings is as inconsequential as the sliced cucumber salad at an Indian wedding feast.

The house would need reorganizing. Robi's things had to be put away, donated, thrown. Hindu rituals were so considerate of ancestors. Even animals in the neighbourhood stood to gain. Cows and crows were fed. But what of the living after the dead? Cleaning up after the departed was pathetic labour. It was labour that couldn't be assigned to servants. Jose and Ramcharan were unwilling to take any of Robi's clothes. Delhi winters were cold. Ramcharan wore a sweater and a monkey cap that covered all but his eyes and nose at night. The watchmen weren't allowed to light fires in this colony and so he wrapped himself in two blankets. Shashi had seen him eye the long wool jackets as he helped pack them in boxes to be sent away but he refused to take anything. His wife had said it would bring bad luck. Jose had followed his advice, though he was not Hindu. 'In death we all believe the same, Madam,' he had told Shashi.

Shashi sorted through the old toys and books in Surjo's and Tara's rooms as well. And the drawers in Robi's study. In one container, she found a cracked seahorse that Robi had probably meant to fix someday. In another, she found dozens of identical perfume bottles with their round glass tops packed carefully. She was open to the possibility of finding gifts and cards from women that might enrage her but nothing appeared as she embarked on a deep-cleaning of the house.

Men and women eat, drink, spill, shit. But the task of cleaning has always fallen on women. It is women who keep the world clean. They're taught its importance early. Is it any wonder that a woman invented the dishwasher and windshield wiper? It starts with their body, restoring itself every month. They wash their faces, homes, memories. They clean their histories to keep the peace. In the Mahabharata, Draupadi is given a boon to restore her virginity at the end of each year she spends with each of her five husbands.

RECOMMENDED JOBS FOR WIDOWS

Nurse

Nutritionist and dietician

Home chef

Wellness industry

Counsellor

Fund raiser

Cultural programming

Religious and cultural re-education trainer

Florist

Teacher (nursery or school)

Teacher (girls' college)

Principal (nursery, school or girls' college)

Hindi language teacher

Other Indian language teacher

Need help with job search or skills training? Call your local Mahalaxmi Seva Sangh (MSS) chapter for support group and guidance.

MSS, HERE TO SERVE.

But is it a boon for her or the five brothers? In the books about Draupadi written by women, it is a curse. That's why they don't like women writing books. It reveals uncomfortable truths.

THE SEVAKS from the Mahalaxmi Seva Sangh came to visit ten days after Shashi returned to Delhi. She had expected them to come but not so soon. They had visited her mother when her father died but back then they only left pamphlets at the doorstep.

It was around 5 o'clock. When Poornima opened the front door, she saw a group of four people. Ramcharan was standing behind them. He knew he was never supposed to let unannounced visitors in, but men who looked holy held sway over him. He hadn't even called on the intercom from the gate.

There were three men and one woman, all dressed in starched white kurtas with the MSS crest where a chest pocket should have been—a white lotus guarded by a pair of hands. On their feet were padukas, traditional slippers with only a platform and toe hold. They seemed uncomfortable in them but senior sevaks rarely walked, they were usually ferried around in white cars emblazoned with the same crest. There were special raths for the seniormost among them—old-fashioned chariots attached to an engine. It was all about a return to Indian tradition.

'Shashiji,' one of the men said, as they walked in to the living room where Shashi was reading on the sofa. Last month, they would have called her Shreemati Shashi Mallickji. But now she was a widow. In Hindi, vidhwa. In Bengali, bidhoba. All of which meant 'separated'; cleaved not just from her husband but also from titles and rituals. She would no longer be part of the Pujo rituals on the tenth day when married women fling vermilion in the air.

The man speaking was the eldest of the lot and they all seemed to take his lead. He walked in and seated himself at the large dining table. The others sat down around him. The woman looked at Poornima and said, no sugar in our tea please, only jaggery, which sent her away to the kitchen.

Shashi walked towards the dining table, unsure of where to sit. The closest the sevaks had appeared so far was in Ramcharan's stories from his village, in newspapers and on TV screens, shouting this or that, decrying something, holding the elbows of distraught young men and women and marching them down a street. They made her feel unwelcome in her own house. She pulled out a chair at one end of the table and sat down. There were gift baskets in front of her. They smelt of apples turning soft.

'Are all the rituals done, beti,' the older man asked, in a kind voice. His thin, fair skin had the clarity of a vegetarian diet. Chunky silver rings studded with emeralds, pearls and other stones that Shashi couldn't recognize decorated his fingers. He spoke about Robi Mallick and his important contribution to society. Reading from a piece of paper, he said he appreciated Shashi's work at the Yuva Vikas Juvenile Home. Women should be in nurturing jobs, he said. Teaching, nursing, counselling, these are blessed vocations for women.

Shashi was grateful for the effort at politeness. Some of the other visitors who had stopped by in the last few days had kept their fruits or flowers on the table and then spoken about troubles in their jobs and the increasing levels of air pollution in Delhi. 'Call us if you need anything,' they had added, just before they left.

'Yes, the rituals are all done,' said Shashi. Only the ashes had to be immersed in the Ganga in Benaras, which she would do once her daughter joined her.

She told them that her son had performed the last rites in New Jersey. Yes, her son had worn the sacred thread for the rituals. No, they were Baidyas, not Brahmins. Well, it depended on who you asked. No, she didn't need any help but it was kind of them to enquire.

Poornima came in with the tea tray. She put it down and placed a coaster in front of everyone. Robi da was very particular about this dining table. It was teak, polished so fine that the grains would show. Robi da's guests would run their fingers over the wood and praise it. 'Not for the veneer class,' he used to say. Robi had shown Poornima how to wipe the table down with a thin film of linseed oil every week.

'Please have your tea,' Shashi said.

'So, is your son going to come here and live with you?' one of the other men asked. He was a young man, who had slipped on the starched white kurta above his office trousers. Must be a professional volunteer, Shashi thought. MSS had those these days for an outlook of modernity.

Shashi explained that her son worked on Wall Street and was married to an American woman—yes, she was Christian—and had no plans of moving back to the country. He loved India and especially Indian food, Shashi added. But his line of work was there. He had investments in India, she told them, in the same consolatory manner in which she explained that her daughter was studying Sanskrit.

'There are banks here in India,' the older man said, and laughed. He had a moustache that moved comically when he laughed, which had a neutralizing effect on the menace he meant to convey.

'I also studied engineering abroad but I came back. I always knew I would come back,' the young sevak added, trying to be helpful.

'Well, beti, tell us how we can help. We are after all here to help. We serve all,' the older man said. 'Your daughter, Kumari Tara Mallick, tell her to focus on the great medicinal texts in Sanskrit. The Charaka Samhita, our ancient tradition of Ayurveda. We didn't just invent plastic surgery, India is also the birthplace of antibiotics.' He pulled out a sachet of Goumutra™ from his jhola as he spoke, tore it open and emptied the cow urine into his mouth. He spoke about cow urine's therapeutic properties, as mentioned in Ayurvedic texts, before dropping the empty sachet on the tea tray.

Shashi shifted her attention to the young engineer's face. While the others nodded, he held his head in a sort of painful stillness. Shashi repeated what she had said earlier.

'By god's grace, I'm well taken care of. I don't need any help.'

The older man laughed. 'Beti, even Goddess Sita needed help.'

The celebrated virtues of the women in Indian mythology were hard to make sense of today, something Shashi had only learnt when she tried to narrate their stories to the children at the juvenile home. The girls always had a lot of questions.

'Beti, Indian culture has always treated its women as goddesses. We didn't put our women in corsets like the Europeans or bind their feet like the Chinese. In India, women have been worshipped for their true nature and form and it is our sacred duty to ensure that can continue. That is our mission,' he said.

'Who's going to live here with you? Where does she stay?' the young sevak asked, gesturing at Poornima with his teacup.

'She's been with us for more than thirty years. She lives here with me.'

'She shouldn't be living here. Two women living by themselves… Beti, we are saying this to help so you are not caught unaware later. You are an educated lady. Are you not following the news?' the older man said. He glanced at the woman, who immediately fished her phone out of her jhola and walked over to Shashi to show her a video of the MSS Lakshman Rekha campaign. The campaign was named after the mythical line that Sita's brother-in-law Lakshman had drawn around their home to protect her. The video said that India owed its women protection. Girls are supposed to be in the custody of their father when they are children, women must be under the custody of their husband when married and under the custody of her sons as widows. It featured a leading Bollywood actor, who said India would be better off if these directives from the Manusmriti, the second century BCE text that carried the wisdom of our ancestors, was followed. It would put an end to rape culture and violence against women. He then said that he would personally live with all the women of India if he could because no Indian woman should have to live alone. The video concluded with a group dance in which the actor was dressed as Krishna, and a female chorus ran in circles around him.

Shashi recalled having seen something of this nature in the papers: an MSS proposal requiring a male family member to live with single women. They were also campaigning to disallow women from living together by themselves. There were small articles buried in the inside pages of the newspapers but like numerous MSS campaigns she expected it to fizzle out when it came to court or parliament.

'I didn't know about this,' Shashi said. 'But I will find out.'

'Which newspapers come to this house?' the older man said, irritated. 'Don't worry, don't worry, you settle down, we will come back later. We will send you all the material.' With that, he wiped his lips on a white handkerchief and got up to leave. He raised both his palms to his chest to bless her. The others stood behind him. As they walked out, the woman turned around and gave Shashi a smile, the kind that Indian and Pakistani soldiers might give each other across a pointless fence.

When Surjo called that night, Shashi told him about the visit. She didn't want to worry him. She told him they had come to give her a pamphlet. But that was enough to worry her son.

AFTER ABOUT two weeks, the guests stopped coming. The flowers, the fruit baskets and the phone calls ceased. Shashi would wear an appropriately light-coloured cotton saree, comb and tie her hair and sit in the living room with a book or photo album and the clock would turn to seven just like that. Time was measured by meals and the tedium of daily chores. Time to water the plants. Time to place hibiscus at the altar. Eat yesterday's sugar pearls and put out new ones for the gods. The long afternoons of dusting and reorganizing. Time to spray the mosquito repellent and shut the windows. Then it was time for Poornima to launch her daily diatribe before dinner. It was the same exchange every evening between the two women. Poornima accusing her of disliking her dal and fish curries, accusing her of purposely filling herself up with biscuits and nimki at teatime. And Shashi telling her she cooked too much every day, that she should learn better portioning. When would she learn? Shashi would say, when she was dead as well? Then there would be tears, from either or both of them. Eventually, they would reach a stalemate, having exhausted themselves of cruel things to say. They would settle down in front of the TV and watch Hindi serials and then go to sleep. Shashi loved them all—the family dramas with cardboard villains, the cases of mistaken identity, of discovering love after an arranged marriage, of discovering you married the wrong brother, the standoffs between mothers-in-law and new brides, the ones with girls overthrowing business empires.

Sometimes they would turn to the news, which was mostly about the same things. Corruption, hate crime, rape, floods, celebrity suicides, a new virus. Lately, the face of one woman made them stop flipping channels: a fisherwoman called KC Meenakshi. A few weeks ago she had been felicitated by the Union Minister of State for Agriculture for innovative practices in India's flailing fishing industry. They had to give her the award because the French government had already given her one. She ruled the news these days. She was in interviews, in advertisements. She appeared as a guest judge on reality shows. It seemed like the nation couldn't get enough of this new celebrity, unconventional in every way. It was less about the tight knot of her hair and the practical cuts of her clothes and skin that looked like roasted brinjal. What made her different from the others was the way she looked into the camera. Her gaze, it was not just searing, it was amused. The ends of her lips curled just enough to say: 'I know I surprise you.' She had political clout. When they showed crowds thronging to her during rallies, it was like a population that had been fed on decorated rice balls had been finally given a full, hot plate of rice and dal. There were even unconfirmed reports that she might contest the upcoming elections.

At Yuva Vikas, 'Kya Meenakshi hai!' or some version of 'You're a Meenakshi!' had become shorthand among the girls to tease each other for their daring.

One day, Shashi and Poornima saw a short documentary on KC Meenakshi, filmed a few years ago. It opened with the forty-year-old mother of three sitting along the Mumbai shoreline at Colaba at the crack of dawn, untangling a mess of nylon fishing nets. She finished the task before her husband and daughter arrived for their voyage into the sea on a single-engine boat. Dark clouds hovered over their heads but India's lone licensed deep-sea fisherwoman was unperturbed as she gave instructions to her husband on steering the vessel and her daughter on laying the nets in a way that they wouldn't tangle again. She has survived rougher times, she told the camera. She was dressed in a salwar-kameez with the dupatta tied tightly around her waist, forming a pocket for small essentials. Her daughter and husband were dressed in jeans and t-shirts. The camera panned to a long shot of KC Meenakshi at sea. The interview continued once the family was back on shore, salt water glistening on KC Meenakshi's face, sweat pooling in the cone of her neck. She flexed her arms for the camera and then threw her head back and laughed. They had a good haul of seer fish worth Rs 25,000 that day. She said they usually went 20-30 nautical miles into the sea, without a compass or GPS device. 'We rely on traditional knowledge,' she said, her fingers expertly removing small, silvery bycatch from the nets and tossing them on a sheet spread on the sand. 'Mumbadevi, the goddess of the fisherfolk, will save us if there's any trouble.' Then the husband was interviewed. He said though women had always been active in the fishing community and fished in rivers, they had never ventured into the sea. It was considered taboo. Women were meant to stay on the shore, praying for their fathers and brothers and husbands till they returned. 'But she's better than me now. She can sniff the presence of a shoal of fish, swim against the current and lay her net quickly. She is better than most men at doing that. She can give us all lessons on the habits and paths of fish such as sardine, tuna, mackerel,' he said. Their daughter also came on the screen and said she was picking up the skills from her mother and also studying marketing communication at St Xavier's College. Then she rushed off as young girls do. It was 8 a.m. and she said she had to bathe and change for college. She held up her salty hair in her fists and smiled, glancing sideways at her mother.

SURJO TRIED to call his mother almost every night, between his job at the bank, his squash sessions and the birthing classes with Laura. Some days, Shashi let the phone go unanswered. She wanted to appear busy so he wouldn't worry so much. Some days it was really because she had no patience with her son's long-distance lecturing. Did she tell him that the hours he worked were making him grey in his mid-thirties? Or that he absolutely must make an intervention in his pregnant wife's low-fat diet? Why, then, should she have to listen to him talk to her about the toxic effects of her few sticks of incense and the benefits of getting a treadmill instead of walking outdoors in the polluted air?

Shashi told herself it was still too early to go back to work. Maybe a guest would show up at home one day. Maybe there was some new official procedure that would take a full day in a government office. In order to have things to do, besides cleaning, she supervised the sliding windows being oiled. Should she get the house painted? Poornima said no. It hadn't even been two years.

Shashi helped with the children's programmes for the Christmas party in their colony every year. She kept their annual contribution for the party ready in an envelope. Robi had always insisted on money being handed over in envelopes. 'The world is not a fish market,' he used to say. But no one came to their house to collect the money or discuss the children's programme this time. 'Out of respect,' Mrs Chadha told Shashi later, dragging on the second syllable to add more weight to the respect. And what would she have done if they had come? She would have had to go to the party. The women would see their future selves in her and become sad. The men wouldn't talk to her because they wouldn't know how to. Besides, Shashi Mallick had never gone to a party alone.

She decided to try new things so she would have something to say to Surjo and Sunita on the phone when they called. She went to the Italian restaurant in the colony market and ordered a seafood pasta and a glass of wine. The chef knew her, as did some of the other diners. He sent her complimentary dessert. When neighbours saw her, they asked her if she'd like to join their table. Their kindness made her wine taste sour.

There were many days when Shashi never left the house. She bathed every day, took a few circles around the house through the front and back gardens and ate her meals on the large dining table with Poornima serving her this and that. She slept in the afternoon. She cancelled the professional gardening service and watered and pruned the plants herself. Either the pinwheel's roots were rotting or one of Poornima's boyfriends had been stubbing cigarettes in them. It had shrivelled; the leaves had become dirty brown. Poornima assured her it was just the change of seasons.

Jose announced his arrival every morning at 9 a.m. Shashi sent him away most afternoons. The dhobi came, the courier boys rang impatiently. The men came and went. Only Poornima was a constant presence, always in the next room even when Shashi thought she was by herself. She had even suspended her Monday golgappa outings.

One evening, Shashi suggested they eat at the dining table, the two of them. How strange for two women sharing air and space to never sit to eat together.

'Bring your plate and come, it's almost time for our TV serial,' said Shashi, as Poornima was ladling out her rice.

Poornima was surprised for a moment, but she was not the kind to show it. 'Eh, I'm not going to spoil my figure by sitting on a chair like you people,' she said, gesturing to the flat cushion beside the sofa where she usually sat. 'Sitting cross-legged on the floor keeps me healthy. Even rishis and sages sit cross-legged, not on chairs!'

'No one will know,' said Shashi, smiling, as Poornima went into the kitchen. 'I won't even tell Ramcharan.'

With that assurance, Poornima returned with her plate of food. She joined Shashi at the table, leaving two chairs between them. Shashi picked up the remote and switched the TV on. The two women ate, bathed in the same blue in the television's soothing light.

*

112

DANGERS OF WOMEN LIVING ALONE

Robbing and stealing

Left alone in medical emergency

Temptation and sensual behaviour

Developing materialistic attitudes

Murder

Rape

Depression, Insanity

Addiction

Cultivating anti-cultural and anti-national hobbies

OCD (Obsessive Compulsive Disorder)

and other nervous illnesses

Loss of control of finances

Money troubles

Selfish attitudes

Loss of maternal feelings

Development of lesbian attitudes

Feelings of suicide and self-harm

Are you suffering from anxiety and depression because you live alone? Become a part of our Lakshman Rekha voluntary scheme. Call your local Mahalaxmi Seva Sangh (MSS) chapter for support group and guidance.

MSS, HERE TO SERVE.

SINCE HER return, Shashi had already visited the municipal office thrice for the paperwork following Robi's death. Robi's longtime secretary had accompanied her on previous visits. But she was by herself this time. This visit would hopefully be the last.

The municipal office was an enormous hall with rows of identical counters. Each counter had a specific purpose. The air smelt pungent. Someone told her it was the Ayurvedic floor cleaner. After a few days of sitting on the cold steel benches, grief can manifest as physical pain. Nobody was in that office for anything good. It was death, divorce, property disputes. The room to collect birth certificates stood on its own, smelling of milk and sugar.

Today, Shashi's lower back hurt. The other time it had been the left side of her chest. It was the way things had happened with Tara that pained her the most. They hadn't been able to reach her in time. Surjo consoled her saying Tara would soften and come home anytime now. But Shashi wasn't so certain.

Shashi had arrived at the office at 9 a.m. She had, over her previous visits, submitted all the paperwork to assert that she was Mrs Shashi Mallick, the rightful heir to Mr Robi Mallick's assets and liabilities.

It was easy to be on time by herself. There was no time spent rinsing out the bathroom sink after Robi had shaved, leaving tiny hairs forming abstract art patterns on white ceramic. No elaborate breakfast to plan, including a plate of sliced—and peeled—apples that Robi ate while reading the newspaper, a nuisance of a ritual that she had inherited from her mother-in-law.

She had had an efficient morning meal of one banana, some glucose biscuits and two cups of tea, despite protests from Poornima, who took this as another affront to her cooking.

'Am I dead that you are eating things out of packets!' she had said, and then stormed off into the garden.

Since her return to Delhi, waking up early had been easy for Shashi. It was falling asleep that was tough. Everything ached, her body and her eyes needed rest, but she lay awake, waiting for the slightest bit of light to seep through the curtains so she could leave the bedroom.

The nights sleep found her, she felt worse. She often saw Lata Jethi in her early morning dreams. It was sindoor khela, the day married women make an obscene show of their marital status, smearing vermilion on the feet of the Goddess, on each other's faces, flinging it in the air. Unmarried girls stay close to the fringes—it's good luck to have some fall on you. In the first Pujo after her wedding, she remembered playing near the thakur dalan. Robi was looking on from a little distance, encouraging her to smear the other women with more vigour. His little cousin Dolly stood beside him and watched mesmerized; she was wearing a saree for the first time but had been told she could not join the group yet. Shashi had looked up and seen Lata Jethi's face in the second-floor veranda.

Shashi had played longer, even though the red powder had begun to sting her eyes. Her mother had told her if a woman did sindoor khela following the proper custom, she would never be widowed.

Robi had seemed like the sort of person who would have had things in place. He was so particular about his all-black wardrobe, his Penhaligon's perfume, his little black numbered notebooks. He trusted only that one barber who came to their home all the way from Old Delhi every month. But it turned out that he had been very disorganized about his finances. Robi had employed a chain of asset managers, and fired them abruptly over the years. He hadn't trusted anyone with all his information. He had made no will. He had probably assumed he had a couple of decades to do that. There was so much living to do. So many buildings to build. So much adulation still to acquire.

On the flight back to Delhi, Shashi had imagined she would bring out Robi's shirts and jackets off the hangers one by one and tear up as she folded and put them in suitcases and cartons. But where was the time?

She remembered the time she and Robi had closed the door behind them and laughed when only a few days after their wedding, Surjo and Laura sat making 'death folders' in the living room of the Delhi house.

'We've lost our son to the firangis,' Robi had joked as the just-married couple prepared folders with their investment and insurance details and a private letter to the other in the event of death. It seemed like a good idea now. For once, Shashi wanted to call her daughter-in-law and say she had been right. A death folder gave the spouse of the deceased the luxury of emotion.

It was finally her turn at the window of the municipal office. The clerk appraised her face. 'So this is the face of a widow in her fifties,' his eyes seemed to say, waiting for some sign of weakness so he could give her a reassuring nod, which he had now begun to think was part of his job: fish out the paper, ask for signature, stamp, nod reassuringly. Next mourner, please. But Shashi's equanimity disturbed his routine. This woman was in a pressed saree and even had a watch on her wrist, which she kept glancing at. When he encountered women who didn't look like they had lost their world after the death of their husbands, it made him afraid. He reminded himself that he must buy jasmine from the vendor outside the Metro station for his wife that evening.

Still, he gave her the envelope gently, sliding it across the counter and pressing his fingers down on it until Shashi reached out for it.

'Thank you,' said Shashi.

'Everything will be okay,' he told her.

Shashi had imagined that when she finally had the envelope with the succession certificate in her hand, she would feel something new. Now Robi was dead to the government as well. He owned nothing in the world. Was a man a man if he didn't own anything?

As she walked out, she saw a young man emerging from the room for birth certificates. His giddiness showed as colour on his cheeks. One more thing in the world now belonged to him.

THE DAYS were dusty, full of boxes and tape. It reminded Shashi of cleaning out her parents' house. To throw away the things a person has touched every day. The handkerchiefs and the underwear, slippers, spectacles, a toothbrush. She didn't want her children to go through that. She didn't want them to grasp in their thirties the knowledge of the bleak afterlife of the objects one shares one's life with.

One afternoon, Shashi pulled out the round plastic tub in which she used to bathe Tara. It was packed with old issues of her beloved *Starglow*. The women had permed hair and shoulder pads on the glossy magazine covers. Everything was shiny. The men wore jeans and sleeveless vests, styled like Rocky. She picked one up fondly, an old friend. For the rest of the afternoon, she dusted the magazines and put them back in the tub. They were a window to another time.

Another window opened soon. There was a long email from Bibek: Robi's closest friend from architecture school, more than a brother, a shadow.

Shashi had known Bibek for as long as she had known Robi. The first time Robi had come to meet her before the wedding, at her father's house, he had brought Bibek with him. The three of them had spoken about Bengali theatre and English movies over tea and nimki. After the wedding, the three of them had gone out together for Bengali theatre and English movies. Bibek and Shashi always voted for horror. When they had gone to see *The Omen* at Lighthouse cinema near New Market, Robi had waited out the entire second half in the hallway. 'Hollywood tripe,' he had said when Bibek had emerged with Shashi, her face pulled and white, like she had plunged it in ice water.

'It is a very lucky man indeed whose best friend and wife can tolerate each other,' Robi had added, looping his arms with the two of them.

'I'm glad she's not like the others,' said Bibek.

It was a compliment but Shashi did not understand it. People were always telling her what she was not.

Robi and Bibek weren't the type of friends who finished each other's sentences. They could sit beside each other for hours without talking; they didn't need to talk to fill the silence. The friendship of men amused Shashi. Women measured their friendships in how much they could reveal to each other. Silences meant distrust.

But when it came to commenting on each other's drafting or Corbusier's impact on Indian Modernism, Robi and Bibek could talk at volumes that would irritate Tapan in his armchair in the living room. Her father-in-law, in the middle of following the latest developments in the tumultuous politics of Bengal, would put down his newspaper, and mouth a resounding 'Ei, hoyeche ebar?' and the boys would take the discussion to the cigarette stall at the street corner.

An old friend is a witness to our life. There are the friends of our youth who choose to walk the wild forest trail while you think it wiser to stay on the road. You promise to meet at the next intersection. One no doubt has to wait for the other; one might have picked up co-travellers along the way. You are both changed. But in an old friendship, you do not spoil the time you have together by talking about the time you were apart. You embrace because you are together again.

Shashi was fond of Bibek for what he was: a reserved man who had inherited his aristocratic mother's fine tastes and almond-shaped eyes and was now out of place everywhere. But she also liked Bibek for who Robi was in his presence. He was comfortable and quiet, like a child who knows he is in the company of people who love him more than they love themselves.

Robi told stories, the ones he liked himself in, too many times. There was that one about the old Italian duchess with her 'elegant fingers and blue diamond ring' who had travelled a long distance to praise the 'beautiful young Indian who had built ingenious extensions to her centuries-old palazzo'. Bibek would listen to the story patiently though he had heard it many times before. Shashi's eyes would wander to the ceiling but Bibek would lean forward and look at every movement on Robi's face like he was hearing the story for the first time.

Robi and Bibek had been roommates in their first year at the Delhi School of Architecture. At first, it was about two pampered boys who'd found themselves in a hostel in Delhi where the winters were colder than they were used to and the rotis thicker. They were the two brightest boys in class. They had even tried to form a two-man band. Bibek played the guitar and Robi did vocals. There were photographs with both of them in bell-bottoms and wide-collared floral shirts. Robi looked the part of lead singer in these photographs, eyes closed, knees slightly bent to get the right angle on the mic. Bibek looked like a boy who had been pushed on stage by a friend.

Bibek Burman had a small inheritance but no home. His father had remarried and he did not feel welcome at his palatial home any more. He had spent the first college break by himself. When Robi had returned to the hostel after two months and learnt of this, he had invited him to Kolkata for the next holiday. It was Pujo. Bibek gathered favour quickly in the Mallick house. Kumudini had another son to fawn over—she told everybody about the noble boy with the thin, pomegranate-coloured lips. Tapan liked that they had minor Tripura royalty in the Mallick house. And there was Robi's cousin Dolly, who followed Bibek around like a pet deer. Soon he was there for every vacation and festival. He was the resident artist of the thakur dalan when the Goddess was invoked. Bibek had a fine eye for detail, textures, colours and finishes. Kumudini did not buy clothes or jewellery for the idol without his recommendations.

After the boys finished college, both took up jobs as trainees in Kolkata firms. And it was understood that Bibek would stay with the Mallicks. It was only after Shashi came into the house as a bride that she realized that Bibek lived there. Her mother was displeased with the idea.

'Doesn't the family have any sense, keeping his bachelor friends around with a new bride in the house?' she grumbled.

There were no other young people in the house. Dolly was only fifteen and had spent the first few months eyeing Shashi from a distance, almost upset with her for taking her Robi da away. Bibek was at home a lot. He kept short hours at the office, and soon quit his job. He said the corporate life did not engage him. He was doing self-study, he told them. 'Easy to say that when you're living off the kindness of other people,' Shashi's mother had pointed out.

So much time had passed since those days. In his email to her, Bibek had written what he had already said twice over the phone while she was still in New Jersey—that he was deeply sorry that his circumstances didn't allow him to fly to America to be with the family. And that for the first time in the two decades since he had moved to the commune near Kanyakumari, so detached from everything, he had regretted it.

Shashi got up to make herself a cup of tea before reading the rest of the email. It was long. She could almost picture it handwritten on three sides of thin blue paper, from back when Bibek would send them inland letters from wherever he was at the time. It would be addressed to the whole family in his voluptuous writing, the crossbars on the t's like a dancer's arms reaching for more. On the last page, he would sign off as Your Friend. He was a friend of the family. He was theirs, shared.

It was beautiful prose, the kind that emerges from the minds and mouths of people who do not speak much. Bibek wrote that he was looking at travel arrangements; he would do whatever was needed but he was especially keen to travel with her to Benaras to immerse the ashes.

This was something Shashi had told him she still needed to do. It was something she had assumed she would do with Tara. But on reading Bibek's email, she decided she would go with Bibek and Tara. How natural the plan seemed. He was an old accomplice of hers. They had come together for Dolly and now they would come together for Tara. And if the sunsets of the last three decades had taught them anything, they could perhaps do better.

If it was possible for Tara to love a man almost as much as she loved her father it would be Bibek. Before each of his visits she used to boast to her friends in the neighbourhood about her big friend and, sure enough, jealous little girls would come over to see him for themselves. Tara, even when she came up only to his elbow, would bring Bibek out from the study, pulling him with both her hands, displaying her valuable possession. She was like her father in so many ways, Shashi thought to herself, and smiled.

Shashi was looking forward to Bibek's visit. She could talk about Robi with him. They were both his witnesses. Her Robi, their Robi. The Robi that Surjo and Tara didn't know. The Robi that his colleagues, the people who gave him awards, the journalists who interviewed him, the women who flirted with him, the trainee architects who idolized him, didn't know.

She could talk to him about herself. People ask, 'How are you doing?' but don't actually listen when you answer. Bibek would listen when she told him how her stomach felt like it had fused with her lungs when the Pakistani doctor at JFK Medical Centre had delivered the news to them. How she had seen Surjo transform in a matter of hours. How proud she was of him. How desperately they had tried to reach Tara in Dharamsala. And the pain she had felt when they had finally spoken. The impasse between them now.

In the loneliness of marriage, when a woman finds a partner but loses a world, Shashi had pondered the idea of human companionship. When a man marries, he gains a wife, her family, her friends. What is it that a woman loses? Why is she in a state of subtraction? Philosophers spoke about the human need to unite, to form colonies. Hegel wrote about individuals straining against the inadequacy of their single actuality. But men seem to reveal no such struggle. They gain and acquire by habit. They mark their territories by spilling on what is not theirs to make it their own. It is in the nature of men to spill, out of their bodies, their homes, their countries.

Bibek was a rare thing, a friend that she had gained in her marriage. Bibek knew her as a girl called Shashi, still practising her new signature on bank cheques. He was a placeholder for that time when life sprawled before her, when it could have become anything.

Bibek's email also reminded Shashi that she would have to plan a visit to Kolkata. After Kumudini's death, Tapan had become too frail to travel. Shashi didn't like visiting the big house any more. The last time she had visited a year ago, she'd seen that Shyam Lal & Sons tea house had made way for a global coffee chain. Durga silk boutique had become a two-floor shopping mall. There were medical shops everywhere and small beauty parlours with photos of Kareena Kapoor. Cycle rickshaws had been replaced by fleets of small cars that distressed pedestrians and street dogs. The oleander tree whose branches fell over her bus stop, shielding her from the morning sun while she waited for her bus to university, had been hacked. That was what had troubled her the most.

HALF
MOON

THE AFTERNOON THEY HAD BEEN UNABLE TO REACH HER, she was in the café. She was still sitting on the wooden bench in the balcony with her back to the room. She was staring at her glass, watching the last of her green juice make rivulets inside it, when Tashi came up behind her.

'The mountains haven't changed you yet,' he said. 'Isn't it serene? Did you know "Dhauladhar" means "The White Range"?'

He didn't look at her. His gaze was fixed on the snow-capped peaks, beyond earthmovers that looked like Lego dinosaurs.

It wasn't a question. He wasn't expecting a reply. It was said to draw a look of demure appreciation that said, 'Wah wah, what wonderful insight.' Tara had imagined the ponytailed café owner— he with his Free Tibet meetings and hacking marathons and posters for social media vigilantism—to have a better opening after all these weeks. So far their only exchanges had been about the merits of the juice-of-the-day. She had gathered that he agented emerging Tibetan artists. There were landscape photographs with price tags on the café walls. And there was an installation in the centre of the room, a cannon fashioned with used monk robes. A plaque mentioned all the places it had been exhibited in.

Male birds of paradise rehearse and refine their mating dance through their lives. Bowerbirds make clearings on the forest floor and prepare soft beds, even tossing in a bauble or two by way of home decor. Out in the piscine kingdom, the white-spotted pufferfish makes rangoli patterns in the sand. The males in the animal kingdom make elaborate shows of beauty and elegance, colour and sound, and most importantly, their housekeeping skills. All so their likeness may live forever. The human male gets away with so little.

Since she had discovered Tashi's Café, a tasteful hideout with reclaimed wood furniture and artisanal coffee served in local pottery, Tara had gone there almost every day. The café was a perfect square, filled with foreigners wearing cardigans over kurtas and talking in quiet voices. She sat in a corner to signal she was closed for conversation. There were always people trying to make eye contact, asking if she was by herself, asking if they could join her. A table for one was a privilege.

But this morning, she had been unable to study or write. She was filled with a strange foreboding. It was Monday, but she hadn't gone to the language centre as she usually did. She'd sat on that wooden bench for hours now. No matter what ropes she imagined pulling the centre of her head to the sky, her body was clay, folding in on itself. She thought it might be her period arriving early. The cold weather did peculiar things. Bath bombs were fizzing inside her stomach. But she wasn't the kind of girl to lie in bed with a hot water bottle. She was a modern woman. Even her painkiller was vegan.

She cast her eye over the book he had flopped, pages facing down, on the table beside her. It was one of those *New York Times* bestsellers about a new history of mankind, very popular these days, with the torso of a man on the cover. This kind of book was one of her Top Ten Hates.

But Tara liked Tashi's Café. She decided to humour the man who owned it.

She looked up at him with a face she had practised many times. She was the *chakit harini* of Sanskrit poetry, one with the eyes of a startled doe.

Tashi smiled at her. 'Are you ready for lunch? We got a good catch of mahseer today. You should have the butter-poached fish with spinach and tomatoes.'

'How soon can I have it?' said Tara.

'Move to a table,' said Tashi, as he strode to the kitchen.

She swung her legs over the bench and moved to a table for four. But she couldn't see Noor.

Tara had made a few friends over the past month and Noor Kidwai, who was researching Tibetan women's microenterprises, had become an easy lunch companion. Tara had seen her around the language centre and, one day, they'd found each other eating at adjoining tables, wearing the same Doc Martens boots. Noor wore them with black jeans and a red turtleneck. A pair of headphones was permanently lodged around her neck. She was from Lucknow. Her parents and her brother were dentists, her younger sister was studying to become one. Noor was the misfit among the Kidwais, she always had been. Even Lucknow's famed chikankari kurtas looked out of place on her. After the meal, Noor suggested that they walk down to the Church of St John. It was a good walk, especially since Tara was wearing sensible shoes and not what Noor called the 'showcase sneakers of the Mumbai chicks'. On reading the epitaphs on one of the graves outside the church, Tara had cried.

This monument is erected by her sorrowful husband in the joyful hope of her resurrection. Henrietta Isabella died at age 26 and 2 months.

'It will pass,' Noor had said, putting an arm around her.

Tara had liked her for not having asked any questions. If she had, she wouldn't have been able to explain. A woman of twenty-five, she had known no great tragedy yet.

That first day they met, they had spent the whole day walking around, talking, stopping twice for ginger tea in a café. Noor had been in Dharamsala for a year. She knew which walking trails to take and where to buy ganja chocolate balls. She said she didn't smoke, not just because of what it would do to her own lungs but because cigarette butts were among the most toxic of plastic pollutants. She believed climate change had a disproportionate effect on women. Tara spoke about how Barthes was wrong, the author never died. You could not separate the art from the artist. Picasso and Neruda and Polanski deserved to be deplatformed.

Whenever Noor disagreed, she leaned back in her chair, nodded, and said, 'Tell me how you arrived there.' This was new for Tara. She didn't have to raise her voice or say something unrelated but venomous to diminish her listener.

By evening, it was Noor's turn to be melancholic.

'It's my sister's birthday,' she said, swirling her tea in a cup.

'Do you want to call her? Sorry, I don't have a phone on me,' said Tara.

'I have a phone… and I don't want to call,' Noor said. 'Love my family but they depress me.'

Returning the courtesy from that afternoon, Tara didn't show curiosity.

'We've been sitting for too long. Let's walk it off,' said Noor.

They left the café and walked one behind the other on the side of the road to avoid the bikes. Tara followed the backs of Noor's ears like tail-lights. They were pierced with many silver studs but Tara could only see the silver screws at the back. After about half an hour of walking in this manner, Noor turned to her and asked her if it would be all right if she kissed her and Tara said yes, and then no, but then came forward and kissed her anyway.

'I didn't mean here on the road, babe!' Noor said, with a laugh.

Then Tara cried, the second time that day, very unlike herself. Noor said they would never do this again. 'Bad for my ego,' she said.

The next day, Noor found and messaged Tara on the library intranet at the language centre.

Are you going to be weird with me now, wrote Noor.

The intranet was a quaint thing. Tara hadn't expected to receive chats on it.

No, of course not. But I am embarrassed, she typed in the chat box.

Don't be. I shouldn't have laughed.

I'm embarrassed you'll think I'm a fence sitter, said Tara. *Also I was surprised. You didn't look like…*

Well, we queer folx don't wear a uniform. We have our own swag ;) Even lesbians from Lucknow. Besides I love fence sitters. Sssoooo full of promise.

Hate to disappoint an optimist, said Tara.

I believe in the radical possibilities of pleasure, babe, Noor signed off with the lyrics of her favourite Bikini Kill song.

They became what old people would call fast friends. Tara had looked Noor up online and her Twitter bio said, 'Muslim, Lesbian, Eco-Feminist, Warrior'. Noor posted a lot of articles about rural entrepreneurs and microfinance with headlines like 'The bestiality of capitalism' and 'Is climate change gendered?' She was quick to get animated when it came to subjects she was passionate about but she wasn't like those girls who were angry all the time. Tara had no patience for those girls, forever playing the victim, complaining, no, whining about things even when things were good, to remind everyone of when they were not good. Tara and Noor spoke about normal things like green smoothie recipes and vegan leather handbags and laughed about Instagram poets. Tara wasn't on Twitter because she thought serious academics shouldn't be. But she thought about what she would put in her bio if she was. To distil herself in four words like Noor would be difficult. She thought of herself as a Wong Kar Wai film with orchestral music, mood lighting and artistic eye makeup.

When the weather was good, the two of them walked higher up the mountain for lunch, where young Israelis had taken up residence. Posters for yoga, Indian cooking and dynamic meditation fought for space on walls. There was an open-air music class where twenty-somethings in pyjama bottoms and tank-tops wrapped their unclean fingers around elegant stringed instruments. It was a population of military kids who had finished their mandatory service and were desperate to learn, to rinse away one set of memories with another.

Tara was here to empty herself. The methodical syntax of Prakrit helped. Routine helped. Running helped. When she emerged after hours of studying, with a headache settled behind her eyes, she ran up the winding mountain roads. She ran till she could feel her lungs had moved up to her throat and till her lips were so chapped from the cold air that it hurt to move them. It helped quiet her mind. She would stop to touch her face and it would be cold and numb, like it was someone else's face.

The afternoons she stayed at the café, she saw Tashi at his Free Tibet meetings. She learnt from Noor that he had a Tibetan mother who had married a local Hindu man, which is why he could run his own café without trouble from the MSS, though she hadn't spotted a single sevak in her month here. It could be that their starched white kurtas were hidden under layers of winter wear.

In the café, as she waited for her lunch, Tashi reappeared from the kitchen with two plates. His ponytail swung as he walked. He was wearing shorts even though it was cold, which impressed Tara. He had bulging, meaty calves—from cycling uphill, perhaps—and the reassuring air of a man who could do useful things in the event of an apocalypse: roll up his sleeves and rappel down a cliff, catch fish with his bare hands and grill them over a fire, have Hanging Garden sex.

Noor hadn't shown up by the time he set the two plates down. He pulled a chair out for himself. Tara praised the buttery fish.

'It's ghee, not butter. That's the trick,' he said.

They ate mostly in silence, with the occasional gesturing between mouthfuls. When they were finished, he signalled to a waiter to clear the plates and went into the kitchen again. A little while later, the waiter brought her a slice of cake with local berries rolling about on a small plate.

Tara ate it hurriedly. She paid and was getting up to leave when Tashi returned.

'How is it that I've never seen you here for dinner?'

'I've had momos for dinner every single night since I arrived.'

'From Lung Ta, I hope?'

'Yes.'

'Come home for dinner tonight if you like. My babies are with me this month. I like them to meet new people.' He pulled out his phone to show her his screensaver with two infants. 'Twins. Surya and Rafael. They're six and a half now,' he said. Tara thought she should say something before he started showing her all the photos of his children that he had on his phone.

'Maybe I can ask Noor too?' she said. 'You know Noor? I eat with her every day…'

'Everybody knows Noor. Sure, come by seven? I'll write down the address.'

'Their mother lives in Berlin,' Tashi added, as she was leaving.

On her way back to her flat, Tara stopped by the Tibetan co-operative to ask Noor. She was always there with the women in the afternoons. But Noor had dinner plans and couldn't come.

Tara's flat was on the top floor of a simple white three-storeyed building with an open staircase that wrapped around the structure, leading to balconies at every level. Tara stood on her balcony as she waited for the clock to go a little past seven, then she went in and showered. The water pressure in the mountains was pitiable. But there was also less to wash away.

Back in Delhi, her bathroom was tiled in a rainforest theme.

Baba had picked for her a rain shower that played birdsong and changed colours to mimic the dappled light on a forest floor. But the tubelight in the bathroom here, the small round mirror in the plastic frame above the sink, these things didn't bother her as much as she had imagined they would.

She took out an indigo maxi dress from her suitcase. It was still folded, with a laundry tag from Mysore. She studied her face in the bathroom mirror and decided to put on mascara. She put her toothbrush and a few other things in her sling bag.

Tara loved male bodies. She had a recurring dream in which all the boys she had fucked were lined up against a wall, naked. Their faces were obscured but she knew them by their bodies. She liked their jaws, the chins with a two-day stubble. She liked the way shirt cuffs sat when rolled on a solid forearm. A wrist that could hold an oversized watch. The bone in the middle of the chest. The deep river of their spines. The hard triangle where the river formed a delta. She liked to cup their ass. Feel muscle flex under the flat of her palm. She liked calves that bulged from exercise. The smells in the corners of their bodies. Not those bright new smells. Old-school musk and amber. She liked the things boys did. The way they strained their faces while they shaved. The way they wrapped a towel low on their waist after a shower. The way they pretended not to notice when she stared. The way she could make them hard with a fingernail grazing skin. The way she could make their eyes soft. The exultation with which they dipped roti in mutton curry, undid bra hooks and zippered dresses. Fingers, except fingers with rings. She loved fingers with neatly trimmed nails.

*

TASHI'S HOUSE was easy to find. He had drawn her a map on a paper napkin, marking it out with the drawing of a plate, fork and knife.

It had a sloping green roof weighed down by a great mass of red rhododendron. Through the metal gate, she could see two children's bicycles fallen in front of the main door in a haphazard manner. As she lifted and dropped the gate's heavy metal latch, it grated against the gravel. The front door opened and Tashi stepped out. He waved with an oven-gloved hand.

'Am I late?' she asked.

'Late for what?' he said, ushering her in.

The door opened without preamble into a living room. The house of a man with nothing to hide. There was never a place to take off shoes in homes like this. There were no ceiling lights: only lampshades that made yellow pools around them. Her mother wouldn't have liked that. On the walls, Tara could see the landscape photographs that were in the café last week. There was an open kitchen with a dining table. Tashi went straight to the kitchen counter and occupied himself with the final touches on a plate of what looked like very tiny chicken legs. She had forgotten to tell him she didn't eat poultry. He hadn't asked.

She heard giggles and feet. A brown mutt, which resembled all the other lazy dogs in the town, bounded in. Two children, dressed in identical denim overalls, followed.

The little girl ran over and put her arms around her father. The boy, practising to be a man, took Tara by the hand and led her to the table.

'This is where I sit and this is where Surya sits but you can sit anywhere you want,' said Rafael. Both children had hair the colour of wheat. They looked nothing like their father.

She looked up at Tashi, who was helping Surya count cutlery from a kitchen drawer. The phone was ringing on a low tone but Tashi didn't pay it any attention. He would probably tell her later that man wasn't meant to be summoned by a machine.

'May I help?' she asked.

She wanted to hide the box of pineapple cream pastries she had brought from the bakery on the market road. They felt cold and cheap. The art director of a good film would definitely have thrown them out for not belonging in the scene. She placed the box on one end of the kitchen counter, hoping it wouldn't be noticed.

'We're ready. Would you mind waiting till they're done?' said Tashi, gesturing to the children. He opened a bottle of barley wine for her.

'Not at all. I'm sorry I'm late,' said Tara. 'I had some writing to finish.'

As they ate, the twins asked her about her favourite fruits and the names of her dogs. They refused to believe there were people who didn't have dogs, or had only one dog. Tara made up some names. When Tashi went upstairs with them to put them to bed, she poured herself more wine and walked over to the bookshelf. She thought it might reveal a peculiar obsession. A girl in her hostel wing arranged books in the order in which she'd read them. She knew someone who arranged books alphabetically by title. The absolute worst ones arranged them by colour. Tashi's bookshelf appeared to be arranged broadly by genre; it had more of those history of mankind books and several books on the Tibetan freedom struggle. There were art catalogues and food magazines. On one of the shelves was a small brass Hanuman with a lotus-shaped incense holder beside it. The incense had burnt to ash and fallen around it. How many days ago? She didn't know. But only a half-Indian boy would have Hanuman on a bookshelf.

Over dinner, Tashi told her about being sent away to live with his grandparents in Canada and returning to Dharamsala in his early twenties. He told her about his spiritual awakening while backpacking across Cambodia. How he had met and married a woman with a half-identity too.

'We are mongrels,' he said, a little too cheerfully, like he'd practised the line for effect.

'How did you know you were meant to end up here?' Tara asked.

'Do we end up anywhere? There is no being, only becoming. My mother used to say that.'

Despite his ponytail and pop philosophy, he was earnest, like an engineering graduate from a second-tier city. He spoke to her about the ambivalence of the Indian government to the Tibetan cause. The many licences required to run a restaurant in the country. The ideological struggle with deciding his children's citizenship.

'When you have children, your way of seeing the world changes. You have to make choices that are best for them,' he said.

He told her it was one of the reasons his wife and he had separated.

He narrated to her in much detail why he had started representing Tibetan artists. 'And why should Tibetan artists be expected to only produce art that is political or about Tibet?' he said.

'...They too should have the opportunity to be mediocre and self-centred,' added Tara.

She took a sip of her wine and laughed. She wasn't sure Tashi understood her joke. He wasn't drinking himself but offered her more wine. She didn't want it. Maybe he wasn't slow, maybe he just hadn't heard her? She already had her doubts about him after he told her that he didn't listen to music with lyrics because they distracted from the melody. She couldn't wait to laugh about that with Noor. She was feeling a pressure in the back of her head. The floor was rising towards her. She saw a lipstick mark on the rim of the glass and remembered it was her own.

Tashi pointed to a slim book that Tara had picked out from his shelf: *Praises to the 21 Taras.*

'Why are you called Tara?' he asked.

'My grandfather named me Nayantara. *The twinkle in his eyes.* It's also a little flower in Bengali. I like Tara. It means so many things… it means "brilliant star" in most Indo-Iranian languages. Tara is also the second of the Dasa Mahavidyas, the great wisdom goddesses: a pretty fearsome one,' said Tara.

'Fearsome? For us Tibetans, she's a patient and peaceful one. The mother of liberation. We believe Tara is greater than a goddess, she's a female Buddha,' said Tashi. 'My mother would read out *Praises to the 21 Taras* on Losar. She would…'

'Greater than a goddess! I assume that's meant to be a compliment like "she drives like a man, drinks like a man",' said Tara.

'That's not how I meant it,' said Tashi.

Tara grabbed the bottle of water on the table and drank from it. She deserved a long night at the end of this long evening listening to this man contemplate life and living. Tashi was now sitting with his brows furrowed and hooking and unhooking his fork with his knife. This was the first time she had had dinner with the children of a man with whom she was on a date. Though nothing about the evening had felt date-like so far. The man just didn't stop talking about himself! Some dates don't make for good conversation. It didn't mean the whole thing had to go badly.

One of her friends had told her that she always waited for the guy to bring up sex in conversation. It made her feel desired. For Tara, being desired was a given. Even a gay man she had once kissed had drunkenly pressed his thumbs into the tops of her shoulders, and told her he wanted her right there on the dance floor at that terrace party. Boys were intimidated by her (some had told her later). And so it was always up to her to raise the red lantern.

Tashi had carried their empty plates to the sink and was now running hot water over them. Steam rose from the sink.

Tara walked over to where he was and leaned over the kitchen counter. She examined the rough granite of the countertop with her fingers. 'I'm allergic to latex condoms,' she said.

Tashi finished rinsing the plates and looked up. 'Oh, I have a friend who's allergic to garlic, can you believe it? So what do you do?' he replied, while looking for a dishcloth.

'I carry my own lambskin ones,' she said. 'It's different but I think you'll like them.' She was brushing something off the front of her dress, admiring how the fabric fell below her waist. She looked up at Tashi. He was wiping his hands, wiping between each finger, with the dishcloth.

'Would you like some tea?' he said, finally.

Tara propped her chin on her hands, still leaning on the kitchen counter. Her face crumpled. She shook her head.

'Listen, it's hard for me to believe I'm saying this,' he said. He patted her cheek like he had patted Surya's earlier that evening.

'Is the wine making you sick too? I don't think I'm going to

140

have this barley wine again. My head hurts,' Tara said. She kicked off her shoes and tried to hoist herself on to the kitchen counter. But the floor was rising towards her again and gravity was an alien concept. She slipped. Tashi helped her on to the counter.

He laughed. Louder than he needed to. Men have a nervous laughter too. It's just not called that.

'I wish I was sick. No, it's my babies, Tara. You don't seem too sure of yourself right now. I have to be careful... I... I can't do anything that could take them away from me. Wait, are you sure you don't want some tea?'

Tara could feel her ears turning red.

She used to have a dream in which her head had become transparent. Her hair, skull, the innards of her brain had all become see-through like the acrylic handbags in old copies of *Vogue*. She woke up from these dreams terrified, her face hot, her neck sweating.

She walked to the chair where she had left her sling bag and opened it, pretending to look for something inside. Tashi told her she absolutely must come by for breakfast sometime because the house was different in natural light. He was courteous. He was making an effort to soothe her, which Tara would appreciate later. But for now she needed to get away.

THE NEXT morning, Noor came around with a bag of oranges.

Tara's third-floor flat had no doorbell. Noor's knocks were always evenly spaced and straightforward, like a policewoman's in a TV show.

Tara had come to Dharamsala with one suitcase and had now

acquired possessions that wouldn't fit into several cartons. She had spilled into the flat tastefully, in various shades of blue. There were Tangkhas and prayer flags on the walls, rugs of different sizes, and tiny pottery items that didn't have any obvious purpose. The functional furniture only comprised a bed in the bedroom and a floor mattress in the living room, on which Noor and Tara talked for hours in what they called their mattress sessions. Noor would usually come over with two ganja chocolate balls and worry her with something new she had read—flowers were changing colour to adapt to rising temperatures and so on. Tara would read aloud Sanskrit poetry with simultaneous English translation, which her punk-music-loving friend had lately become fond of.

No one ever came over except Noor, not even anyone to cook or clean, so Tara barely paid attention to what she was wearing. When she heard the knocks, louder than the pounding in her own head that morning, she wrapped the quilt around her to answer the door. The small electric radiator she had rented was just enough to keep her warm while she was in bed. She was wearing pyjamas with mangoes printed on them; and flip-flops with pom-poms.

Noor's long black hair was braided in several places and then gathered high. Under the jacket that she had now shed, she was wearing a shirt that carried its freshly washed status like pandits on the streets of Benaras. It made Tara wish she wasn't in her pyjamas.

Noor dropped her satchel on the floor. She took the oranges with her to the kitchen. She had brought a business magazine with her that had a cover story on KC Meenakshi. 'Changing the Tide', the headline read. 'Read some news once in a while,' said

Noor, flinging the magazine on the mattress. 'Babe, this woman's a champ,' she added, from the kitchen. 'She's a fishing magnate from Mumbai. I'm trying to organize a talk with her for the women in the co-op here.'

'Will she bring fish when she comes? I miss fish,' said Tara, suddenly sullen.

'Didn't you have a big dinner last night with mister chef? How was it?' said Noor, returning with two bowls.

'It was grilled quail. I'd never had quail before.'

'A change of menu for you! Is your name Miss Nayantara Mallick?'

'I am still off poultry. Quail is a game bird, so it was not wrong to eat it,' said Tara.

'And then what happened?' said Noor.

'Nothing happened.'

Noor narrowed her eyes. 'Liar,' she said.

'You know we might fail our own Bechdel Test,' said Tara.

'Why? We don't only talk about your boy stuff. We talk about other things. Last week we spoke about the historical significance of graveyards,' Noor said, laughing. 'Besides, I'm not interested in talking about the boys. I'm interested in talking about the sex.' She was peeling oranges, spraying the air between them with a Mediterranean drizzle. She held up one she had finished peeling for Tara.

'Ode to the Orange,' said Noor.

'I don't eat oranges,' said Tara.

'You order orange-carrot juice at Tashi's all the time. How can you refuse the fruit of faaa-yeeerrrr!'

'It's too early in the morning to argue Neruda with you.'

'Whatever your thoughts on the man, it's a beautiful poem. And both things are true.'

'I don't know how to eat an orange.'

'You peel them and put them in your mouth,' said Noor, demonstrating the act of eating, and licking her lips obscenely.

'My father used to peel them for me.'

'I am peeling them for you.'

'No, he'd peel that thin skin and fork out the insides too.'

Noor put her hands up. 'This explains everything. You must be disappointed Tashi didn't carry you around in a palki, Your Highness Princess Nayantara of your own esteemed Himalayan Kingdom.'

Tara stuck out her tongue at Noor. She picked up an orange segment from the bowl and bit into it. Pulp squirted on either side of her lip. She hadn't brushed her teeth yet. The citrus waters washed her tongue in unfamiliar ways. She walked over to the dustbin in the kitchen, pressed the pedal with her foot, and spat it out.

'Noorie, I've decided I'm going to come to your yoga class this evening,' she said, returning from the kitchen.

'Babe, you don't need yoga. What you need is an Ikea fuck. Off-the-shelf. Easy to assemble. No defects.'

The girls burst out laughing.

Noor's phone rang but she let it ring out. She went over to where Tara was standing and fed her a mouthful of orange pulp with a spoon.

They were interrupted by someone at the door. There were shuffling sounds, some fumbling with the latch and then finally a loud thup-thup on the wood.

It was the old woman from the reception desk at the language centre. She had walked up the three floors and her breath was caught in her throat. The girls asked her if she'd like to sit. She couldn't, she had left the reception unattended. Tara got her a glass of water while Noor stroked her back. She still didn't say anything. Noor's phone rang once more. There was never a good signal in Tara's flat. She picked up her jacket and satchel and ran down the stairs, signalling to Tara that she would come by later.

THAT WAS how Tara received the news. On a slip of paper in a spidery scrawl: 'Father died. Call Surjo.' The message reached her in this manner because she had not responded to the many messages left at the language centre the day before.

The woman remained silent and gave her two other slips of paper. They were as redundant as romance novels were these days. 'Urgent from New Jersey. Call.' 'We are trying to reach you. About Baba.' She handed her the notes with the same equanimity with which she conveyed messages when Tara missed her mother's calls. Tara was never particular about calling back. When she did, her mother had the same questions about money, sweaters, covering her ears while running, eating enough rice. She rarely made any calls to her family from Dharamsala unless it was to tell them to transfer money or courier her books. The woman held Tara's hands, closed her eyes and said a long prayer. Before Tara could say anything, she had turned around and left.

Tara's first instinct was to look out from her balcony. There was the sky, the pagodas of the Dalai Lama temple rising in the distance, the big deodar spreading its limbs like men on public buses, the tea stall opposite the road, and even the Pahari cow with colourful beads around her neck who parked herself there daily. The cycles chained in a row to a metal railing were not there. It was past nine now, and they had made their way into other streets and lanes, their destiny yoked to their owners. The world, with its order and rhythm, was in order. Only her father, older than her world, was gone.

As children, Tara and Surjo would laugh when they heard servants use the word 'expire' for deceased relatives. Medicines and packaged foods expire. Can a human being finish his purpose, literally cease to be useful? As a child she had found the misplaced usage funny. It seemed cruel now. But the democracy of death in the English language seemed unfair. A terrorist could be dead in an encounter. A rogue elephant could be shot dead. And now, her father too, was just dead. In Indian tongues, a common criminal and her father would sway the verbs to conjugate differently.

She saw Noor's braided head bobbing down the road. Should she shout from across the road and tell her what had happened? If Noor hadn't come around that morning, she would still have been sleeping and missed this altogether. None of this would have happened. No, calling Noor would confirm the matter. She would look into her eyes and put her arms around her and that would make her cry. Maybe there had been a mistake. Whose father did the notes refer to? It must be Laura's father. Poor Laura. She would call and console her. But why would Surjo call him Baba? They had only one Baba. There had to have been a mistake, but she couldn't work out what.

She put on her jacket, which was hanging on a hook near the door from last night, and started walking towards the language centre. The grocery store in her lane, where she bought her bottled water, had a phone. But it was too loud in there. She would have to walk to the language centre and use the phone there. It was ten minutes away. It would be quiet and she would be able to hear Surjo and then they would laugh about the confusion. Then her father would snatch the phone from Surjo and say something clever.

The sun hadn't gained in strength yet and Tara's jacket flapped about her knees as she walked. She stopped to start buttoning it but her fingers were stiff. Then she realized it was her feet that were cold. She was wearing flip-flops. She would have to walk fast and get this over with—what if she ran into Tashi in this outfit of mango-printed pyjamas, flip-flops with pom-poms, and an elegant silk jacket? Still, she made an effort to acknowledge everybody she usually smiled at on the market road. She crossed the man at the momos counter at Lung Ta who gestured to his momo pot and seemed to be asking why she didn't get dinner from him last night. She nodded at the woman who tried to sell her a silver jewellery set with turquoise stones every day. She smiled at the boy selling cut fruit and a group of students she always saw at the centre but had never spoken to. When the language centre loomed just ahead, she slowed down. Suddenly she regretted having walked so fast. She felt hungry. She hadn't had breakfast. Why didn't Noor bring something more useful than oranges? She turned around and walked back to the fruit seller and asked for a bowl of cut fruit. He gave her pineapple, banana, watermelon and a few strawberries on top. She asked for more slices of pineapple. It would take time, she'd have to wait while he cut a new one. She would wait, she said. She buttoned up her jacket properly as she waited. After she was done eating, she walked towards the centre again.

The language centre looked minimal from the outside. Inside, it was gaudy. White tubelights lit every flaw. A round of global grants had enabled a new library wing, and a coffee counter in the lobby. Students usually crowded around that. But the lobby was deserted today. The coffee machine was not making its usual noises. It was Christmas break and a large number of foreign students had gone home. It was just the monks and her. A young monk in crimson robes was making a call, so she waited in line. He always seemed to be around the phone. Weren't they supposed to give up the world? Who did he call? When he finally finished, she wiped the receiver with her sleeve and called Surjo. Laura picked up. She said she was sorry for her loss.

Tara felt like she had when she had been on a rollercoaster ride for the first time. There had been a thrill when the ride started, going straight at first then curving upwards in a large semicircular loop. Baba had been beside her in the coupe. It had always been like that: Baba and her, Ma and Surjo. These were the family teams even when they played carrom. She had held on to his arm through his shirtsleeves, her little-girl nails digging into him. They had reached the top and she had got a glimpse of the entire amusement park— how small the people looked! 'And you, Tara rani, are on top of the world,' Baba had said. 'You and I on top of the world.' She and Baba had looked at each other for a moment, and screamed. But when the ride went past the loop and started a downward spiral, the hollow sensation in her stomach had caught her by surprise. All her insides had been scooped out. She was skin and heartbeat. She didn't know if it was thrill or fear. 'Ekhuni shesh hobe, Tara rani,' she had heard her father say over the collective screams of children and adults. This would be over soon, all she had to do was hold on tight to the railing in front.

Now, Laura was telling her she was sorry for her loss. This would be over soon, Tara told herself. Then Surjo came on the line and started giving her details. She heard a jumble of words. Heart failure. Monitor. ICU. They had tried reaching her over the weekend, but the language centre was closed. On being unable to get her to call back even on Monday morning, they had gone ahead with the cremation. How soon could she come? She tried to register all this. She was beginning to feel angry but then Surjo's voice became brittle and cracked. She felt tender towards her older brother. He had never been good at showing emotion. He dealt with crises by retreating emotionally, obsessing about logistics, and sometimes by physically demanding work. When their dog Mishti had died, he had polished both the family cars with a piece of chamois leather, something he'd never done before. He was telling her about death registration in New Jersey and other complicated things that she made no effort to understand. Then her mother came on the phone. Her voice was high and low, she was sobbing. 'We had to do what was practical,' she heard the voice say. It made Tara spill over. She started screaming into the phone. No known words. Just sounds she didn't know she had inside her. The old woman who had handed her the phone now gave her a glass of water. She didn't gesture to her to quiet down like she usually did when Tara laughed into the phone while speaking to her friends from Delhi.

Surjo came back on the phone and told her that if she wasn't coming to New Jersey, she should prepare to go to Delhi to be with Ma, who would be returning in two weeks. The milky sponge of sibling affection between them had dried up after Tara had made all that fuss about his wedding. Surjo knew his sister was headstrong but even he hadn't thought she would go that far. 'Weddings are an instrument of perpetuating regressive patriarchy,' she had emailed not just him and Laura, but also the extended family. Shashi and Surjo had tried to reason with her. Then Robi had said it was unfair to force her to do something she didn't want to do. Tara had proceeded to walk in and out of the house in running shorts while silk-clad guests roamed the garden and corridors for various wedding ceremonies, looking at her with both mild disgust and awe. She had participated in the lunch feast on all days, however. Poornima had told her the fish croquettes were too good to miss.

But the bond between siblings is old as life itself. Perhaps they leave messages for each other on the walls of the womb. She started to cry as she was talking to Surjo. He was the only other person who could share her precise sentiment. Surjo told her again that she should stall her Dark Ages retreat, and go to Delhi. She and Ma would need each other.

It was an absurd suggestion. Seeing her mother would make her father go even farther from her reach. Ma was always telling him not to take something up, not to go somewhere, not to meet someone, not to change things in the house again. When she was seven, the old Italian duchess her father spoke so much about had invited him over again. A global congress of architects was being put together to plan interventions to save Venice from sinking. He would be her nominee at the congress. It would involve moving to Italy for at least two or three years. Her mother had put her foot down. The children's schooling would be disrupted, she had said. Italy was not like England, Singapore or America. How would

Surjo adapt to a change of school just years before college? Surjo
was old enough to think about the appeal of girls in bikinis and
their powdery deodorant smells. He wanted to go. Tara wanted to
go because she saw how happy her father was. And she'd fought
with Diya in school that day over glow-in-the-dark stickers. Shashi
had involved Robi's parents and triumphed. They had stayed in
Delhi all their lives. Her father went away on projects for a few
months at a time. He never brought up Italy again.

Tara put the phone receiver down and sat in a chair in the lobby
of the language centre all afternoon. Her foreboding yesterday at
the café was a rehearsal for today. She thought Surjo would call
back and say this was all a mistake. Your father didn't die, someone
else's did. But no such call arrived. The old woman left for lunch
and returned. The few students who had been hidden so far in
the rooms started pouring out by 4 p.m. Days ended early in the
mountains. Finally, Tara too peeled herself away from the chair
and walked out into the fading sunlight. Vendors were wrapping
cloths around their wares. The fruit seller was discarding the day's
peelings in a large bin. The birds were flying low. Lost tourists, as
usual, were trying to match what they saw on their phone screens
with signs on the road. Tara was in the habit of going over and
guiding people even when they didn't know they needed help.
Today it was a family comprising a young couple and a little girl,
must have been five, holding on to the hands of her parents, linking
them to her and one another. While the adults were busy, the little
girl pointed to the pom-poms on Tara's feet and smiled. She lifted
the pom-poms hanging at the ends of her winter cap to show Tara.
But there was nothing in common between them, Tara thought.
She was jealous of the child. The parents were calling out to Tara,

asking which way Mountain Bliss guest house was, but she turned and started to walk away.

Tara thought about her father's hands. Hands around her hands, teaching her how to brush her teeth. Tying her shoelaces—no, that was probably Surjo. Hands on the bicycle handlebars. Once, when she still had a bicycle with trainer wheels, he had picked her up from school and taken her in an aeroplane to Kolkata because Dadu was to have a minor surgery and had demanded to see his granddaughter. The flight was full but they had let her travel on her father's lap. She had sat facing him, put her head on his chest and slept. Baba all to herself, no Surjo, no Ma, no Zeenat-Daya-Khosla-Cyrus, no phone calls from the office. His chest smelled of a faraway lemon, not the kind they squeezed on tomatoes and cucumber at lunch. After she had woken up and eaten a giant cheese sandwich, her father had told her to go up to the front and ask to meet the captain. He had told her what to say. The air hostess had pulled her cheeks and taken her to the cockpit. They had all called her a smart girl. Pretty girl. Daddy's girl. They had given her tamarind sweets with so much sugar that she could feel the grains grind in her mouth. When they got off the plane there was a commotion. A huge crowd had gathered and her father was trying to push his way through—she was holding on to one of his fingers with both her hands. It was a maze of legs and sweaty, damp clothes. She could see the skin on women's backs where their saree blouses ended, the leather belts strung into the loops of men's pants. Somebody stepped on her shoe. Metal buckles from bags poked her now and then. One uncle put his hand on her bum. She let go of her father's finger. It was only a few minutes before her father found her and lifted her up. But those few minutes had felt dark like she had never known darkness. She had cried and cried and her father had wiped her face with a checked handkerchief and promised her he would never let go again.

As she walked towards her flat, Tara was cold once more. She had missed lunch but she wasn't hungry. She needed to go to the loo. She had been sitting on that chair all afternoon. Her head was spinning. She stepped off the market road to enter a narrow lane and walked along it. She saw a compound with an open gate. Inside, there was a garden patch in front of a house with a few low plants. Tara stepped into the mud and pulled down her pyjamas. The vinegar smell of piss filled her nostrils. It felt good to squat low, to see the world like that. As she was getting up, an adolescent boy entered the gate. He looked at her with an expression she couldn't name. She tied an elaborate bow with her pyjama strings and walked out of the gate. She wasn't cold any more so she walked slowly, lifting each foot like it was made of sticky tar. She made her way back to her flat but the idea of changing out of her pyjamas, showering, brushing her teeth, or even eating, all of that felt unnecessary. The only thing to do right now would be to hold Baba. To put her arms around him and inhale his Penhaligon's smell, her cheeks touching his chest through his thin white cotton panjabi, his palms cradling her face as if it was made of glass. If it was so important, so essential to her very being, why had she not put her face in his palms more often? Why had she left home at all? Why didn't she call home more often? Why had she come to Dharamsala? Why wasn't she with him now, in New Jersey, with whatever physical form of Baba was still left in the world?

*

TARA HAD always been second in class. Her teachers complained that sometimes she purposely left the last few questions unanswered. No one liked the girls who came first. The boys avoided them, and it made the other girls talk about you with their hands cupped to their face. Her report cards said she was an 'all rounder'. The juniors worshipped her. They all wanted to be Nayantara 'Tara' Mallick. She won gold medals for the school in track: hundred and two hundred metre sprints only. She didn't enjoy long-distance running. Tara and her best friend Diya had managed to get the entire Class Seven Division C expelled midway through a school screening of *Chitty Chitty Bang Bang* for 'the shameful act of littering the school auditorium with popcorn kernels'. These things go down in school history as heroic acts but still stay within safe realms. Tara wasn't rebellious in the way some other girls were, wanting to get piercings or tattoos or having older boyfriends who waited for them outside school on bikes. Her rebellion had come instead in the choice of her undergraduate degree, when she opted to study Sanskrit instead of English Literature or Psychology or Economics, as her friends had. She picked a small, nondescript department in Delhi University even as her parents had been counting on her to go abroad, like all the children of their friends. Surjo had assured Shashi and Robi that it was a phase she would outgrow. But to their surprise, after a master's degree, she had found her way first to an obscure research fellowship and then a doctoral programme in a small town that didn't even have its own international airport. She had insisted that the Indian Institute of Languages and Literature in Mysore was the best place for her to pursue doctoral studies. She told them she had a long-term plan.

Some of her discipline came from kathak. Twice a week, every week for fourteen years, putting on the uniform of white churidar-kurta with a green dupatta, braiding her hair and tying the ghungroos on her ankles.

Her kathak Guruji was an old man with paan-stained teeth, a white kurta-pyjama and a pair of canes. A soft one for the little ones. A hard, long one for the older students. He called her Tara kumari. But the stick knew no such honour. A little misstep and he would hit her ankles just above where the line of the ankle bells were tied. She remembered being hit only a few times in all those years, but her ankles carried the memory brightly. All she needed was a slight movement of the stick in his hands to gather everything in her body and mind and fall into step. She had always fallen into step. *Tat-tat Thun-thun.*

Her friendships knew no such discipline. People went in and out, bonds soared and soured. 'Are we allowed to talk about Diya today?' Surjo would say over breakfast to tease her, and Tara would throw her spoon at him.

Diya and Tara had been inseparable since they were six years old. They went to the same school and the same kathak class. They would often board each other's school buses without telling their mothers and alight, fingers locked, at either one of their homes. A few weeks after Tara's seventeenth birthday party, when the Mallick house had been taken over by a gaggle of girls for a weekend, Tara had said Diya should never be mentioned again. Then Diya went away to Trinity, and they never spoke again.

Once every year or so, Tara would say she was breaking her

heart. The process of breakage and restoration usually lasted a week. After Senthil, it had lasted several weeks. She vomited everything she ate even though her mother cooked her favourite foods and took her out shopping. Her father had stayed home all weekend. Finally, on Sunday morning, he had said, 'These boys are not worthy of you.'

'And if I'm forever alone?'

'Study, write, travel, learn to play the piano I bought for you, spend your weekends in museums. Live with us in the house you've always loved.' He had held her face and pulled her to his chest. This will always be here for you, that had said. Without the real estate of her father's chest, Tara was without home.

Her father had taught her to carefully wax the bottoms of paper boats so she would win when they raced the boats in puddles of rainwater. When the cement was being poured in front of the Delhi house, Surjo and Tara had been told not to walk on it. But she had walked over the wet cement with Mishti. Tara prints and Mishti prints still marked the front porch. Robi had never filled over it.

Who would love her like her father?

TARA WALKED up the stairs to her flat. When she put her head on her pillow, it felt like she hadn't slept for days. Her eyelids felt sticky, like sugar syrup had been poured over them, but she couldn't get to the boiling point of sleep. Her mind wouldn't stop turning. In the silent meditation retreat she had attended when she had just arrived in Dharamsala, the teacher had pointed at clouds and said those were her thoughts. That day, they were soft and frothy. Another day they could be dense and ominous. But clouds always pass, the teacher said. She had to remember that she was the vast sky.

She was at a table with everyone's faces turned towards her. In front of her was a large bowl of oranges. She was trying to peel them, but the skins remained stuck. Then she saw her father across from her at the other end of the table and asked him to help her. But he remained still. He didn't move at all. As she stared at him, crying helplessly, he started to melt like a grotesque Dali artwork.

When she woke up the next morning, the sky was the bleak grey of hospital furniture. She felt as hungry as she would after a long run. She dropped her clothes on the floor and walked into the shower. She turned the water lever to very hot. It burnt her skin, making red splotches where it arrived. When she put her hand under the hot water, she felt the burning in her thigh. When she turned to have the hot water run down her back, she felt her feet burning. She was grateful that her nerves were disordered.

She heard steady knocks on the door. At first she thought she wouldn't open it. She would let the whole day go by and then tomorrow she would call Surjo and her mother again. But the knocks came again. They were Noor's. She couldn't see her face in the bathroom mirror. It had fogged up. She put on a clean pair of pyjamas and opened the door. The clothes clung to her wet skin. She had forgotten to dry herself. Noor was with Tashi.

'Sonam from the language centre told me. I didn't know what you might need so I got Tashi along,' Noor said, as she went towards Tara to put her arms around her. 'I'm so sorry, babe,' she added. She gave Tara a flask. It looked like an old woman's flask.

'Sonam,' said Noor. 'I told her I was coming here so she gave me the flask. Want some tea?'

Tashi had his eyes down. He was fiddling with his motorcycle keys. When the girls untangled, he looked up and asked if he could book her a taxi to Delhi? Take her suitcases down? Drive her to the bus stop or airport?

'There's nowhere to go right now,' said Tara. It was the first time she had spoken since the phone call and her voice startled her. She was surprised by the simple act of speaking. That her lips could part, her lungs pump air, her mouth form words. All of this astonished her. Noor saying she was at a loss for what to do astonished her.

'Have you had anything to eat?' said Noor.

Tara nodded.

Tashi left to bring them sandwiches from the café. Noor had brought her laptop and books with her. Tara sat down, not beside her, but at some distance. She was angry with the intrusion but as she sipped the salted tea from the cap of the flask, she warmed up to it. From time to time, she glanced at Noor, facing away from her to read. She could see the knobs of her spine through her red turtleneck.

Noor was deeply engrossed in her reading, underlining things with great purpose.

'Shall we go to the cemetery?' Tara said.

'Anything you want. After lunch?'

'Now.'

At the cemetery, Tara read the epitaphs again and cried. This time, Noor didn't say anything but she cried too, turning away from her friend as she did.

TARA SLEPT a lot in the days that followed. She told Jigme she would not be attending the Prakrit classes for a while. After breakfast, Tara and Noor would sit in the flat and study. Tashi would usually bring or send lunch or they would make a salad. In the afternoon, Noor left for the Tibetan co-operative workshop and she usually returned with the ganja chocolate balls. The hard part of the day was after their mattress session, after they had finished eating their momo dinner, and Noor had left for home.

On one of her runs around Dharamsala—before she had chosen to become housebound—she'd taken a leafy mountain trail and chanced upon a patch of fireflies. She stood there as it grew darker and the fireflies brighter. But when she walked towards them they dimmed, or disappeared. She was in the presence of fireflies but it was hard to understand where they were and where they would be the next moment. She tried to touch them with her hands but they seemed to recede when she did.

Tara tried to write things down, hoping the ruled pages of her journal would order her mind. She wanted to record everything about her father. She imagined she was composing an elaborate obituary. There must have been a few in the papers but she didn't want to read them. She wrote down the things he spoke about. The blurbs from his magazine interviews which she had read many times:

A building is immobile but it doesn't mean it doesn't have the capacity to move. It's the way that light enters, the way that air circulates through the space, that gives it movement.

Architecture is the precise manifestation of what it means to be human. The role of an architect is to set the internal human creative impulse in concrete.

But these were not private memories. They were not hers alone. She switched to making a list of personal recollections. She wrote down the stories he repeated often: the hostel escapades with Bibek, the time that Dolly Pishi had gone missing, the tsunami while he was in the Andamans. Can you remember a whole life in neat lines? How does one choose what to remember? A life isn't a play that you can review. There are no fixed seats.

Tara had seen a play in Mysore on the life of the city's eighteenth-century ruler. When the play opens, Tipu Sultan's court historian is talking to a British officer who has asked him to write about the sultan's last days. As they recall the final siege when Tipu Sultan was killed on the ramparts, fighting alongside his soldiers, the court historian says, 'I remember thinking, I will never forget the look on his face. But I have. I cannot remember his face at that moment. It's such a betrayal.'

If remembering is love, what is forgetting?

Her Didu, her mother's mother, had asked her grandchildren to call her by her name, because there was no one alive who called her by her name any more. She was afraid it would be forgotten. Her name was Indubala. Little moon. She was born when the moon was a thin sliver.

What was the song Baba had sung when they were on the deck of the cruise and everyone had asked him to sing a Bollywood song? What was the title of the bedtime story he had written and illustrated only for her because Mishti had destroyed her favourite book? What had finally made them speak that time they had fought and not spoken for four days? They fought often, but what was that fight about that summer when they were going around in the vaporetto in Venice? She remembered his clothes while disembarking the vaporetto, bright as a full-colour advertisement. Was that before he started wearing only black?

Tara had unwrapped two new notebooks. But she had filled only a few pages so far. The words and scenes to describe her love for her father, they were not pouring out as she had expected. They were lodged in her throat, in her eyes.

Just a few months ago, she had been a far more fluent chronicler. She had made an inventory of all the times she and AD had made love. Encounters as scenes, as she imagined a film script might read. Snatches of conversation as marginalia. She had written down the things he had said to her, the names he had given her: 'Walking distance, risky unit of measure, isn't it?' 'Do you dance?' 'Ginger kumari.' 'Bhartrihari's bride.' 'Hansini.' The memory of him made her touch the back of her neck. Before he came, his hands reached the back of her neck to pull imaginary hair. There was never enough of it to hold after she had cut it. Hansini, he called her, swan-necked. She had written everything down. When you're in love, you want the feeling to last forever. Eros strangles Thanatos. The synaesthesia is total. A person is a colour. The sight of a white shirt can make you weep. The ceiling fan's whirring can make you throb. It was a wonder to her that new lovers kept their food down. The Persians were on to something when they spoke about emotion being stored in the liver. There was a constant uneasiness in her stomach, or butterflies, as old people called it. It was more like half a dozen hummingbirds flap-flapping their wings as though spring had arrived. When she saw him in the lecture room; when she walked beside him on campus; when he walked towards her, dropping his trousers by the bed, the feeling stayed. It was only when he bit her earlobes, made his tongue hard and circled her nipples, when he ran his fingers on the insides of her thighs, when he was inside her, when he pushed her knees to her chest or pressed against her shoulder blades, when he held the back of her neck and came, and later, as he slumped back on the bed and lay with one arm folded behind his head, his glasses on his nose, seeing something on his phone, that was when the flapping of the wings stopped.

She had had sex since she was seventeen. But what was it about this time with AD? Was it because Bilhana's verses had introduced her to what the poet called *the hot taste of life*? The ancients understood heat. That's why they tried to learn ways to quell desire. The fasting, the meditation, the chanting, they were all only attempts to tame heat. It was a disease that could burn your skin and your insides. Make your brain become cotton. Why else would Bilhana's hero compose verses of passion on his way to the executioner, preferring the certainty of execution to separation? Why did Bilhana start each of the fifty verses of the *Chaurapanchasika* with *adyapi*: even now? Does a lover never stop looking back?

Even now
I think your feet seek mine to comfort them.
There is some dream about you even now
Which I'll not hear at waking. Weep not at dawn,
Though day brings wearily your daily loss
And all the light is hateful. Now is it time
To bring my soul away.

Even now
I know that I have savoured the hot taste of life
Lifting green cups and gold at the great feast.

Just for a small and a forgotten time
I have had full in my eyes from my girl
The whitest pouring of eternal light.
The heavy knife. As to a gala day.

The things they had said to each other, she could recount it all so clearly. But there was no one to say it to, not even Noor. She didn't have the words. Her body was sick, bloated with secrets. He had thrown her in the sea, and she had gulped salt water in greedy bursts, not knowing she could drown one day. She studied the fifty stanzas of *Chaurapanchasika* not for form or metre, but for its words. She was afraid her own would slip away. She was that mad woman on the beach, hair flying and buttons undone, picking up all the shells she can see before the waves claim them.

A deft weaver was weaving the strands. The man she was trying to remember, and the one she was still too full of, and needed to erase. When she wrote about her father saying, 'Ekhuni shesh hobe, Tara rani,' she could hear AD whispering, '*Keep doing that.*' Their names for her: Nayantara. *Hansini.* Tara rani. *Ginger kumari.* He said she was the best Mallick creation. *He liked her nose, almost aquiline; her lips, full and bow-like; her breasts like palmyra fruit.* Tara rani was the best chef's apprentice a man could have. *The colour of her skin he adored—like flat, golden beer.* Smart girl. *Lovely girl.* Daddy's girl. She loathed herself for it but the weaver had handed her the loom and in her hands the threads were liquid, giving into each other like milk and tea.

Inner Peace workshop

BATCH 1: UNDER 35
BATCH 2: AGE 35-42 (EXTRA BATCHES)
BATCH 3: AGE 42 PLUS

Do you suffer from stress and anxiety? This 7-day workshop teaches you to tackle the evil triumvirate of greed, ambition and desire that is poisoning women's minds and bodies, leading to hormonal imbalance. Learn how to cure PCOD, fibroids, infertility and early menopause. Ancient relaxation and meditation techniques like Yoga Nidra and Lotus meditation will help you find deep inner peace.

Do you live alone? Become a part of our Lakshman Rekha scheme.

Visit LakshmanRekhaForAll.com to upload your video and make your voice heard.

Call your local Mahalaxmi Seva Sangh (MSS) chapter for support group and guidance.

Free
recipe booklet for calming, Ayurvedic teas.

MSS, HERE TO SERVE.

WHEN ROBI had the stroke on Friday night, it had been too late to call Tara. The reception desk at the Tibetan Culture and Language Centre, the only number they had for her in Dharamsala, was closed on weekends. Early on Saturday morning, the Pakistani doctor had told them that Mr Robi Mallick was no more. She was sorry for their loss. On the report, it said Dead on Arrival. 'We wanted to be sure there was nothing we could do before we told the family,' the doctor had said, placing her gloved hand on Shashi's shoulder. Shashi was grateful for the hand on her shoulder. But she also wanted to slap the doctor. She raised her hands from her lap, but they fell back down like the limp branches of an overwatered plant.

They had sent emails to Tara, placed call after call. After many attempts to reach her, when it was Sunday night in New Jersey, and Monday morning in Dharamsala, they had finally been able to speak to Sonam at the reception desk. Shashi had cried to her to give their messages to Nayantara Mallick as soon as she came to the language centre that day. It would be soon, wouldn't it? Yes, the same Tara, the tall one. Curly hair like noodles, yes. But it was only very late on Monday night, when they were all asleep, that Tara had called back and they had managed to speak with her.

They had had to tell her everything at once. Her father had already been cremated. Tara would have had to take a flight or a taxi down to Delhi. But however much she hurried, it would have been a couple of days before she arrived. Surjo had decided it was best to cremate his father without waiting. The priest had also said the cremation should take place as soon as possible for the soul to transition with ease.

'How could you not have waited for me? He was mine too,' Tara's words rang in Shashi's ears.

They had told her to come to New Jersey as soon as she could, even fly First Class if needed. She may have missed the cremation—it had been quick, in an electric crematorium where they didn't even allow them to carry incense. But there was the memorial the coming weekend. The shradh on the thirteenth day, the niyom bhongo the day after that. She was to eat only boiled vegetarian food until the rituals were done. Eat only food that was cooked with rock salt.

But Tara had said she wouldn't follow the rituals and that she wouldn't come. She called and cried into the phone sometimes but she didn't want to see any of them.

'We had to do what was practical,' Shashi had told her over the phone. She regretted saying it. You can get a new husband or a son, but not another father. Shashi thought of her own father, a simple, frail man who had not prepared her for the world. But now was not the time to fault him.

The rites had happened. Tutu had presided over everything with the efficiency of a woman who once managed large teams in the workplace. The travel-agent priest was habituated to people asking for express versions, symbolic gestures for the real thing. He had been born and raised in New Jersey and had never seen the Ganga himself. For Tutu, he had had to revise some lessons, and check with his father (who had bathed in the Ganga many times). But everything had gone well. The memorial too had been beautiful, even though Surjo had got drunk in his bedroom at the end of it. New tickets for Shashi's return to India had been bought. But Tara continued to close herself off from the family. On her return to Delhi, Shashi had left more messages for Tara at the language centre. She had typed a long email with two fingers. She had explained what the specialists at the JFK Medical Centre and Doctor Joshi had told her. Tara would want to know.

But Tara was in no hurry to make amends. To the young, time is unstopped. When you see your husband die, you negotiate time differently.

Her little girl, Nayantara, *the star of her eyes*. She had told Robi they would name the baby that if it was a girl. She had wanted a girl. She had always wanted her daughter to shine, to be fierce, to be unafraid, to pull her shoulders back when she spoke. From the time Tara could walk, her mother-in-law had asked if they had found a good dance class for her in Delhi. Women must have grace, they must know how to move, Kumudini had said. Shashi had found a kathak class but she had also found a karate class. Tara had to do both, bolstered by tall mugs of Horlicks twice a day.

Surjo had been an easy child. He was born on the day, and almost to the hour, that the doctors had said he would be. He was the right size for her to carry and deliver. For the nurses in the Kolkata hospital, even the right gender for a firstborn. It was only when she was pregnant with Tara that she learnt that children carry their temperament right from the womb.

Shashi had waited for Surjo to reach middle school before enrolling in an MPhil programme at Delhi University. Her proposal was to situate Hegel in the context of Indian philosophers like Sri Aurobindo and Jishnusarathy, whom Bibek had introduced her to. She was still grieving her mother. She had resumed her studies in part to address the feeling of loss after her mother died. All her life, her mother had told her what to do. She had lived and moved with her mother's voice in her head.

She had come across a Ladino proverb: 'Mother and daughter

are like nail and flesh.' There were so many sayings about a mother's love for her son, a son's love for his mother. So little about mothers and daughters. Was it because it was men who chronicled proverbs? The only one she found was in a dying language. And she wasn't sure what it meant.

It had not been the right time for Shashi to conceive a second child. It was a surprise. Robi was travelling so much at the time—Lisbon, Toronto, Sydney—they had not even been planning another child. It had been almost nine years since Surjo.

And this time she was alone in Delhi, without the comfort of her mother's nagging or Kumudini's kitchen. Poornima, who claimed she had helped birth numerous babies back home and knew all about cravings and labour pains, sank into a peculiar melancholia as the months progressed. When she was carrying Tara, Shashi vomited every day, she couldn't eat eggs or, god forbid, jackfruit.

Robi tried to turn down travel at the time but there was a commission in Sweden that needed him to be away for three weeks. Shashi had insisted that he take it.

It had happened while Robi was still away in Sweden—'my last trip and then I'm here'—and Poornima was taking her afternoon sleep. Shashi was in the kitchen making tea. It was her eighth month but she had had to stop going to the university already. She was bloated with fear. She had just strained the brew into a cup, when, without warning, every inch of her stomach twisted into burning knots.

With a first child, you are giddy and ignorant. You know there will be screaming and pain, but everyone goes through it, how bad can it be? With a second child, with the pain, there is foreboding of pain. The loss of control, muscles that feel like someone else's muscles, the apathy of the nurses, the hurried cuts, the knives and scissors, the blood and mucus. The terrifying cries of other women. The bland food of the hospital. The overbrewed tea. Family members you can't recognize, greeting each other by the bedside, their breath smelling of onion and garlic, while you are sore and aching to sleep. While she was carrying Tara, she had been sensitive to each twinge, each shift of tissue. She had hoped it would build slowly, give her enough of a warning of what was to come. But it surprised her how sudden it all was. She held on to the kitchen counter and cried out till Poornima rushed to her side. Her waters broke, coming in a warm gush down her legs. Poornima and Jose took her to the hospital. They called Robi from there.

It was a full day of labour. Nayantara Mallick was born several weeks early.

But their daughter had waited for her father to arrive.

'Too much in a rush to see the world, molukutty molukutty,' a nurse had said.

'Already fighting with your mother,' an aunt had joked.

To a new mother, tired and confused, this had pricked more than the needle and the stitches. Ever since she had learnt she was going to have a daughter, Shashi had been buoyant with a different kind of joy. A girl, her own girl, to shape and to mould. She would learn how to swim and drive. She would go to a school that had a blazer in its uniform. She would wear sleeveless dresses and go to a disco. She would be good at maths. She would know how to get what she wanted. She would have so much to choose from.

When she had first seen her, underweight and a little blue, Shashi had been seized with fear. She had lost a part of herself in making her. She held the baby to her breast at the slightest cry. It took Tara a long time to take to the nipple. Shashi held her patiently to her breast till her arms burnt. When they went home from the hospital, Poornima massaged Tara with warm mustard oil twice a day and held her in the sun. By the age of three, Tara's paediatrician had declared her overweight because of Shashi's paranoid overfeeding.

'Mrs Mallick, now when did Bengal start sending entries to Sumo competitions?' Dr Nair had joked.

'Girls need to be strong,' Shashi had said, with a calm confidence.

'They do, but we women should know that strength resides anywhere but in flesh and bone,' Dr Nair had said, giving Shashi a look that reminded her of Professor Mitra, when she'd seen her for the last time.

Kumudini had taken the train to Delhi to stay with them for a few months. She had helped Shashi make the transition from fattening Cerelac to mashed rice and fish. She had left only after Tara's mukhe bhaat ceremony at five months, when the baby was fed solid food for the first time. Shashi loved those photographs. Tara dressed in red and gold, an infant bride. Small dots of sandalwood paste on her forehead. A little crown made of shola. Most children had to be forced into eating a little from each bowl for the ceremony. But here was her girl, jubilant, her fingers smeared with payesh, her feet kicking the silver thali with its many little silver bowls. In another photograph, Shashi's brother, Shona, was holding up the platter from which Tara was supposed to pick an object that would decide what she would grow up to be. Surjo had picked money. Everyone had said he'd be rich. What would

Tara pick: the powder puff or lump of earth, money or the pen? Shashi couldn't remember what she had picked. Kumudini had changed the story so many times based on who she was speaking to that it had clouded Shashi's memory as well.

A year later, Kumudini had to come down again to help Shashi wean her daughter off the bottle. When they succeeded, Shashi was relieved but also forlorn. Her daughter, that helpless, wrinkled creature she had birthed, was on her way into the world.

And now that creature had the power to reduce her mother to tears. When do daughters become monsters that their own mothers fear? Nail and flesh. Flesh and nail. The flesh nourishes. The nail protects. Where one ends, the other begins. Who was who in the Ladino proverb? She longed to find a Ladino woman to ask her if she knew.

The prospect of meeting Tara weighed heavily on her. But she knew they needed to meet before they were forever divided by the death of the man who bound them.

She would have to be gentle. Tara had had a difficult year. The months at Mysore had seemed eventful. She was always 'in the middle of something' or 'still in the lab' when she called. She said she loved the library, she spoke about the 'awesome biryani' at a restaurant near the campus. She had cut her hair again, herself this time, she had told her. She had volunteered for a project but after the initial flurry, she had stopped talking about it.

Robi had been wary of the Mysore plan at first. But father and daughter had quarrelled once again, there had been a week-long impasse, and finally the old had surrendered to the young.

Once he agreed, Robi went overboard. He had insisted on going with Tara to Mysore, taking the flight with her to help with

171

four large suitcases. He agreed to send her own mattress there in a removal van. When Shashi had expressed her horror at the idea, father and daughter had made their case as a united front.

'Hostel bedding won't do.'

'I can only sleep on my own mattress.'

'How will she study if she can't sleep at night? A new mattress will take months to break in.'

'Ma doesn't love me. She never did. She didn't even want me.'

There it was. It swayed between them always. An errant thread that unravelled the weave. The recklessness of having been honest to her mother-in-law. 'I was surprised,' is all she had said to Kumudini. But if conceiving her daughter had surprised her, now it was her daughter who surprised her again and again. Like Robi had, when they were newly married. Because after all of that, after taking her own mattress to Mysore, Tara had taken a semester off and gone off to Dharamsala.

'Too much fire,' an Ayurved had told Shashi about Tara. When he saw her worried face, he added: 'Nothing to worry, very intelligent.' Robi was fire too, he said. 'Put ghee in their food. Ghee is "sita", it cools the body.'

Even when Tara was in Mysore, and had a phone, she rarely called her parents. There were things Shashi wanted to ask the hostel warden: Does she look happy, this spoilt daughter of mine? Do the other girls tolerate her? If she falls ill, might they sit beside her? Does she keep warm when she goes running early in the morning? Does she fill up her plate in the canteen?

Now in Dharamsala, she was totally cut off from her family. Shashi and Robi had been worried about their month-long trip to New Jersey coinciding with this deviation in the life graph of their daughter. 'Something is wrong,' Shashi said aloud, every morning, at some point between waking up and finishing her first cup of tea.

Shashi was reassured by the knowledge that Tara was like her father. The passionate and confident ones who do well in the world. Quick to fire, but quick to settle. They like to think they are radical, but they chase comfort and adoration. Not the mark of rebels.

Robi blamed his father for filling Tara's head with 'ancient nonsense'. He could still accept that neither of his children was passionate about architecture and wouldn't join him at Mallick Architects, but Sanskrit? He had hoped that she'd pursue art history at least. He had tried to inculcate an interest in her from a young age. He knew the curatorial heads of several international museums. They could create a position that was suitable for his daughter.

'Ei meye, if this was about shocking us you could have just coloured your hair purple again,' Robi had joked, though Shashi knew that some part of him was secretly proud. Some of their close friends had rebuked Robi. It didn't send out a good message. 'Why Sanskrit? It's so regressive. The MSS will believe you're falling for their return to Indian tradition spiel.' Robi had dismissed those concerns. He wasn't going to stop his daughter from doing what she wanted to do because of how it made him look.

Like Mysore, Dharamsala was a strange setting for their turbulent daughter. What was she in search of? Why had she chosen to go there? How much did she even know her daughter?

One of these days, when Shashi's cleaning and reorganizing efforts in the Delhi home had begun to wane, Sunita called to ask when she was returning to Yuva Vikas. She told her that Friday was Leaving Day.

'It's a good day for you to start again, no,' said Sunita on the phone.

'As good a day as any,' said Shashi.

'Enough with your staying at home now, no arguing. I will pick you up tomorrow morning after I pick up the samosas.'

'Jose can drop me. He has nothing to do these days.'

'He can follow my car. Because I can't drop you back. Surinder and I have to go to a party… you know how it is, I have to rush home and change. And this Surinder, he can command an entire police force but he can't put his own clothes together. These Indian men, they're always… you know how it is…' Sunita stopped abruptly. The line was silent.

Shashi tried to laugh to ease Sunita's discomfort. 'I know how it is. I'll be ready at nine,' she said.

Leaving Day was always a day of promise. One of the teachers usually offered to get samosas and jalebis—the administrator said they didn't have the budgets. Even the humourless canteen manager participated in the festivities by adding more sugar than usual to the chai.

It was Asha's Leaving Day. Shashi had been fond of her from the day she had come to Yuva Vikas a year ago.

What should we read in class today? Asha always raised her hand and said 'Love across the Salt Desert'. She had seen the movie version with Kareena Kapoor and that had interested her in the short story. When Shashi read, she watched Asha's eyes dim and glow with every trial and victory of the young lovers. In Spoken English class, she had worked on hardening her sibilants. She said *sugar* and *shake* properly now.

She was seventeen when she had been brought in. Asha Yadav's

174

crime was that she had stolen a waxing machine from a beauty parlour where she used to sweep the floors. The children were not supposed to discuss their case files with teachers but English Composition always meant Shashi knew more about the children than the other teachers.

'It was a machine that not work not work and lie on flour for 2 week…' she had written. The essay was meant to be about The Day that Changed My Life. Asha wrote that she had washed the machine carefully one day and had wrapped and kept it aside. She had waited for two more weeks. When no one noticed its absence she thought it was safe to take it home and see if she could get it repaired. The beauty parlour madam, who owed her two months' salary, had reported her to the police and they had picked her up. Only for a day, they had told her. The police lady had been nice to her and given her two thick sheets to sleep on and half a tube of Odomos to fight the mosquitoes. In the morning, they had given her tea and biscuits. She had washed her face and brushed her teeth with her fingers and been taken to the sub-inspector's office to phone home. Her parents had refused to come and get her. They had no daughter named Asha, they said. The officers got busy, they had other things to do. They called again that evening and got the same answer. Asha always believed that there had been a cross-connection with the phone lines.

She was sixteen. They couldn't release her unless it was to a family member, and so she spent time in a number of short-stay homes for girls and women. At one of them, she had learnt how to make bhel puri with crushed packets of Peppy from the canteen and stolen onions and potatoes from the kitchen. She sold the mix for five rupees. At another, where they made them stitch twenty gunny bags every evening, Asha and two others had tried to sweet-talk a construction worker into helping them get away. But they had been caught and finally wound up here in the juvenile home. Asha was eighteen now. She wanted to have her own beauty parlour someday. Yuva Vikas had facilitated her beautician training. She had a certificate now.

The samosas and jalebis arrived. Asha was such a favourite. Her friends and some of the teachers had gathered in front of the gate. When she came to Shashi, she said, 'Call me to do henna when Tara didi gets married. Promise, ok?' She had added glitter extensions to her hair that gleamed in the sun.

A man who simply went by the double honorific of Sir ji had come to pick her up. He was a middle-aged man affiliated to MSS and other social organizations and was frequently seen around Yuva Vikas in his all-white outfit and oversized rexine pouch. He was familiar with the Yuva Vikas administrators. While Asha said her goodbyes, he opened his pouch and pulled out a string of Goumutra™ sachets. He tore one open and emptied it into his mouth, and offered one to the administrator standing beside him. He had a kindly manner about him. He always told the teachers how valuable their work was in preparing these children to rejoin society, which he helped them do. He walked with Asha to an autorickshaw, letting her slide in first. He held her little hold-all in his lap. Asha stuck her face out from the other side of the rickshaw and waved as it pulled away, raising dust in its wake. She squeezed her eyes shut but continued to wave. Colourful bangles moved up and down her wrists, creating a blur of colour. Her hair caught the sunlight.

Asha's Leaving Day had rejuvenated Shashi. Another one of

her students was rehabilitated, and she had played a part in it. She left Yuva Vikas with the jalebi's sticky sweetness still in her mouth.

A FEW weeks after he had sent her the long email, Bibek called Shashi to say he was reaching Delhi in two days. He would arrive in the middle of the night, like always. Shashi asked Poornima to keep a meal ready in case Bibek wanted to eat when he arrived.

'Let's buy pabda at the market,' Poornima said.

'Nobody eats fish at that hour.'

'You always say that and then Bibek da eats everything I put before him. He must miss his fried river fish in Madras. Poor man, they must be giving him dry vegetables every day there.'

Bibek always said that the way he lived couldn't be explained to those who couldn't think beyond doors and walls and gates and fences. 'Make your home the centre, not the boundary for your affections,' his guru Jishnusarathy had said. The commune he was part of sought to build a new world order. They tried to live without money; everything was bartered. There were too many artists already, they needed architects, educationists and the medically inclined. Bibek had designed and supervised the building of several houses in the commune. The inhabitants owned the houses but not the land they were built on. When you died in the commune, what you owned died with you. There was no one to pack your boxes after your death. No concept of inheritance.

In the mail, Bibek had told her that he had been busy the last few months designing expansions for community areas: an indoor play area for children, a music room, a naturopathic hospital. There was no one over seventy in the commune. Not yet, but they had to insure their own future. They needed to. Most of them had either cut ties or been disowned by their families.

The commune was situated in the hills near Kanyakumari, all the way in the southern tip of the country, where the three seas—the Bay of Bengal, the Arabian Sea and the Indian Ocean—met. The hills were renowned for their medicinal plants and the commune's primary source of income was processing herbal oils and powders and naturally dyed fabric, which they sold to buy things they needed: building material and tools, books, computers. They grew and harvested their own food. Somebody had loaned Bibek an old motorbike, and he wore veshtis and shirts stitched by one of the women he lived with. He had everything he needed while he was there. It was only once he stepped out of the leafy compound, thick with the smell of therapeutic oils, that the inconveniences began. He avoided restaurants and movie theatres. And it was hard for him to travel. Always an early morning train. Or a late night flight. The cheapest tickets.

When he had first moved to Kanyakumari two decades ago, Robi and Shashi had visited him at least once a year, usually just before the mild winter set in and the part-time commune members arrived from Europe, deeming the weather now suitable to ponder a new world order. When they walked around with him on the unpaved roads, passing mothers riding bikes with babies in a sling, and the man offering buttermilk to every passerby from his steel flask, people beamed beatifically at them. Everybody was in a permanent state of greeting, their faces glowing in anticipation of the Truth. Bibek had explained that there were no charlatan routines, no idols, no psychedelic drugs, no group sex in the commune's daily practice. Nothing was banned outright, however, except anything that could distract from your search for the Truth. Living arrangements were simplified so you weren't weighed down in this journey by petty concerns of money or fidelity.

It was a delightful place to visit as a guest. The commune had its own abundant farmland, and everything was cooked communally in a central solar kitchen. Surjo and Tara loved it as children. Bibek had taught Tara to ride her first cycle here. Most people they met were potters, painters, children's book illustrators. Their bodies were beautiful, glowing with sun and oil.

But outside of Kanyakumari, and especially in Delhi, Bibek looked like an apparition. His cotton veshti, sturdy sandals, the dot of sandalwood paste on his forehead, the fashionable rubber watch on his wrist, the fair and noble face—he was neither artist, nor guru. People couldn't place him. Bibek was aware of this, which made him defensive and overly critical of what he called the 'sickly urban lens'. Had both Shashi and Robi not been so deeply fond of Bibek, the friendship might not have lasted.

After their TV serials that evening, Poornima fried the pabda fish in mustard oil, and made a cauliflower curry with potatoes and peas. She was relieved that Bibek da's arrival wasn't interrupting their daily TV schedule.

It was 3 a.m. when Jose rang the doorbell. The train was several hours late. He didn't have a suitcase to bring in. Bibek travelled with very little. He usually wore Robi's panjabis when he stayed with them. Shashi hoped he had brought some clothes this time.

There he was. His skin stretched more tautly over his cheekbones than she remembered, making the slants of his eyes more pronounced. He entered the house, kept his jhola down and moved around the living room, drinking in the details of the curtains, the arrangement of furniture, the photo frames on the sidetables. He always did that when he first arrived. He would look around and point out changes. Sometimes he would miss something significant and Robi would tease him about losing his architect's eye. He didn't point anything out this time. He walked up to Shashi and held her hands between his palms.

'You will eat, won't you?' said Shashi.

'Is it home until we have eaten?' said Bibek, with a smile that didn't mask the weariness in his voice.

But when Poornima brought out the food in a large steel plate studded with small steel bowls and placed it before him, he couldn't eat much. He asked her to cover it and leave it on the table. He would eat later. He sat on one end of the sofa, at a right angle to Shashi, so he could reach out and hold her hand again if needed, but so she couldn't see every tremor on his face. Poornima was lingering by the kitchen door. She shut it and went inside.

'I'm sorry for arriving so late,' he said.

'You must stop with the apologies. You've always been with us,' said Shashi.

'I lost… I lost a part of me when Surjo called. I wish I could have flown to New Jersey to be with all of you.' Bibek stared at his clasped hands on his lap, his nostrils flared. A lump formed in his throat like the small rice balls his mother fed him when he ran around as a toddler, refusing the food in her hands, in the cruel way that children do.

Shashi said she was grateful he had come when he had, at a time when the tide had waned. The tourists of despair were gone. The two of them could mourn privately. It was like taking a cool bath after a day at the juvenile home. She told him about Tapan, who had taken ill with the news of his son's passing. He had begun to muddle things up. Perhaps the mind forgets so it can protect the heart. One day he called and cried to Shashi about Surjo's death. He told her he knew what it felt like to lose a son. He had lost a son too, many years ago, he told Shashi. His son had died in a rickshaw that had toppled, he said. And where was his Nayantara, when would she come to meet her Dadu? He'd finished reading the last set of books she had given him. Why had she forgotten him?

After Kumudini's death a few years ago, there were only Tapan, Lata, Swapan and Sree in the North Kolkata house. They had closed off a large part of the house. Renting out to strangers was too middle class. They lived in rooms beside each other on the ground floor now. Babloo da stayed in a room behind the kitchen, sleeping most of the day, tormenting the new hired help when he was awake, regaling them with stories of when the house was full and when lunch was made every day for around fifteen people; when notun bou Shashi made tea in her small copper pan, when Robi shona stormed into the kitchen looking for bananas after his swim, when Bibek babu—he was a real rajputro—stirred the payesh, and when Dolly stole amloki from the jar on the high shelf.

Shashi and Bibek knew Robi when he was a tall, skinny young man who loved Ayn Rand without irony. Before he won the National Award, before he wore success like a perfume that drew some and repulsed others.

They spoke about him for hours. Memory comes in jagged shapes. There was no train of thought, no tracks to follow. When a loved one dies, the best memories stand as beacons, casting shadows on the ordinary ones, wholly obscuring the less favourable.

'Remember that song he used to sing?'

'Ei, and that tree house he built for Tara as a surprise.'

'Those suitcases full of local liquor he would lug back from his trips?'

Robi was devoted to those who were devoted to him. For those who looked up to him, he shone brighter. They spoke about gifts he had made, chosen, bought. His handsome face, his perfectionism, his freehand sketches, his knack for picking the right verse for the mood, for making people feel like they could conquer everything when they were with him. It was easy to write the legend of a man like that. He had accompanied Bibek to the labyrinthine offices of the local courts day after day, first to battle the bitter dispute over the division of his father's ancestral property; later, for his divorce with Rupu. He had encouraged Shashi to enrol in Delhi University for her MPhil. He had helped her overcome her nervousness at starting college again. The things he said, the things he did, his glamorous all-black wardrobe for public life, these things made him larger than life. For three decades, Shashi had been told she was lucky to be married to a man like that. The last few weeks those words had pooled in her mouth like too-sweet rose syrup. It was unpalatable when it came from others. But she believed it too.

'Do you know, when you were visiting your mother once, your jasmine had died. He called me at the ashram, as if I could revive a jasmine long-distance,' Bibek said. He laughed. It was a relief to laugh.

Shashi said she didn't know. She had never known this.

'He went hunting around all the nurseries in South Delhi. He looked for days and days to find one that looked similar so you wouldn't know.'

Shashi looked at her left wrist. The priest had asked her to remove her wedding bangle during the cremation. But she could see it on her wrist still, gold that had lost its lustre over the years. When she was newly married, there were two other bangles. Red coral and white shell. Kumudini had said she needn't wear them apart from special occasions. Only servants, with husbands back in the village, wore them all the time.

'Bibek, are there other things I don't know?' she said, still staring at her wrist. It looked misshapen.

Bibek got up from the sofa and paced in front of her, his fingers clasped behind his back.

He sat down slowly again, as if his movements might disturb her.

'That is not like you, Shashi.'

'Why are people always telling me what I'm not? When your husband of more than thirty-five years dies, how can you know any more who you are?'

Bibek took her hands in his. 'Give yourself time.'

'Not all of us have the luxury to renounce the world and look at the sky for answers.'

'We don't look at the sky. We look within,' Bibek said gently, letting go.

Water pooled in Shashi's eyes and spilled. She didn't call it crying. Crying should have sound, should involve a crumpling of the face, a deformation of features. It should involve hand-wringing. An expression of grief needs to be witnessed to be called grief. Shashi rarely cried. It seemed too self-indulgent. Almost selfish. She only spilled salted water from her eyes like boiling milk spilt over the sides of a too-full pan. Her breath became barbed. Her lungs seemed to collapse into her stomach. But it was not crying.

She put her hands over her face. Robi's voice came to her.

'Why do your fingers always smell of garlic?' he would say. 'You should rub lemon over them.'

'So there are things I don't know?' said Shashi.

'There was never anyone else, if that's what you're asking,' said Bibek. 'Robi Mallick was too much of a narcissist to shatter his own image as a good husband, an ideal father, the perfect man.'

Shashi had imagined that was the answer she had wanted to hear. But it made her bury her face in her saree. The sound of her own breathing was loud in her ears now. She could hear Bibek pace the floor in front of her again. She could hear the whirring of the fan above her, switched on despite the pleasant weather to keep mosquitoes away. The sounds married each other and became the sound of her breath, moving up and down her chest like burnt, used oil. It was too much of an effort to keep her head buried. She wiped her face and looked up.

'It was easier for me to think there were others to blame for why we didn't have what you're supposed to have. You had it with Rupu. Don't tell me it doesn't matter. It's harder to think there's no one to blame,' said Shashi.

All these weeks, Shashi had hoped to chance upon a biscuit tin with notes and cards, with photos. She told Bibek that she had hoped to pause her grieving and turn scornful instead, if only for a few hours.

'You had a good marriage, Shashi,' Bibek said.

'Robi had a good marriage. I was a small part of it. I mourn him. But I also mourn me,' said Shashi. 'And now there's no chance of it.'

Bibek was quiet. There were things he wished to say about contentment and truth. But he didn't say anything then. Jishnusarathy had taught them not to preach to the pained. He had sent Shashi everything he had read of his guru. Had she not absorbed any of it? Even if she had, reading and living is not the same. Jishnusarathy taught them to pursue a deeper meaning in everyday life. That's why he had brought the commune together—so people could live his philosophy, bathe in its light every day.

Bibek longed to be able to console her. But there were things that couldn't be said.

Shashi switched off the table lamp beside her, put on her slippers and walked up the stairs. With Bibek, there was no need to explain where he was to sleep, where the blankets were, or that the geyser needed to be switched on fifteen minutes before, even though it said Instant Water Heater in bold letters. She pulled her shawl closer to her body as she walked up the stairs.

When she came down the next morning, Bibek was reading the newspaper on the sofa. The elections were ongoing. But even otherwise, when he visited them, he read the newspapers front to back with the diligence of a newly arrived foreign correspondent. There was an empty plate and a cup on the centre table. Poornima gestured to her from the kitchen door that breakfast and tea had been served. She had handled everything.

'Don't even think of entering the kitchen, Didi. I'll bring your tea,' said Poornima.

Shashi peered inside the kitchen at what looked like preparations for a feast. There were pieces of mutton sitting in curd, halved onions-tomatoes-potatoes rolled on the chopping board, the smell of fresh coriander filled her nostrils. Shashi frowned at Poornima, who smiled at her and closed the kitchen door.

'Can we borrow her for a few days at the ashram? She'll set the new entrants straight.' Bibek laughed. 'Ei, she told me the MSS sevaks were here. No trouble, I hope?'

'They have no reason to come again,' said Shashi.

'Reason!' said Bibek with the scorn he reserved for air conditioning. 'The fall of reason is what births movements like the MSS. It is a virus that is spreading in the world slowly, and it's more deadly than those we blame civet cats and pigs for carrying. It does not come as fever and congestion but as a speck in the eye that makes us see the world differently. They had started with pamphlets telling you what to eat, what to read. All of you looked the other way thinking the virus would never reach you in your homes with your doors and your gates.'

'Bibek, trust me, we are safe from that lot,' said Shashi.

'Even if you are, what about the others? You have a daughter. What about Tara? I hear they're in college campuses these days.'

'When she moved to Mysore, she told us they check the cupboards in her hostel. They sprinkle goumutra in the corridors. She finds it amusing.'

'It won't always be funny.'

Shashi folded her palms together. Her lips were a crescent moon. But a frown was beginning to form on her face.

'Is there room in your commune for all of us? Can we all be saved from the many viruses spreading in the world?' she said.

'We think of the ashram as the centre, not the boundary for Jishnusarathy's teachings. It's preferred but not everyone is expected to live in Kanyakumari.'

'Only the truly courageous?' said Shashi. Her voice carried the slight bit of menace it was capable of.

For years, Bibek had pressed upon Robi and Shashi to move to

Kanyakumari too. They had discovered Jishnusarathy together in Kolkata, visited the ashram the first time together. But as Bibek fell more into it, Robi's career soared. Shashi was busy with Surjo and Tara. There was homework, karate class, cricket coaching, dance recitals. It would be selfish of them to make their children give up familiar comforts and move there. It would be confusing for them all. It had been hard for them to reason with Bibek because he only spoke in extremes in that period. The competitive education system was ruining children, one tripped electricity line was a dark sign of decreasing power resources, Poornima's addiction to TV was proof of 'digital opiates'. He told them to have more courage. But Shashi knew that Bibek would never have moved to Kanyakumari himself had it not been for everything that had happened with Rupu.

Rupu had entered his life after Robi and Shashi's wedding. Rupu was dazzling, the kind of girl who played Portia in college productions. She worked in an advertising company, and wore sleeveless blouses with a large bow at the back like the actresses from Bombay. He had married her in a daze. As Bibek spent his afternoons in libraries and evenings at poetry meets, he handed over everything he called his own to Rupu. One day he learnt she had been cheating him. There were only thirty thousand rupees in his current account. She had also taken loans from his father's second wife with the understanding that she would convince Bibek to give up his princely title. The deceit of the body was so insignificant compared to this. She had robbed him of his pride, his ability to trust, to share. It was then that he had moved to the commune. It was easy to talk about the merits of not owning anything when you truly didn't own anything. But he had made himself believe it had been a choice. Now, sitting beside Shashi, he could no longer lie to himself.

In the commune, they viewed nuclear families as selfish units. One man lived with two or three women, and their children, if they had any, because there were more women than men there. At first it had bothered Bibek, but he told himself it was needed for practicalities like establishing paternity. Besides, what mattered was the higher purpose.

The women at the commune appeared free of worry. They did house and farm work, danced, made love and nursed their infants with a muscular conviction. He could see their breasts and their slender waists, sometimes the darkness of their crotch, through their thin cotton clothes. Their bodies were strong, their eyes were fixed. They would never ask questions like Shashi was asking him now, shrouded in tentative words, drowned in soft sobs. But they were all very young. Maybe the questions in a woman's life only arise later. At the commune, there were men in their fifties and sixties. But only young women came. And they left young too. They sought something the commune couldn't provide.

Bibek let Shashi's anger drain. And then he returned to the newspaper he was reading. 'Here they say the Lakshman Rekha proposal by the MSS might be drafted as a bill?' he said.

'I'll be surprised if it is,' said Shashi, taking a sip of her tea. She winced because it tasted bitter. 'They're all about the noise. They've had many campaigns. Never goes anywhere. I doubt they even want them to. Actioning these proposals would require real effort which I don't think they're ready to put in.' She placed her cup on the centre table and stirred more sugar into it.

'But what does this mean? Women can't live by themselves? You can't live here? You'll move to the US?' said Bibek.

'It'll never come to that. We know enough people, Bibek. They won't dare to harass Robi Mallick's wife,' said Shashi.

Bibek studied her face for concern. It would help with what he wanted to say next. 'Shashi, leave all this. Come to Kanyakumari, come study Jishnusarathy like you always wanted to,' he said.

Shashi had expected this to come up but not so soon. She and Robi had always turned down the idea of moving to the commune with reasons that were firmly rooted in the physical world—children, schooling, office, ease of access to an airport. Those reasons were no longer in her way. The truth was she had become disenchanted with Jishnusarathy over the years. Besides, the two decades hadn't altered Bibek. For all his searching, he still thought that what he believed was the only thing to believe.

'It's not so bad. I'll just have to get used to their occasional intrusion,' said Shashi.

'It is no measure of health to be well adjusted to a diseased society,' said Bibek, quoting his guru.

'Bibek, my work at the juvenile home is important to me. I can't just pack up and leave,' said Shashi. 'Does my work not matter?'

'That's not what I'm saying. We need teachers there too, Shashi. You are a student of philosophy. You are meant for… There you can study and teach, both,' said Bibek.

Shashi gathered that Bibek had put thought into this, prepared answers to possible objections. The strategic assault by her friend injured her. Robi would have known what to say on behalf of them.

Bibek saw the hesitation on her face and softened. 'What's coming in your way?' he said. 'Tell me. I'll understand.'

How was Shashi to explain what it would take for her, a woman in her fifties, to begin again. It was so much easier to take the road that had been planned, for which obstructions had been cleared, the soil prepared, the concrete poured and compressed. A road that even had pygmy palms planted on either side for an illusion of symmetry, a token of beauty. Even his years in the commune hadn't prepared Bibek to understand.

'Robi,' said Shashi.

As an answer, it was whole and complete. Bibek put away the folded newspaper, resigning as easily as he had stepped up. He looked at Shashi's slippered feet, the border of her pale yellow saree grazing the floor. The colour of seasons turning. Of spring, of new blooms, of beginnings. What was so wrong in asking what he had?

'All right. Let's talk about Tara,' he said. 'What do you want me to do?'

The light caught Shashi's face again. Bibek was one of the few people who could touch her daughter's wounds. There was something in raging temperaments like Robi's and Tara's that made them seek stillness in natures like his.

Bibek would help her reach Tara. Just like all those years ago, in the big house, he had helped her reach Dolly. Dolly's story bound them to each other. She was their shared triumph and their shared guilt.

'Come to Dharamsala with me,' said Shashi.

WAXING
GIBBOUS

When Tara reached Mysore Palace Hotel that Saturday night, the lobby was quiet except for two families with their suitcases, waiting for taxis to take them to the airport. They looked like versions of the family shown in local tourism advertisements. The husband wore a pair of trousers and a collared t-shirt, revealing the slight paunch of corporate stress. The wife was in a salwar-kameez, with neat hair and a powdered face. A boy in elasto-waist jeans and a girl in an oversized frock.

Today would not be a good day for sitting casually on the sofa and overhearing their conversation, picking up cues from their accents, making up backstories about their lives. It was nearing midnight and Tara had something to accomplish.

This was what they called a family hotel in Mysore, and the man at the reception desk would not take kindly to Tara, who was not a guest at the hotel, walking straight to the elevator late at night. Any other day, she could have passed off as a member of one of the families—a daughter that the parents were waiting to find the right boy for through classifieds in the newspaper. But today, her mascara was smoky and her lipstick was vampire red. She was wearing heels, and they gave her an affected walk. Besides, she did not know Amitabh Dhar's room number. She would have to involve the receptionist. She picked up some magazines from a table in the lobby, arranged them in a stack, and walked up to the reception desk.

There are things she had learned being Robi Mallick's daughter. There is a body language, a gaze that powerful men carry. A gaze that doesn't pierce ordinary people but bypasses them entirely, reducing them to the unseen. It comes from a childhood in which they've seen servants move around like tireless phantoms; servants who've hand-fed them and cleaned their commodes, but whose full names they've never known. It comes from being bowed to and greeted so often that acknowledging each instance is an effort. Even when such a man is temporarily shorn of his car or clothes, like in a spa, the privilege rests deeply in his features. It is a privilege born of his birth, education, wealth, extraordinary faculties, or all of these, and it shows in the faint arch of his brows, the sure lines of his unsmiling lips, the clarity of his English diphthongs. It shows in the way he doesn't contract his nose, but looks unmoved when presented with unwanted ideas, sounds or smells. Acting powerful doesn't necessarily come with being powerful. It takes years to perfect. You have to work at it.

Tara slammed down the stack of magazines on the receptionist's desk, tapped her fingers on them, and asked for Amitabh Dhar's room number. She looked around at everything except the receptionist. Guruji used to make them refine their bhav batana while seated on the floor, using only the torso, hands and face to show loneliness, fear, hope, ecstasy. The nayikas in the thumris they danced to were highly indecisive. These heroines jumped from one emotion to the other. They were all like Radha, the archetypical heroine of classical Sanskrit poetry—consumed by longing, playful, sulking, jealous and tempestuous. Radha flies into tempers, rails at Krishna, but always consents and finds joy with him.

The receptionist apologized for the delay as he walked her to the elevator and held open the door. As he stepped in and pressed the button to the right floor, Tara could smell the sweat on his uniform. She smiled at him and at the button lit up in green.

When she knocked on the door, AD opened it in a ridiculously ornate dressing gown, something that resembled Victorian upholstery. She could not read his expression; there were too many other details to absorb. The gown matched the curtains so she gathered it must belong to the hotel. She was feeling giddy now. It was hot, and blood had rushed to her ears and feet, both of which throbbed. She felt like a hot air balloon that was slowly deflating. A cold ginger soda—two cubes of ice—would be nice. It was unwise to have come here when she was angry, and her body registered its protest. There was a sharp pinprick in her chest. Her stomach felt unsettled. All she wanted to do was to tell him off.

AD made way for her to enter the room and she promptly put the stack of magazines on the bedside table. She parted her lips but found that her tongue had gone limp. He went and sat in a chair by the desk beside the window. He was smoking, which made the room with its heavy drapery unbearable. There was an open periodical, his notebook and silver pencil on the table in front of him. There was a glass and a bottle of whisky. Cheap, blended stuff.

Her father would never drink it. Amitabh probably wouldn't drink it in public either. There were old Hindi songs emanating from the general direction of the TV but he had put a towel over it so it worked like an enormous radio. His face was soft, perhaps from the music. Having inserted herself into this scene, she didn't know what to say or do and it couldn't be said that AD was helping in any way. He was looking at her with a kind of amused curiosity but he didn't ask what had brought her there or even why she had brought him a bunch of old magazines.

When Tara said she wanted to use the bathroom, he pursed his lips and gestured towards the bathroom door. He had still not said anything since she had entered the room, which she thought was rude. Tara stepped into the bathroom and closed the door. There was a razor and a face towel near the sink. She could see tiny hairs clinging to it. *Alaqah*, she thought, the Arabic word for the second stage of love, 'that which attaches'. She giggled to herself for having come up with that. There was a piece of alum too, like the one her Dadu rubbed on his chin after he shaved. She had never seen it anywhere else. The bathroom smelled like an old man's. The old man smell is a real thing. She had read about it: old men make more of an unsaturated aldehyde called 2-Nonenal, which is also a component of aged beer. Limp clothes hung where the towel should have been. She was feeling muddled. She decided she needed to drink water. If he wasn't going to say anything then she wouldn't either. She would just drink her water and leave.

When she pulled opened the bathroom door, he was there in front of her. She had never seen him so close. He rested his palms on the bathroom doorway and stood there. He must have just bathed. His hair was wet and combed across his forehead like a schoolboy's. He was wearing his glasses low. She could see the light from the bulbs above the bathroom sink reflected in them. The bathroom was at a step rise and he had placed one foot on it. His dressing gown parted slightly at the thigh. He looked almost obscene, like a '70s Hindi movie villain. He was missing the visual effect of a cigar but she could smell the tobacco on his breath.

'Why did you come here?' he said.

His manner was accusatory, menacing even. It perplexed Tara. She had expected gratitude from him, like she did from boys. Soon, he was looking around the room, like her answer didn't really matter.

'I have come here because I did not like what happened in the office this afternoon,' Tara said.

'So this is an apology?'

'No... I'm here because I don't like feeling this way.'

Then it all happened very quickly. Amitabh lifted her up and placed her on the bed. What unfolds over weeks or months in small increments of intimacy was condensed to a few minutes. Had she imagined them together? Had she had fantasies of getting naked with this man? She couldn't remember at that moment. She knew that she had wanted him to say 'That's brilliant, Tara' and 'You must come to Chicago, Tara' as they shone like two torchlights in a coal mine. She had wanted to command his attention in the lab, in the canteen, at the dean's dinner party. That was important to her. But that was different from this. This, she had not quite pictured. Maybe it would come to her slowly, like the letters during a test in the optician's chamber.

He tugged at her bra fastenings. He was breathing heavily, his lips roamed her body, his fingers probed. He bit her earlobes.

197

When she lay on her back, he could not penetrate her. So he put her on top of him, and held her hips in place. Tara felt her body become pliant. She was letting it be moved here and there. She was not usually like this. Maybe it was the beer? She didn't have the vocabulary for all that was happening. A lot of it was muscle memory. When you're thrown in the sea, you swim towards the sky. She looked down at his face, there were lines like vermicelli on the sides of his eyes. His lips were brown and chapped. He had pursed them and narrowed his eyes, like she was being given a test of some sort. As she straddled him, things started to fall into place. She felt a familiar sense of thrill. But also something else. Her fingers had lost sensation. Her ears were burning. She told herself it would be over soon. After some time, when he moved her on her back again, she became rigid, put her hands by her side, hoping that he would notice and stop to say something. Instead, the full weight of Amitabh Dhar was now on her. She felt uneasy and thought it might be what she had eaten. She considered asking him to stop but she also felt a sense of power in making his body hungry for her. His eyes were closed and there had been no words exchanged since they had moved to the bed. Maybe this was how old people did things. The TV-turned-radio was still playing. An old Hindi song cackled between them, completely wrong for the moment. *Phoolon ka taron ka*, a song about a brother's love for his sister. Tara started to laugh.

When she woke up the next morning, AD was at the desk. His glasses were in their usual place, low on his nose. He had a newspaper cracked open. There was coffee, a bowl of fruit, his laptop. His morning had started and she was not part of it.

Soft light was streaming into the room through the half-drawn curtains. Tara sat up. She saw her mascara had left black streaks on the hotel's whitest-white pillowcase and turned it around. She thought it might be late because AD looked busy. She picked up her watch from the bedside table, where it lay amidst a gleaming pool of her jewellery. It was only just past eight.

Tara Mallick had no idea what the proper code of conduct was. She wanted to do things correctly. With her boyfriends, she would have fished out her top from the night before and put it on. They would have kissed over morning breath, and immediately had a long discussion on what to get for breakfast. But something more elegant was called for now. Movies had set such a high bar with women wearing oversized shirts and lounging around the morning after, looking effortless. She tried pulling at the coverlet to wrap it around herself but it was tightly tucked into the sides of the bed. Her clothes lay crumpled on the floor. She looked up at AD and their eyes met. He signalled to her to come to him—moving his hand the way people guide bus drivers as they reverse. She got out of bed and walked over to the desk. He put one arm around her naked body and kissed her waist. For the first time since she had entered the room the night before, he smiled at her. It was as easy as that. All she had to do to be near this man was to do as he said.

Divine Love Workshop

Mira, Radha, Sita.
Learn from the heroines of Indian History
how to love selflessly and surrender yourself to
experience true love and the divine touch.

Learn how
to overcome
Ego and Vanity.

Small groups only

Call your local **Mahalaxmi Seva Sangh (MSS)** chapter for support group and guidance.

MSS, HERE TO SERVE.

It was Monday, the first of Amitabh Dhar's special lectures. Tara had left Mysore Palace Hotel after breakfast the day before because he had to make 'goddamn slides' for the lecture.

Too many people had registered for the inaugural lecture and so it was in the main hall instead of the seminar room. There were two men in security uniforms on either side of the stage. A few MSS sevaks were standing in the aisles of the hall. As she walked in, Tara collided with one who was fidgeting with his phone. Dean Patnaik had given the sevaks free rein on campus. They were particularly interested in the activities of the Sanskrit department and even displayed piety at the mention of Sanskrit. One of them had tried to touch Professor Goyal's feet while he was walking on campus, and the nervous man had jumped out of his skin. He had rebuked the sevak about the social media messages they had been sharing in order to get more people to study Sanskrit. 'Unqualified people are calling the department. The phone doesn't stop ringing,' he had complained. The messages they had circulated said that the study of Sanskrit was the only authentic way to understand the ancient glory of India. 'We are linguists. I'm interested in grammar, not gotras,' Goyal had said. The man had called him Guruji nevertheless and left without a promise to retract anything.

From the time Professor Amitabh Dhar's visit to IILL had been announced, the sevaks had been agitated. Why had the Indian government welcomed a troublesome figure who routinely dishonoured Hindus? How could he call himself a Brahmin? Tara had seen senior sevaks in their padukas come in for meetings with Dean Patnaik. AD had not met any of them personally yet, or he would have told her and Ajay. From the way the fidgety sevak was speaking into his phone, playing it back, testing audio, she understood why he was there.

Tara took a seat in the third row. Close enough to read the slides properly but not too eager. All Sunday, she had had time to think about things. She had claimed him. Now she would claim the seat of her choice.

After a delay appropriate to the importance of the occasion, AD walked out of the wings with Professor Goyal. There were two women from the Indo-French Culture Council—the council was sponsoring the lecture series—who walked on stage and gave Professor D-a-a-r a bouquet. The French women were dressed in sarees, which looked alluring but misshapen on them. They reminded Tara of the time her mother had worn a kimono when they were holidaying in Japan. And how she and her father had laughed.

Professor Goyal took the mic to make a short introduction. He would remain seated quietly for the rest of the event. Tara always found this part amusing. Saying 'This man needs no introduction' and then introducing him for ten minutes.

She scanned the crowd. Tara often had a dream in which she could X-ray people. Find lust in their toes. Envy in their intestines. Fear in their kidneys. But there was nothing here. Just greasy hair and printed kurtas, and black or brown slippers that were grey with dust. The tap-tap of pens on notebooks.

'Professor Amitabh Dhar has published over fifteen books, most of them on Hinduism and Sanskrit literature. The Sanskrit and Indian Textual Traditions Chair from the University of Chicago, he has translated the Kama Sutra into English, as well as an anthology of hymns from the Rig Veda...'

AD took the mic. Tara looked at his fingers wrapped around the wireless microphone. She missed the first few minutes of his talk as she thought back to Sunday morning. The way he had put his arm around her and kissed her waist, fed her an apple slice from the bowl in front of him.

When she came to, AD was saying, 'There are many different forms of Hinduism, including Hindutva, which is to me just one branch of a very large tree. The trouble with Hindutva is that it says it *is* the tree...'

Tara looked at the fidgety sevak. He was typing into his cell phone. But she had more important things to worry about. The French women were sitting in the first row. Tara watched them closely for any sign of particular interest in AD. One of them was laughing too much, the other was adjusting her saree. But these women, this lecture hall full of people, they were here to adore the man she had gone over and fucked on Saturday night. She tried to focus on what he was saying. She pulled out a notebook and a pen from her bag. She took copious notes but couldn't grasp their meaning. There was a throbbing in her head, in her chest, between her legs.

The lecture was on the Sanskrit idea of *slesa*, which in medieval Sanskrit poetry was a literary device where language lent itself to double, or even triple, meanings.

'Polysemy, as students of language will know, is the capacity of a word or phrase to have multiple meanings, usually related within a semantic field. It is different from homonymy, which is an accidental similarity between two words... As a literary device, *slesa* was used by Sanskrit poets from the sixth century to as late as the twentieth. Does anybody know who used it first?'

Amitabh looked around the lecture hall. Tara looked around too. She didn't want to be the only one raising her hand.

'The poet Subhandu, in the sixth century,' said Ajay Iyer, from the first row.

Amitabh nodded. 'That's right, Ajay.

'About a century after that, *slesa* was part of most narrative poems. By the early eighth century, poets were merging the two great Sanskrit epics, the Mahabharata and the Ramayana, with plot parallels. When the male protagonists, Arjuna and Rama, are seduced by non-human females, both men spurn the women; Arjuna humiliates the apsara Urvasi, a beautiful celestial nymph, and Rama's brother Lakshman cuts off the rakshasi Surpanakha's nose to punish her for her sexual advances. When the two epics were fused, poets came to embrace a new aesthetic ideal, in which telling a single story was no longer the goal for a work of narrative art.

'In recent times, Sanskritists haven't touched the subject. Few living scholars have actually read a bitextual poem,' said Amitabh. 'An understanding of *slesa* is not just important for appreciating Sanskrit poetics but for understanding our philosophic tradition. You must understand that *slesa* was much more than a rhetorical ornament, it was a cultural phenomenon. And this ability to see in multiples is something we have lost. You can see it in…'

Suddenly, there was a microphone problem. One of the guards immediately climbed on stage. Tara shot a glance at the MSS sevak who was still typing into his cell phone. Amitabh tried speaking without the mic but Dean Patnaik signalled from his seat in the front row that it wouldn't work. The sevaks asked the students to start leaving in a single file. The French women hurriedly went on stage, touching their cheeks to AD's. They tried to do the same with Professor Goyal but he covered his cheeks with his hands and looked alarmed. Was she supposed to stay back after the talk to speak to AD? Everyone was leaving the hall and so she had to leave as well. She had work in the lab, which was now almost set up. She moved between the lab and their office all day but AD didn't show up. Ajay asked her if she was feeling unwell. She hadn't slept much the last two nights. She smiled involuntarily. She refused coffee when the peon came at 4 p.m. She remembered, while playing with her earlobe, that she'd lost an earring on Saturday night. She had tried looking for it in the morning but abandoned the search in case AD thought her too girlish and said something disparaging about baubles and trinkets.

She composed imaginary messages to him. Finally, in the evening, after dinner in the hostel canteen, most of which she left untouched, she decided to send him a text. They had all been given each other's numbers on the day the project had started but no one had needed to call anyone so far.

That lecture? Nothing you haven't written about already, she wrote.

This is Tara, by the way, a second message followed.

My attentions have been elsewhere, he responded immediately.

Tara rolled in her bed. She had nothing to say. She wasn't sure why she had messaged at all. But he wrote back again.

That was grand Miss Mallick. Nothing so grand has ever happened to me.

Tara felt a heat rise up her throat like acid. She sat up in her bed.

Liar, she wrote.

It was the only thing she could type. But she hoped that she was wrong. Then she turned off her phone and kept it in her cupboard. She had learnt that from a magazine in the beauty parlour.

She went to bed feeling pleased with the exchange. She replayed everything that had happened. She had got into an autorickshaw and gone to his hotel. There, she had flirted with him. She had seduced him. She had made him her lover. And now he had said it had all been grand. He was her conquest. He was a poor communicator—she would change that. Soon, she would be in Chicago. She'd become the youngest person to get tenure in the Sanskrit department.

The idea of boyfriends felt childish. Those young, eager boys, who got hard too easy, whose eyes melted too easy. They were too affectionate, too transparent, too needy. This must be the real thing, what Bilhana called *the pleased intimacy of rough love*. The insides of her thighs ached. She could feel the tiny hairs on the nape of her neck standing up, waiting for instructions.

She fell asleep thinking about the dancer who had played Arjuna in the dance drama on campus. His body contorting into beautiful shapes, his fanning hands. What was the lure of old flesh? Of skin that had lost the pliancy of youth? A heart that has conquered and been conquered?

Many years later, she would see that she had confused her longing for her place in the world with her longing for this man. Sometimes sex is just another way to be close to someone you admire. Had it been a girl her age, perhaps they would have gone for runs together, swapped clothes and argued about which musician was the greatest.

That entire week in the lab and office, Tara was subdued. AD was perhaps a little more curt and formal than usual. Tara began to go over to his hotel almost every evening. She was careful to use the staff gate of the campus always, careful to keep her room light on through the night, careful to return early in the morning and shower so the girls would see her there.

She was careful not to sit too close to him or touch his arm by mistake or hold his gaze for too long.

The distance in public was worth the time they spent together in his room. The time Tara really had all of him was after sex, when he lay in bed with one arm folded behind his head. In those minutes, she could access the part of the man that remained shuttered to her on campus. They quoted poets to each other. He was generous; he let her correct his occasionally inaccurate Sanskrit pronunciation. They spoke about their mothers' cooking: fried river fish and the sweet dishes of their childhood made with milk and sugar. Once, he ironed her shirt when it was too creased and she had to go straight to class. Tara, who had never ironed her own clothes, was touched by this.

One day, in the room, he read out the six virtues of an ideal Indian wife from the *Niti Shastra* of the Telugu poet Baddena.

'I worry. You don't make the cut, Hansini,' he said.

'Marriage is for old people and unaspiring fools,' said Tara. 'Anyway, tell me why.'

Amitabh read aloud from his laptop:

Karyeshu Dasi: works like a servant;

Karaneshu Mantri: advises like a minister;

Bhojeshu Mata: feeds like a mother;

Shayaneshu Rambha: pleases in bed like the apsara Rambha;

Roopeshu Lakshmi: beautiful like Goddess Lakshmi;

Kshmayeshu Dharitri: having patience like Earth.

Tara drew her knees to her chin as she laughed, rolling over on the bed.

'Why are you reading this garbage?' she said.

'The head of publications at MSS wants a foreword for a new translation,' said Amitabh.

'But they can't stand you. You're a dishonour to Brahmins and all that.'

'Well, I am the best man for the job.'

'You're not seriously considering fraternizing with those clowns, are you?'

'I'm going to decline but only because with the lab and the new book, I simply don't have the time. The *Niti Shastra* has some good advice. That's what the foreword would say if I did write it, that the contemporary reader should see context and take what she will. You kids these days will blacklist Baddena for a few passages you don't agree with but you must remember this was written in the thirteenth century.'

'Fine. What does it say about the virtues of an ideal Indian husband?' said Tara.

'A man… is born,' said AD. He laughed, in that menacing way that occasionally surfaced.

Tara raised her eyebrows. He moved closer, pried open her thighs and went down on her, hooking her knees over his shoulders.

TARA HAD begun to decode the mystery that was Amitabh Dhar. He sprang into the shower soon after sex, while Tara liked to lie there wrapped in sheets. The women in Bhartrihari's verses wore moonbeams after lovemaking. Here she had the dim yellow halos of the bedside lamps and the hotel's whitest-white bed sheets.

'Catholic school upbringing,' he had explained, about the shower. She learnt that he was estranged from his second wife, Sophia, who had left home with their son a year ago. Tara was never jealous when he spoke about Abigail, his first wife. Amitabh and Abigail were friends, he spoke of her like one would about a beloved neighbour with whom one once shared a backyard. But Tara was curious about Sophia. She wondered what it might be like to have access to all of this man everywhere, not just in the confines of a hotel room.

AD was always distressed at the mention of Sophia. When Tara had first seen a picture of her, with her lustrous copper-coloured curls, she had been filled with wariness. But something AD had said had comforted her. 'It doesn't matter if she looks like Salma Hayek or the witch from Hansel and Gretel. When man and woman fight, you don't see beauty or reason,' he said.

She didn't know what that kind of anger meant for a couple. AD had told her that she was too young to understand that those who spend years drifting in a calm sea would give anything for the sounds of each other's hateful words or the sight of each other's naked bodies to arouse something in them.

The person she was really envious of was his son, Zaffran. When AD spoke about him, his features seemed to lose all their sharpness. He was a soldier returning home, to a place where you know you are safe.

She signed into his personal email several times in this period. She had guessed his password after a few tries. It was easy with this kind of man—it was usually the title of their first book, their youngest child, or some other creation with a two-digit number of some significance at the end. It was a trim inbox, organized into folders. There was one on Cricket Essays, one called Srinagar. Some emails from friends warning him to be careful about the MSS caught her eye. In the folder for Abigail, there were notices from lawyers and emails about club memberships and car insurance. The folder titled Sophia Figueras had pictures of her and Zaffran. She found one of Sophia lying naked and face down on a sunbed, took a photo of it with her phone, and looked at it whenever she was upset with AD.

What did AD talk to Abigail and Sophia about? How had they made love? Did they amuse each other? If the three women were going to die in a burning building and he could only save one, wouldn't he certainly save Sophia and not her? It seemed foolish to be having so much sex with someone who would later allow you to burn to death.

Tara had articulated her anti-marriage views to him. A single, separated man was a good audience to practise on. She told him she had boycotted her own brother's wedding, and not just because marriage was an instrument of perpetuating regressive patriarchy. It was not for her because she wanted to study, travel and live her life as she wished. She did not want to become her mother.

After she left a spare toothbrush in his hotel room, she started to feel more at ease with the affair. They brushed their teeth at the same sink, shared the same brand of toothpaste, hence she was equal to him. Some days she even felt she had power over him: when she entered the room, dropped her bag and put her feet on his lap, demanding a massage after her run, she was Omphale and he was Heracles, spinning wool at her feet.

Early in his teaching career in the US, Amitabh had had a few affairs with his graduate students. Sophia had briefly been a student of his. They had become involved at the height of his stardom, just when the first murmurs of his book ban had begun. Marrying a graduate student twenty years younger than him had only added to his legend. Abigail had taken the news relatively well, even though their divorce still hadn't come through.

Abigail Katz was a lawyer. They had met soon after Amitabh moved to New York. He was exotic to her, and they had married and moved into an apartment on the Upper West Side owned by Abigail's family. They were married twenty years, fourteen of them good. They had parted amicably. He was reassured by the fact that her parents had never approved of him anyway and that they would soon set her up with a suitable man from one of the families they regularly summered with.

The marriage with Sophia, despite the passion and their similar area of work, had been tumultuous from the start. Sophia was suspicious of his students and her jealousy bore down on him. He blamed her for the delay in completing the sequel to his magnum opus. Zaffran's arrival created an additional strain. One day, after he hadn't come home for three days, she had left home with Zaffran. They were not officially divorced because Sophia would have to go back to Argentina if that happened, and she would take Zaffran with her. Amitabh had no family except a sister in Australia, no country he called home. This boy, with his cinnamon eyes, and dark brown curls falling over his forehead, was his own. The women he could replace, his son he could not.

During his stay in Mysore, AD seemed to be having a difficult time with Sophia. She called at unreasonable hours. After these phone calls, AD would retreat. His body would look like a different man's body. 'Our bodies store emotion,' Guruji used to say. 'We speak with our bodies. Now fill your lungs with air, let your neck stretch like a peacock's, and show the world that you are proud.'

She felt sorry for him. While he was still asleep one day, she studied his face. A brown spot under his left eye. A rough spot on his chin from decades of shaving in the wrong direction. The weak morning light was coming into the room and his skin was thin as paper. On his earlobes were the faint remnants of a piercing. Was it from a Brahminical boyhood or a hippie youth? How much did she know him? When she asked him pointed questions about how he was feeling, he crinkled his eyes and gave her a half-smile. As he lay there with his eyes closed, she wished she had verses for him. There was little to transpose to her present circumstances from Sanskrit poetry, all so taken up with breasts and waists and rainfall and deer.

The act of sex with him was not what she craved. She craved what came before and after. The things he did, the things he said, felt better than tongue on skin. After his shower, she would straddle him. '*Mother of the Stars, give me your feet to kiss,*' he would say, quoting the *Chaurapanchasika*. Where else would she find another person in the world interested in the eleventh-century poem she was studying? She would ask him to make little odes to parts of her body. She had wanted to do this ever since she had seen Brigitte Bardot do it in a movie. She didn't ask AD if he had seen the movie. She wanted it to look like her own scene.

What did you and Abigail talk about after you had sex? she texted AD one night, with a photograph of her feet on her purple bedsheet.

Everything and nothing, he responded. *People don't discuss Baudelaire in bed.*

We do, she wrote back.

Because we are lovers, he replied.

So what do husbands and wives talk about in bed?

Who would refill the handsoap dispenser was a favourite of Abigail's.

The picture of the great Amitabh Dhar refilling handsoap made Tara smile.

Why do people get married?

Because you can't live in poetry, he wrote.

I plan to.

AD didn't reply for a while and Tara went to sleep. When she checked her phone in the morning there was a message from him:

Would Panini have written the Ashtadhyayi if he lived in poetry?

TARA DIDN'T know who to be around him any more. It was hard to plan who to be if you were going to spend a lot of time with a person.

Not content with writing under his own name, the Portuguese poet Fernando Pessoa had dreamed up some seventy-five others. Pessoa said he wrote as other people because it enabled him to go beyond the confines of his self. 'I break my soul into pieces,' he had written.

Tara wanted to be Pessoa. *I want to be different people so I can reach different parts of you.* She typed and deleted the text. She was aware of how ridiculous it would be to him. She spent so much of herself thinking about him when they were apart that she was often exhausted when they met.

Once, when he was drying off after his shower, he said she should make an ode to him instead.

213

'Don't be embarrassing,' she said, making a show of looking away dismissively.

But despite her verbal protestations and her attempts at appearing unattached—she never shared a blanket with him, not even the hotel's double one—she did begin to think of them as a couple. She thought maybe they would become the kind of couple who only fought about innocuous things like the air conditioning temperature or whose anniversary gift was better.

THE LAB, meanwhile, had been fully set up. Ajay had selected twenty-two graduate students as transcribers and after a short training programme they had begun to input data. The coders and web developers came in every day, making their own tribe in a corner marked by tumblers of filter coffee. Amitabh, Ajay and Tara spent most of their time at a long table in the centre of the lab: to approve text, design or problemshoot. The students had queries that needed to be answered, there was the day's input to check and clear for upload. After lunch, Amitabh would retreat to the office on the floor above. At first, Tara avoided going up there when it was just going to be the two of them. Ajay always seemed to be absorbed by what was on his screen, but he was watchful.

Then Amitabh began to summon her to the office in the afternoons. Tara resisted at first, there was work in the laboratory, and certain queries that Ajay was unable to resolve. But he wrote her a persuasive haiku. Sent her emails with the subject line 'academic emergency'. She would excuse herself from the lab and tell Ajay she had something to discuss with Professor Dhar. Soon, she spent less and less time in the lab though she ensured that she attended to queries over email from the floor above. She began to order lunch for the two of them in the office. Sometimes, she took a nap on the sofa. They never locked the door or even locked fingers. But the air was intimate enough for the peon to hurry out after he gave them their coffee.

Tara did not remember when she and AD began to walk around the campus alone together. When they started leaving the office, walking over to the library, going to the canteen without Ajay. They never walked in or out of the campus in each other's company, Tara was still careful about that.

When they ordered a dosa in the canteen together, with everybody watching, she felt they were in the light.

When clandestine lovers walk side by side there is a shift in the air, palpable even to the foolish. They make more of an effort to walk with some distance. They try not to laugh at each other's jokes. For a while, they make a third person feel very special. Ajay didn't know what had befallen him. Tara asked him if he wanted more biscuits with his coffee. AD smiled at him and complimented his work.

One day, the peon spilled some coffee on Tara's fingers while putting her tumbler down on the table. It wasn't too hot, she didn't say anything, but AD took out his handkerchief and wiped her fingers. Tara shot him a look. He had been out of the country and become unfamiliar with its ways. The peon apologized to Amitabh and left the room.

Another day in the lab, while Tara was packing up her laptop to go up to the office, Ajay handed her a strip of pills.

'Give this to Professor Dhar if you're going up. It was among his papers,' he said, with his hands extended, eyes still on his screen.

Tara took a look at the pack and dropped it back on the table. 'He finished this antibiotic course last week.'

She only realized she had said something she should not have when she caught the look on Ajay's face. His breath, it appeared, had stopped.

That's how it happens. A little bit of what the peon saw, a bit of what Ajay heard, what a girl from the hostel imagined. All of it is enough to send out perfectly formed tales into the world. Especially if it's about someone who has always looked at those less endowed with barely masked condescension.

DEAN PATNAIK walked into Amitabh Dhar's office. It was a rare event. He usually sent peons to summon the professors he wanted to meet. He'd only been seen rushing around the corridors with great excitement once, several years ago, to announce that IILL had got the neurolinguistics grant from the Education Ministry.

It was after lunch and only Amitabh and Tara were in the office. The dean knocked and entered without waiting for a response. Tara was sitting on the sofa near the window with her feet up on the centre table. Amitabh was at the seminar table with his laptop. Seeing the dean walk towards her, Tara swung her feet to the floor. The dean sat down beside her on the sofa. Amitabh hardly seemed to take notice of the man's presence. He didn't favour the intrusion. After a cursory nod, he pushed up his spectacles and continued to look at his laptop screen.

'So, Miss Mallick, looking forward to Chicago?' said the dean.

Nothing had been formally communicated to her yet. But she had assumed she would be picked as the IILL fellow for Chicago.

She was best equipped to articulate the project. Besides, when had she not got something she wanted? When she had not been picked for the group dance for annual day in school because she was 'too tall', her father had called the principal's office and offered to construct a bamboo shamiana in the school grounds as a gift from Mallick Architects. He had said just that. But the principal had asked the dance teacher to programme a solo recital for Tara Mallick.

With the dean looking at her, she didn't think it would be appropriate to answer. Replying in the affirmative would be too brash. She smiled instead. She couldn't feign a Miss-India-like 'I'm so surprised'. She was not surprised.

'Come over for dinner one of these days. Both of you,' he said. Then he walked over to Amitabh and spoke in a low voice for what seemed like a long time. There was a lot of gesturing at the laptop screen so she assumed they were discussing the progress of the project.

After the dean left, Tara took a deep breath and sucked her cheeks. Her face was flushed. Amitabh wouldn't have ordinarily noticed but he had come to smoke near the window. He put the cigarette back in its case and touched her arm. She pulled away.

'He invited us to dinner together. Why did he do that?' said Tara.

'Too late to think about that now, Hansini,' he said. He was silent for a few minutes, which made Tara think he was concerned as well.

'Should I go speak to him?' she said.

'You will do nothing of the sort. Don't prove yourself to be a child, Tara. Your work is all that matters. Just do your work,' he said, adding, 'there are real issues to worry about. The MSS has asked Patnaik to take me off campus till they conduct an "enquiry" into my ongoing research… whatever that is, goddammit.'

AD sat down at the table again and clicked his silver mechanical pencil several times as if to erase the conversation from the air.

After some time he said: 'I don't get why Patnaik even gives them an audience. They're not the government, they're not even quasi-government.'

For the rest of the afternoon, he avoided her gaze. Before he left, he told her he was expecting important phone calls to discuss the MSS enquiry. Tara didn't go over that evening. The next evening, he said the Goyals had invited him for dinner. It was a lesson for her not to bring up things he didn't want to talk about.

Professor Amitabh Dhar, the Sanskrit and Indian Textual Traditions chair from the University of Chicago, visiting celebrity on the IILL campus, the man of myths and legends, remained the same. Seeing how easily he slipped back to work, how he could speak to her and Ajay two hours after they'd had sex, like they were the same to him, began to perplex Tara.

To her it seemed like her whole life, its rhythms and waves, had been upended. She had been lying to people around her, losing sleep, losing focus in her thesis work. She had stopped going for her morning runs, stopped her afternoon reading at the bench outside the library. She'd lost even the slight connection she had with the girls in the hostel: Can I borrow your shampoo, Tell canteen-anna to hold a plate for me, Do you have my Sanskrit–Hindi dictionary?

She didn't doubt that he cared for her.

'You are like me,' he had told her.

But he hadn't had to give up any part of himself for her. When the project was over, he would leave campus the same man. But the way the peon looked at her would have changed. Were a few weeks of passion worth months of pain? She believed they were. People sniggered when she went to the canteen by herself. The girls in her hostel, who were always hostile to her, had watered down their hostility to aloofness, which was worse. When Thulasi saw her in the library, she turned away.

When gossip travelled through salons and courts and letters, it got diluted along the way, its strength and flow distorted by time and memory and tongues. It didn't land like an acid attack, its menace gaining power through numbers, multiplying over text forwards.

Now that she was seeing less of AD, she opened her eyes to other things. She learnt there was a text broadcast group on campus called Mr and Mrs Kamasutra. She told herself ignoring it showed strength of character. It was what her father called the petty banter of the mediocre. She learnt of the degrading nicknames for her in the lab and the hostel. One day, her canteen card was already signed as 'Bitch'.

Her father had called Daya an uppity bitch. Daya Chaudhari was a former colleague and a close friend of his—she often accompanied them for weekend visits to the museum. She wore all black like Robi Mallick, but with bright necklaces and thick lines of kohl.

'What has happened, Ma?' she'd asked her mother, after Robi had spent an entire afternoon speaking about the 'uppity bitch' to various people on the phone.

'Your father is surprised,' her mother had said.

It was in the papers the next day. Daya Chaudhari had won the National Award for architecture. Robi would only win it two years later. The Mallicks never saw her on Sundays anymore.

Tara had no one to speak to about her anxiety. She could only confide in Amitabh. But he made an exasperated face and said he was too old for her teenage troubles. He told her she was reading too much into things.

'Ostracism is inseparable from the heroic nature of passion,' he told her.

'Camille Paglia?'

'Walter Benjamin as quoted in Paglia's book, yes. You kids these days don't read the source texts, do you? It's always essays about the text. Such a derivative generation.'

Age hung like a quiver of arrows. Every now and then, he would draw from it to shut her down.

ONE DAY, when she and Ajay were sitting together in the lab, the peon came for his usual morning round and missed handing Ajay a coffee. Ajay sighed. 'I guess I'm invisible to everyone,' he said. Tara felt sorry for him but she wasn't going to allow him to make her feel guilty about Chicago.

She had nothing to defend. But she wore armour nevertheless. It comprised uncharacteristically bright lipstick. She took care in picking her clothes every day. She tried to laugh in conversation with canteen-anna and the graduate students. She went for runs late in the morning when everyone could see her in a purple running kit that clung to her body. It was a cold war, a deadlock. Campus vs Tara Mallick.

She wasn't prepared for a confrontation. Not now, when she had just managed to stretch her neck and stand tall.

Tara was putting up a poster for a feminist reading group on the notice board outside the canteen, when Thulasi came up behind her.

'What texts have you identified?' said Thulasi.

'Oh, it's a long list. I can email it to you. The idea is to focus on language and feminist thought,' said Tara. She was relieved that Thulasi was speaking to her. Tara had started the reading group in her first month on campus but abandoned it along the way. Restarting it was part of her new resolve. Like the coral lipstick she was wearing that day.

'There is reading ideology and living ideology. They are different things,' said Thulasi.

Tara was pushing in the fourth pin on the poster. It had been another night of staying up and arguing with AD and she had hoped for a big plate of poha and two cups of filter coffee to make up for lost sleep. She had certainly felt buoyant when she walked out of the canteen after breakfast, with the poster in her hand.

'There are different approaches. Not everyone needs to set the streets ablaze,' said Tara, trying to keep her voice steady. 'Or light fires online.'

'This is a time for action. Not theory,' said Thulasi. 'Why haven't you made time to attend a single one of our action group meetings?'

'That's unfair,' said Tara. She put her hands on her hips but changed her mind about that and let them hang loose.

'What is unfair?' said Thulasi.

'Not everyone needs to fight for the same things. Your meetings are about reservations on campus and I wouldn't be allowed to speak in the meetings, would I?' said Tara.

Thulasi's face did something she had never seen it do before. Her eyes widened as she threw her head back and laughed. 'But you're allowed to listen. And you should. When you question your Brahmin privilege, you'll see it's the same thing. Patriarchy does the same thing to women, to queer folks, to Dalits, to Adivasis, to the dark-skinned, to single mothers, we're in this together...'

'I'm not Brahmin,' said Tara, cutting her off. 'So you could direct this elsewhere.'

'You are Brahmin enough for me. It isn't just Brahmins who practise Brahminism. It's the construct,' said Thulasi, drawing a square with her hands.

Tara was taken aback by the turn in their conversation, though Thulasi seemed relaxed through her tirade. Part of it was delivered as she bent down to retie her shoelaces. This is how she spoke to everyone. Her father would have probably called Thulasi an uppity bitch. Thulasi didn't have Daya's posh boarding school cadence but she had all the right words.

'Keep your hands off the notice board. Leave something for the others,' said Thulasi.

Tara looked appraisingly at the poster she had made, listing the texts she had identified, scanned and uploaded for the reading group.

'I'm not here for all this. I'm here to study,' said Tara.

'Yes, *that* we can all see,' said Thulasi, as she walked away. If she had stayed true to her scholarly convictions so far, now she seemed no different from the sniggering girls in the hostel. It was a fresh wound on skin that was raw.

As Tara saw Thulasi's retreating figure, her head still shorn, her body perfumed with the heady aroma of the righteous, she forced out of her mind everything she had heard, some of which had even made sense to her.

*

AMITABH DHAR had a week left to go of his stay in Mysore. The MSS enquiry seemed to be over as abruptly as it had started. The dean had said he could return to campus.

The team in the laboratory had made over half a million inputs and a beta version of the generator was being tested. They were still working on the error messages, which frequently showed up. But the bulk of the work had been done. The project was a success with a relatively low investment—IILL had essentially supplied free student labour. Amitabh would never have been able to carry out this project in such a short span of time in Chicago. The students here were not only competent, they took direction without too much questioning, and didn't complain about the hours they put in. Plus, it had turned into a grand PR exercise at various levels. He was rather pleased with himself. Another accolade for the office wall.

The food hadn't been as terrible as he'd expected either. He'd identified a Himachali chef at Mysore Palace Hotel who made him mutton rogan josh and fried spinach the way he liked a few times a week.

Besides, what a surprise it had been with the girl. The last time he had felt this alive was in the months after he had met Sophia. After he had told Abigail about her and moved out, the curtains had fallen on the magic. Abigail had denied him drama, which had hurt him. Sophia was a different species—you only know a woman when you live with her. Where he had only seen her passion, now he saw the focus and ambition that buttressed it. When Sophia had an article due, there could be a storm outside and she wouldn't know. When Sophia decided she wanted a baby, she wanted one right away. Even when he had had a harrowing day defending paragraphs from his book to enquiry committees, she didn't let up. She gave him cleansing juices to drink, set alarms. The bathroom counter was strewn with kits and thermometers. There was urine in shot glasses when he went to the sink to brush his teeth. She had stopped calling him her hero, her voice didn't change any more when she spoke to him. There was no poetry, in Spanish or Sanskrit. He began to have dalliances during book tours and seminars. He assumed Sophia knew, but her focus on getting pregnant had overshadowed even her natural instincts of envy. He enjoyed the fooling around, the few nights here and there. But none of it had been as grand as the full-hearted devotion of this girl here in Mysore. She was so young, so feisty, so viscerally intelligent. Her skin was burning milk. Her body was the land he'd left behind. But unlike the land that had disowned him, the girl had come to him herself. A cherished plot of earth at his doorstep.

He remembered a time when as a young boy, he had visited cousins in a village on the outskirts of Srinagar. His mother had warned him not to go near where the shepherds grazed their sheep. While playing cricket, the ball had fallen beyond the grazing fields, at the mouth of a forest. The forest was new to him. He had entered only briefly. The girl's body had the darkness of those forbidden forests, the fragrance of flowers on the forest floor. She carried their strange, decadent alchemy.

Tanvi shyama shikharidashana pakwabimbadharoshthi.

Madhye kshama chakitahariniprekshana nimnanabhi.

Dusky of skin with sharp teeth and lips the colour of ripe bimba fruit.
Thin of waist, with the eyes of a frightened deer, deep of navel.

He would think of her every time he read *Meghaduta*. Kalidasa was the greatest of all Sanskrit poets and the girl was fierce in how much she disliked him. She was amusing, so full of opinions, so quick to make up her mind, quick to take offence, quick to be pleased—that part was exhausting for a man his age. Still, the girl had done him a favour. He felt again like the man he once was. She reminded him of Sophia. They had the same lustre in their eyes, a beating heart that wanted to keep time with the world. The idea that they could be anywhere at any given moment but were yoked to you instead was thrilling. The ferocity with which this girl told him she despised the idea of marriage made him look forward to returning to his own. To take Zaffran to feed the ducks in the park and to hold his beautiful wife, to kiss her wrists, crush her hair in his palms. To bring them back to the home where Zaffran had arrived from the hospital, where his bed with its dinosaur-print sheets now lay empty.

But there was still the last instalment of his lecture series to wrap up. And the meeting with the committee to discuss the relay of the project back to Chicago. Several students, including those whose existence he had barely registered in the lab, had sent in applications for the fellowship. He admired their determination. The formal English that Indians reserved for academic applications. It reminded him of himself as a student in Srinagar.

It was a Friday morning; the last weekday in the last week of his stay in Mysore. If the project got more funding, as expected, he would be back soon. There was much fuss made about his departure. He had been invited to several lunches, been gifted books, spices, sandalwood.

The students of the Sanskrit department had been asked to gather in the main hall again. Tara sat in her usual spot in the third row. Amitabh's final lecture was to be on 'Gandharva unions in Sanskrit narratives'. She had eaten a large breakfast because she knew this would be a drawn-out morning. There would be a vote of thanks. Flower bouquets and cartons of bottled water had been seen going into the hall. The French women from the council had arrived again, dressed in salwar-kameezes this time. She would be called on stage. She wore the pink shirt she'd worn to the airport.

The lecture was particularly fascinating. Gandharva unions were one of the eight classical types of Hindu marriage. He illustrated his talk with slides, showed miniature paintings, photos from temples in Madhya Pradesh and Odisha. He finished to much applause.

The graduate students had prepared a dramatic reading of the episode of *Shakuntala* from the Mahabharata to resonate with the theme of the lecture.

The part of the epic they performed narrated how God Indra, terrified of the power of the king-turned-sage Vishwamitra, who was known to possess the splendour of the sun, commissioned the apsara Menaka to seduce him. Indra and the celestial nymph Menaka contrived for the wind to blow open her skirt made of moonlight, and a fragrant breeze to blow through the woods when she stood before the sage. And so the strictest of seers saw

Menaka nude and lusted for her. He asked to lie with her, and she was willing. Shakuntala was born of this union, after which, her duty done, Menaka took flight to return to Indra's assembly. Shakuntala was brought up by the sage Kanva. King Dushyanta, a dynast of the Pauravas, came across her while out on a hunt and asked her to make love to him as per the Gandharva rites of union, which required no rituals or witnesses. Shakuntala agreed but not before extracting a promise that if she bore a son, he would succeed Dushyanta as king.

The students narrated only a part of the story, and their pronunciations needed work, but Tara was impressed by the choice of passage. The women in the Mahabharata cherished their autonomy, argued for their rights. This was part of the reason she despised Kalidasa's singular popularity. In his version, he had altered the story of Shakuntala for the purposes of dramaturgy, changed genres, demoted her from a heroine of kavya to a heroine of nataka. As the idea of multiple narratives disappeared, so did the version of Shakuntala from the Mahabharata. The Shakuntala that remained was Kalidasa's—an ingénue reliant on magic and miracles to get her due.

Dean Patnaik came on stage after the students. 'The past few months have been an example of how IILL can collaborate with leading universities around the world. Today it is Chicago that has funded a lab here. Tomorrow it could be IILL giving scholars on loan to institutions abroad. We have a great history of knowledge exchange in our Indian culture. The Goud Saraswat Brahmins from the Indo-Gangetic plains were invited by the kings on the Konkan coast, the Brahmins from Kannauj became the Brahmins and Kayasthas of Bengal...

'We thank Professor Amitabh Dhar for championing this exchange. And all the graduate students who were part of the laboratory. Finally, Mr Ajay Iyer and Ms Tara Mallick for working closely with Professor Dhar to see the project to its fulfilment.'

There was a round of applause. Tara looked around the hall. Some people were whispering to each other.

'There is still some fine-tuning left to do, and at IILL we believe in perfection, so we will not be unveiling the generator till we are 200 per cent ready.

'As you all are aware, a committee comprising Professor Dhar, Professor Goyal, Professor Hegde and myself was set up to select one student representative to relay this project to Chicago as part of a six-month fellowship. This student representative will relay the processes employed here to guide teams there to create other linguistic generators,' he went on.

There was a murmur in the hall. It was the collective sarcasm of those who are never singled out.

'I'm happy to announce that Mr Ajay Iyer will be relaying the project back to Chicago. Mr Iyer, will you join us on stage please.'

Ajay was seated in one of the middle rows, behind the aisle that allowed people to walk across. When the dean announced his name, the students turned to look for him. He was talking to a friend next to him. Caught by surprise, he hurriedly straightened his shirt as he stood up and walked towards the stage. Tara felt like she was reading a novel. These things were surely happening to other people, people who were not Tara Mallick, but they felt real. Her body brought her back to the present scene. Her temples were damp, she could feel the heat of her breath and she was sure her ears had turned red. She clapped because that was what everyone else was doing. She made her face break into a smile. She tried to catch Amitabh's eye on stage. When he got up to shake hands with Ajay, she ran her palms over her hair, tucking a stray lock behind her ear.

She had felt so much in her body in the last two months. Discovered new muscles, new surface areas for touch: the skin behind her ear, the back of her neck, the webbed skin between her toes, the crease behind her knees. With this expanse in receptivity—the ability to feel slight shifts in temperature, a finger hovering above skin, sounds softer than breathing—she had also developed the ability to feel other things she had never felt before. Shame, guilt, humiliation, impotence. Now, her ankles were stinging like they had tasted cane.

Ajay walked up to the stage by her side of the aisle. He walked slowly, in a manner that people would appreciatively describe as humble. Her eyes caught the bottom of his beige trousers, his slippers. She looked at the stage, trying hard not to let her eyes focus on anything. People continued to clap. It was easy to clap for Ajay. When he went on stage, he was almost in tears. He had not expected this, he said. It was not only a tremendous honour, it would also be his first trip abroad. She couldn't help feeling happy for him. She knew he would call his Amma right after the event and she would make him listen to her prayer bells over the phone. That had happened when he had called her the day the lab was inaugurated.

As Tara clapped with the others, she could feel eyes on her. It was the low heat of a vessel that has burnt and would continue to release its malodour until it is thrown in the sink. It is not a heat that has the power to burn. It only fouls the air.

The dean announced coffee and biscuits in the foyer. Tara filed out with the others and stood in a long queue for the milky coffee that she would not drink. It was something to do.

Ajay came out to look for her. He had overcome his surprise by then and believed he deserved what he had been awarded. He found Tara in the line and told her he wished both of them were going. It should have made her feel better but she felt worse.

Professor Goyal found her in the line and asked her to join him at the head of the queue. There was a tray of cream biscuits just for the professors. He picked two biscuits and placed them in her saucer.

'We were going to pick two students, you know. Then the budgets were cut,' he said, as he stirred sugar into his coffee.

Tara told him she understood. 'These things happen,' she heard herself say, as she dipped her biscuit into the coffee. She held it for too long. It became soggy and dropped into her cup.

She saw Amitabh and the dean walk out of the hall, towards the coffee. Professor Goyal turned to speak to someone else so she put her coffee down and left, trying to walk at a normal pace. She sat on the bench outside the library for some time, then she went to her room. But the tears didn't come.

The lab was supposed to be an open house that day. Students and faculty from other departments had been invited to come over and try the generator. She told Ajay she had a submission for a journal to write and stayed in her room through the afternoon.

The few times she stepped out of her room to go to the bathroom or fetch something from the refrigerator in the corridor, she went past girls in their rooms with the doors ajar. They were doing the things they usually did—studying, talking on the phone, folding their clothes, applying nail polish. They played a game where they knew the rules. It was only she, Tara Mallick, who had walked guilelessly into a harrowing, foreign playground.

In the bathroom, when she went in to wash her face, one of the sevaks came up to her and stroked her back. She had a kind, plump face.

'I heard what happened. You wanted to go to America for that fellowship, no. You've been working so hard. Working all day and night, we have all seen that. You must be sad,' she said.

Tara felt tears starting to form and tried to stop them. Stop it. Stop it. How much could she even reveal to this woman?

The sevak searched her jhola and produced a shrink-wrapped laddoo for Tara.

'It's not fair,' said Tara, her voice quaking. She tried to keep herself from crying. Tara Mallick rarely cried.

'If you have complaints about the selection process, you should write an official letter,' the sevak said.

'It's too late. It's over. I'm not going to beg,' said Tara.

'You have every right to question their crooked American systems. I can ask the sevaks from the research wing to help you. Let me tell you something. They have paused their enquiry on this Amitabh Dhar but it's not over. Things are not quite right with him and his research for the next book. And some graduate students have already complained about the inhuman hours in the lab,' the sevak said, adding, 'I'll be outside the warden's office if you want to talk.'

Tara had to splash her face with cool water all over again.

*

In the evening, Tara hailed an autorickshaw and went over to Mysore Palace Hotel.

When Amitabh opened the door she saw his suitcase on the bed. Shirts and underwear were stacked in neat rolls. An Indian man who's been without a mother or wife for a while, she thought, and laughed.

This propensity to laugh at the wrong time, the comedy act she had going on in her own head, confused others. The corners of her lips curled into a smile even while her eyes burned. It wasn't that she was afraid to speak her mind. In her teenage years, she had had obscenities ready, a hand to slap—the cousin, the attendant at the medical store, the man at the traffic signal. It wasn't fear that stopped her, but habit. It was exhausting to be enraged all the time. She had learned to ignore the small violations, counter them with good manners.

Her problems were peculiar to her. They were not problems that others considered warranted. She was never the recipient of praise. People fell over themselves praising those lesser to her. But she had to be the very top of the class to be called a good student. She had to win the 100 metres track race every time to be called a fast runner. She had been awarded the prestigious dean's scholarship for a fully funded doctoral programme at IILL, but the faculty and other students seemed to begrudge her that. Everyone assumed Robi Mallick's daughter had it easy. People didn't see her victories as her own.

But AD had told her he saw her. He had told her he admired her scholarship and her ambition. He had told her she was like him. And the man loved himself.

It was her rage that came out as laughter.

'Would have helped to have some advance notice,' she said, as she walked in. She went over to sit on the chair by the desk, still laughing.

Amitabh continued with what he was doing—wrapping his slippers in newspaper—but looked at her briefly like she had just had a haircut, wondering what was different about her face.

'About Chicago? Didn't think it mattered to you. You never brought it up. You can always go to Chicago, if not now then later,' he said. He zipped up the flap of fabric on one side of the suitcase and patted it to check that it was packed tight.

'It's not about a free ticket to Chicago,' said Tara. 'It's about having Chicago on my resume.'

'Well, in that case, Ajay Iyer put in the hours and you spent more time in this room than in the laboratory. You compromised your position. He had more facetime with the students,' said Amitabh.

He shut the suitcase and cleared the bed, before walking towards her.

'Besides, why mix grammar and pleasure,' he said.

'My career's a joke to you?' said Tara.

'Be reasonable. How do you think it would have made me look if I had picked you? Don't worry, Patnaik, Goyal, Hegde, they all voted for you.'

'That's supposed to make me feel better? That you gave me up?'

He held her chin with his fingers. 'Having you in Chicago would be a terrible inconvenience.'

The sun was coming in through the sides of the curtains in sharp, slanting bars, like the lightsabers she and Surjo played with as children. She remembered AD entering the dean's gate for his welcome party the day he had arrived. He had looked like a man without shadows.

The tears that streamed down her face were a relief. They cooled her cheeks. Amitabh sat down on the edge of the bed, facing her.

'Trust me, I'm doing you a favour. You'll have other opportunities. You're young. Grief, loss, disappointment, these things help us grow,' he said.

Tara kept her face still. The tears were clearing the way for something else.

'And listen, if all goes well, I'll be back in a few months. That's what you really want, don't you. You want to be around me?' he said.

Tara could see her rage seated beside her. It had been a third presence in the room, but now it was billowing like smoke, occupying more space, making it hard for her to breathe.

'Amitabh Dhar, how is it possible for a man to be so consumed by his own arrogance? It's no wonder that Sophia left you. That your sister has cut ties with you. Not everything in the world is about you!'

Amitabh shot down what he called her dramatic monologue with two swift poison arrows. First, he said she sounded like a hysterical TV heroine. Then he called her a conceited little bitch.

Tara stormed out of the room just like she had stormed in all those weeks ago. None of Bharata's nayikas did this. In the classical treatises, in the paintings in the museums, or the dance ballets Guruji taught her, the women sulked and pouted, suffered and raged. But they never left. Only apsaras left. Those celestial nymphs were always taking flight. But unlike mortal women, they were made of cloud and water.

*

Tara knew what time his flight was on Sunday. She had made plans for how they would spend their last two days in Mysore. They would order Kingfisher Strong at the café, shop for gifts at the state emporium 'like tourists' and perhaps walk by the lake.

Instead, early on Sunday morning, she had her green smoothie, put on her purple running kit, and went for her run. She circled the library building, the central building, wound around the professors' quarters and went all along the staff quarters, coming back to her room when her t-shirt was soaked through with sweat.

There is something curious about a woman's anger. A spark can set alight a whole forest, once wet and green. And it burns and burns, fuelled by the memory of injustices borne not just by them but the women before them—their mothers and grandmothers, sisters and aunts, friends and maids, the women in stories, witches, rakshasis, princesses and goddesses.

As Tara ran through the campus, snatches of Thulasi's email— which she had received the night of the encounter by the notice board—had come to her. She could almost picture Thulasi standing in front of her and saying: 'We can have this conversation when you understand what it is like to have something denied to you for reasons beyond your control.'

There was still time for the breakfast bell. Tara changed her t-shirt and walked to the Kukkarahalli Lake, a couple of kilometres away from the campus. She sat by the lake and looked at herons swooping into the rotting wood of an abandoned boat. Boatmen were soliciting tourists for early morning coracle rides. Many of them asked her, offering a discounted rate for their first ride of the day. Perhaps a ride by Goddess Lakshmi would make their fortunes turn that day? She was not a tourist, she lived in Mysore, she told them. They didn't believe her. She answered in broken Kannada to reassure them, which confused them even more. 'Witch,' she heard one of them mumbling under his breath. Tara laughed. It was amusing how men, all men, were surprised when they didn't get what they wanted.

They had come here together. The coracles reminded AD of the boats on Dal Lake.

She saw a boatman do a delicate dance to push the coracle off the banks. The muscles of his body seemed to be engaged in the effort but his face was relaxed, his eyes looked straight ahead—he caught her staring at him and looked away. He didn't want trouble.

When they had come here together, AD had managed to get a boatman to give him his oar. No Indian tourist ever wanted to row themselves and the boatman didn't understand why this man wanted to row and sweat when he could just sit with his arm around the girl and talk in English. AD had tried to row standing up as though he was in a gondola. He had told Tara that to row well while standing you needed to keep your eyes off the water. If you kept looking down at the water it wasn't as good an exercise or as pleasurable. Her mother used to tell her that while making mutton curry, if you kept opening the pot to check the meat, it never cooked as well. You had to put everything in and let it stew. 'When you grow older, you will be confident enough to resist the urge to open the pot,' she had said. She missed her mother's food. She was hungry now. She looked at her watch. She had been sitting here for so long that breakfast at the canteen would be finished by the time she returned.

She spotted a shining tinsel sword by the grassy banks of the lake. There were other things that remained from the Dussehra celebrations. Even this town named after the buffalo demon Mahishasura celebrated the event of the Goddess piercing a spear through his heart. Good versus evil. Her Dadu had told her that many believed Mahishasura was a good king, so powerful that the gods couldn't defeat him. He had a boon: he couldn't be killed by a man. And so the gods created Goddess Durga to do their bidding. On the tenth day, her work done, Durga is immersed in water. There is goat curry and libation. Married women smear vermilion on each other, moving their bodies to the beat of the dhaak. But what is it that they are really doing? Why do they celebrate the drowning of one of their own?

A heron came to sit in front of her. The lake extended into a bird sanctuary and herons, painted storks and pelicans frequently made an appearance. She didn't know the names of these birds. AD had identified them for her. She was too much of a city girl, he said. She threw a lotus seed from a packet she had bought from a vendor towards the heron. It seemed disinterested, looking at something far away. What noises can a girl make to catch a heron's attention? She threw a few more seeds and a group of crows came down and started picking at them. The heron flew away. But she had wanted the heron. She had wanted only the heron.

Tara was used to falling in love. This was the first time she had been thrown out of its salted waters. She longed not so much for him but for the longing she once had for him. She longed for who she was before she went to Mysore Palace Hotel the first time.

She picked a faraway coracle as a point of focus. She wanted to be able to remember the good things. What had AD said when they had come here together? What was she wearing? Why did he hold his newspaper that way, with the top right dog-eared as if he was expecting an impending distraction?

He had quoted a verse from the *Chaurapanchasika* as they watched the birds, recited it in Sanskrit, then English:

Even now
I bring her back to me in her quick shame,
Hiding her bright face at the point of day:
Making her grave eyes move in watered stars,
For love's great sleeplessness wandering all night,
Seeming to sail gently, as that pink bird,
Down the water of love in a harvest of lotus.

'How fateful that you'd pick Bilhana, a poet from Kashmir, for your thesis. You will have to think of me every time you read this,' he had said, planting a pestilent seed in the fertile grounds of young love.

Are we altered by love in the way astronauts are altered when they return from space? Tara realized it had played tricks with her memory.

She felt deceived by her own self. She had come to the lake not to get away. She had come here to water her memories. She had to believe that the hurt she felt now was, in the same measure, once something else.

It is hard to hold on to a feeling. The moment you try to solidify it, it crumbles. You play a memory again and again. But the more you play it back, the more you forget. Each forced recollection loses a fraction of the original. It leaves a scratch on the record. What you have are only perfect bits and pieces. Words without syntax.

Memory does not live only in the mind, the body stores it in its own ways. Simple movements had begun to overwhelm her. When she did her lunges and high knees before her run, she remembered him. She went for long-long runs to create aches that would distract from the ones she carried.

She had made herself believe that AD had been her conquest. She had picked him. All my life I have been chosen, and now I choose you, she had said to herself. And yet, why was she the one who felt refused? When had she lost her power? Why couldn't Omphale hold on to Heracles? Why did Tagore have his proud Abhisarika ridden with smallpox? She tried to think of him ageing further, his skin becoming the crinkled skin on top of milk.

It was sadder for a love to end than for a love to be lost. What she felt was not just sorrow, but a sting. What if their time together had ended for no reason other than that it had finished? She had opened a jar and greedily drunk up too fast.

She didn't doubt that AD had cared for her. But in his vast life stretched between continents, awards, books, marriages, and a son he spoke to in his sleep, she was a glass of water. For her, he was the sea you encounter for the first time. He had made her lose parts of herself that she would never see again.

ECLIPSE

Shashi was roused from her afternoon sleep by the sound of Chanda's bangles.

Chanda came to the Mallick house early in the morning. After a cup of Babloo da's tea, she sat on her haunches to grind masalas for the curries that would be made that day. Kumudini would usually decide this, but Babloo da took over the task of bossing the maids around any chance he had. Chanda rarely went up the stairs unless it was to deliver tea and nimki to the rooms. It was Radha mashi, an old, bent woman, who swept and mopped the rooms, once in the morning and once before the men returned home in the evening. Radha mashi was a quiet presence, sweeping dust like her life depended on it, partially disappearing under the large beds, dusting behind the almirahs. 'Never hire a young woman to clean your rooms,' Kumudini always said.

Chanda was a surprising presence in the room. She was looking behind the bedroom door. She even bent and looked under the bed.

Shashi had been married two months and waking up in the

mornings was already a smooth ritual. It started with a single cycle rickshaw's tooting horn. Soon there was an entire fleet. The sound of vegetable and flower vendors tempting morning shoppers added to it, forming a full orchestra of sounds. She woke up when the light came as rods through the barred windows. Then there were Lata Jethi's prayer bells from the floor above. She turned to face Robi while he was still asleep, admired the lines of his face. Soon he would open his eyes. This was how every day began.

It was a particularly hot afternoon, and Chanda had made a noisy intrusion. She was looking behind the clothes hanging on the aalna. Shashi sat up and adjusted her saree. 'Dolly is nowhere,' said Chanda.

'Why would she be behind the aalna?'

'She used to hide here when her dance moshai would come when she was little.'

'But she is no longer little. Do you think a fifteen-year-old girl can hide behind the aalna?' said Shashi.

Tapan's younger brother Swapan was a devoted sibling. Men like Tapan needed men like that around them. Swapan worked as an assistant manager with a fan company. He kept fixed office hours and made himself available when his Dada needed him. Every time she had an argument with Kumudini, his wife Sree would sulk and talk about moving to their own house in Alipore. But both Swapan and Sree knew that would never happen. He didn't make enough money to move out. And Sree wanted three new sarees for Pujo every year.

Their daughter Dolly was something beyond their understanding. Goddess Lakshmi incarnate, a visiting priest had told them.

She was fifteen when Robi and Shashi got married. Shashi

often looked at Dolly and wondered what it might feel like to be a truly beautiful woman. Dolly was mostly seen in the blue and white pinafore she wore to school, her hair braided into tight plaits and then looped around her head. What would it be like to have people turn and look when you step into a room, to feel the need to talk softly, to walk quickly, to avoid being noticed? Every morning, and then again in the evening, Sree would sit behind Dolly on the first floor veranda and pull at her hair. Dolly usually maintained a patient grimace. The red ribbons her mother tied at the ends of her plaits—a requirement of the school uniform—made a mockery of her. They were a reminder that she was still a child. But she was not. Anyone could see that. Even Babloo da didn't treat her like a child any more.

Shashi tucked her saree around her waist and joined Chanda in the search. They went to all the rooms on the first floor. Then the rooms on the second floor. Chanda told her she would run up and look on the terrace, grumbling about her backache. And then she grumbled about her drunk husband in the village. Any grouse Chanda had always led to her drunk husband in the village. As if to say, not only did she have to redo the masalas or string the mosquito nets tighter because they weren't to Kumudini's liking, but she had to do so with the knowledge that her drunk husband in the village still inhabited the world.

Shashi parted with Chanda and walked down to the courtyard, where everyone had assembled. Tapan was sitting in his armchair, talking in a low voice to Bibek and Lata Jethi. Swapan was consoling Sree, who was in tears. Kumudini seemed to be the only person working—dispensing instructions, looking into a phone book.

Lata Jethi had made herself indispensable in the Mallick house. Not only was she Tapan's trusted minister, but she ruled the tastebuds. At the end of summer, she would pour boiled and sweetened mango pulp into the stone plates she carved all year. After the requisite time in the sun there would be aamshotto, thin layers of mango leather. In the afternoons, while every member of the household slept, she cut potato and bitter gourd to a hair's thickness with her floor-mounted blade to fry and store in jars. Tapan couldn't have a single meal without these. After Pujo, she would gather old sarees and start her season's quilting. Sree and Kumudini had tried to help but their needlework never matched Lata's.

Shashi was alarmed by the scene. She glanced at the clock: it was almost 6 p.m. Dolly was usually home from school by 3 p.m. But when the servant had gone to fetch her that day, as he always did, she was not in her usual waiting place by the gate. He had waited for an hour and come back.

Now he had returned with news. In the streets, there was some talk of the Mallick girl being seen on a cycle with the Mondol boy. Further investigation along the route revealed that they were seen going towards Outram Ghat.

Built in the late nineteenth century by the British in memory of Sir James Outram, the ghat along the banks of the Hooghly was a popular picnic spot. Young families sat on mats and ate chanachoor. A cinema box at one end kept children occupied while their parents spoke about things they couldn't speak about in their joint family homes in North Kolkata. For decades, it had been where romantic songs from Bengali movies were filmed. In the songs, the heroes sang about being unable to read women's minds; and heroines with high cheekbones challenged the men to walk away from the crowds with them.

Shashi went to the kitchen where tea was being made. One look at Babloo da and she knew she wouldn't have her special tea today. He handed her two plates piled with butter biscuits. The biscuits from New Market were usually brought out for guests. The guests had gathered already—several neighbours were already in the courtyard commiserating with the Mallicks. Bibek tried to soothe things in his gentle manner, now speaking to the wailing Sree, now nodding at something Tapan was saying.

Tapan asked for Robi to be sent for from the club. Swimming could wait when family honour was at stake.

Kumudini was worried about this interruption to Robi's schedule. She wanted her son to get his exercise, so she could stuff him again. She believed it was her duty to feed her son till he could physically eat no more. Robi always protested but Shashi suspected he liked it: he would leave his breakfast plate a little unfinished and his mother would carry the plate and run behind him—this was the scene every morning—begging him to finish the food. It was all new to Shashi, who had seen her little brothers rinse their own breakfast plates before they left for school. After Babloo da handed him his briefcase, Robi would acquiesce to a few bites. It was a private mother and son moment, as if to make up for the fact that he no longer slept in their room. She would feed him two mouthfuls and then he would touch her feet and leave.

Shashi placed the plate of biscuits on a stool near Tapan and sat on a chair. Nobody was sitting though several chairs had been laid out. She decided to stand up in solidarity. Since Robi would take a while to arrive, Tapan asked Bibek to go for the retrieval mission to Outram Ghat with the servants. Bibek nodded to Shashi as he left to reassure her that everything would be handled with the least cruelty. Shashi looked longingly towards the biscuit plates. Nobody was eating. How could she be the first?

After about an hour, Bibek, the two servants, Dolly, and a thin, scared boy with glasses and a sliver of a moustache appeared. Nitin—Shashi had seen him in their house for Pujo—was the shy kind who didn't get to bat in gully cricket till everyone else had had their chance or was tired.

Dolly was ceremoniously held by the elbow and taken up to their first floor room by her mother. The room was locked from outside. Everyone below could hear the latch creaking. Sree joined the group downstairs. She wanted to be there for the interrogation. Nitin was sitting on a chair and everyone was glaring at him. Robi had arrived by now and stood beside Tapan with his hands on his hips. Bibek looked at Shashi and then looked down. They were both trying to hold in their laughter.

Finally, Tapan spoke. He was surprisingly gentle. 'Where were you going?'

'Outram Ghat,' the boy said. He was shivering now and looking at his feet.

'Why?'

'To sit.'

'And do what?'

'Talk.'

'What on earth would a fifteen-year-old girl have to talk about with a seventeen-year-old boy. Have you no shame!' Sree interrupted. Her lips curled as she glared at him. Some of the

248

gathered neighbours joined her in admonishing Nitin.

Tapan asked Robi to take the boy home. 'Take the Buick,' he hollered. It was to be a message to the lower-caste Mondols when the magnificent car rolled up in their narrow street. Our daughters don't belong on your streets.

In the serious discussion that followed after Robi left, it was decided that Dolly was to be taken out of Loreto House and enrolled in Nivedita Girls' School, a Bengali medium institution ten minutes from home. A car would drop and pick her up. It was also decided that her dance classes would stop—this was Lata Jethi's touch. She didn't need any more preparing to be a woman.

Now that most things were settled, and the butter biscuits were still untouched, Shashi walked towards them. She was just about to pick one up when Tapan's eyes fell on Shashi and his face lit up. 'You are a young woman. Go talk to Dolly,' he said. Then he looked at Bibek. 'You too. Young people. Talk to her,' he said. He was feeling sorry for his Dolly now. She wasn't his child but he didn't have a daughter and thought of her as his own. It was he who had called his business associates to get her into Loreto, though her school marks were not so good.

Shashi and Bibek walked up the stairs to the latched door. Shashi expected a sobbing mess. But Dolly was listening to the Beatles on the old record player Robi da had given her. When they entered, she latched the door from inside and sat on the bed.

Dolly started giggling.

'Where was he taking you?' said Shashi, trying to sound authoritative.

'Did you see his face?' said Dolly in answer.

Shashi didn't understand.

'Shashi di, *he* wasn't taking me anywhere,' said Dolly.

'Where did you get the idea to go to Outram Ghat?' said Shashi.

'*Teen Bhubhoner Parey.*'

They had all seen the movie on TV last weekend. Outram Ghat was the scene of the actor Soumitro's romantic declarations.

'I wanted to see the place myself so I wouldn't be surprised when a boy actually took me there.'

'But he's a boy too,' said Shashi.

'Nitin's not the kind of boy I will marry.' Dolly turned to look at Shashi and Bibek. She narrowed her eyes and started to unbraid her hair.

'The one I fall in love with will have Soumitro's soul and Uttam's hair,' said Dolly. Then she looked at Bibek, suddenly bashful. 'And he will be like Bibek da in everything.' Bibek, who had been quiet so far, blushed a deep maroon and rubbed his forehead.

Shashi's friend Ritu would joke that any sampling of Kolkata boys at the time could be divided into those who aspired to be the chocolate-boy hero Uttam Kumar or the intellectually inclined Soumitro Chatterjee, with his faraway look and angular charms. Shashi was more an Uttam girl but at Jadavpur University, saying she was in the Soumitro camp was a better idea. All the girls in the Comparative Philosophy department agreed. Uttam looked like he hadn't read a book in his life.

Shashi pulled Dolly out of bed and towards the window. She turned up the wooden slats. It was late evening now and there were no children playing. Men were returning from offices, servants were walking swiftly with heavy bags of shopping and some young boys were dressed for the evening, possibly looking to hail a ride to take them to Park Street.

'Dolly, see, they are all either Uttam or Soumitro. Do you want to play a game? I'll point at a man and you say which is which.'

'Okay,' Dolly was cheerful, her unbraided hair now a halo around her face. She had thought Shashi di was here to reproach her.

Shashi started easy. She pointed at a boy, perhaps just twenty, in a large collared shirt. He had an exaggerated lock of hair that he kept touching for effect, as if to check it was still there.

'Uttam, Uttam,' said Dolly.

'Good.'

Next, she pointed at a weary-looking boy studying his watch, his shoulders drooping with a bag of books. His trousers were even more high-waisted than was the norm then. But there was a gentle grace to his walk. A cigarette dangled from his long fingers.

'Soumitro?' Dolly said with some trepidation.

They continued like this for a while.

'Why are we playing this?' asked Dolly.

'What I'm trying to say is you cannot have everything.'

'I *can* have everything. I won't marry a man unless he is both. Unless he is all of them together.'

'Do you know people like that?'

'Yes, Bibek da, Robi da. I will only marry a man like Bibek da. And when I'm sick, he will feed me payesh made with jaggery.' There was a decisiveness in her voice.

'Who eats payesh when they're sick, mad girl!' said Bibek, laughing.

'I do, and I will.'

'Ish, we shouldn't have let you watch those movies,' said Shashi.

Bibek remained silent but nodded in agreement to everything

Shashi said, his face blushing maroon every time Dolly mentioned him.

'No, no, please don't stop them. I have nothing to do. Robi da used to let me listen to records in his room but...' said Dolly.

Shashi felt a pang of apology. Her entry to the household had separated Dolly from the cousin she worshipped. They left Dolly to the Beatles, and Shashi said she'd bring her some dinner in her room when it was time.

Shashi floated in an air of self-importance that evening. She was the only mediator the Mallick household had to understand the mind of their adolescent rebel. Even Robi was struck by her hauteur. When Sree asked her what had transpired in the room, Shashi said she would tell them all together at dinner. She did not think it wise to reveal that Outram Ghat had been Dolly's plan all the way but she said enough so the matter didn't escalate to disinviting the Mondol family to the Pujo that year.

These were the terms Shashi negotiated on behalf of Dolly: Dolly would be happy to stop the dance classes. But if they changed her to the Bengali medium school she would stop studying altogether, which would be embarrassing for the family, especially for Tapan. She was all right being dropped by car at school and picked up, if her best friend was dropped and picked up on the way as well. Everybody was tired and relieved and all her terms were agreed to.

Clever girl, Shashi thought. She must learn a few things from this fifteen-year-old. But she had already won something. That night, Robi asked her if she wanted the light on longer to read.

*

THE YEAR after Robi and Shashi moved to Delhi, the Mallicks launched an urgent search for a suitable boy from the Baidya caste for Dolly. They had been unable to control her exploits. Dolly had responded by eloping with her forty-year-old tutor, an embittered alcoholic who could not comprehend how a girl like Dolly had landed up with him. He beat her because her beauty enraged him. He brought another woman home, and Dolly, unable to suffer the ignominy, tried to kill herself. But two-storeyed Kolkata homes weren't built for jumping to one's death. And so she lived, paralyzed from the waist down, with the added burden of the neighbourhood's pity. Dolly's fate was a revenge of the world against wilful beauty.

When Shashi had heard of Dolly's accident, she had called Bibek and teared up over the phone. Both of them felt complicit. They had facilitated Dolly's visits to Outram Ghat with boyfriends, telling Kumudini and Sree they were with her. But that was before Dolly had made the real mistakes.

THE
ILLUMINATED

SHASHI ASKED BIBEK TO HELP WITH THE RENOVATION WHILE he stayed with her in Delhi.

There was little that could be structurally altered in a Mallick Architects design but Bibek replaced the blinds in the rooms with thin cotton cloth from Delhi Haat. Both Jose and Ramcharan found occupation in this project: measuring the windows, buying fabric, dropping and picking it up from the tailor, sliding the new curtains through the long curtain rods. Life at the commune had made Bibek unable to sit on a sofa for long to talk, watch TV or nurse a single malt. When he wasn't meditating in his room, he was up and about. He made himself tea even before Poornima came into the kitchen in the morning, much to her indignation. He received a few visitors: friends from architecture school, a nephew who lived in Delhi, women from the commune who were now married and settled in the city. His presence gave Shashi and Poornima more to do. They planned elaborate meals and went more often to the market.

It was when they were returning from the fish market one day that Shashi encountered Asha.

'Shashi Miss, Shashi Miss!'

Shashi heard the calls from the storefront of a small medical and general supplies shop just beside the entrance to the fish market. She immediately recognized Asha, who was waving at her energetically with her hands above her head.

Shashi walked up to the shop. A man who seemed to be her superior at the store was asking Asha where something was stocked. A glass counter at waist height separated Asha from Shashi but Asha lifted one end of the counter and stepped out. She looked radiant in a floral-printed salwar-kameez. Bangles jangled on her wrists. She had a red bindi on her forehead.

'How are you, Asha? You work here? This is not a beauty parlour!' said Shashi.

'I'm married now, Shashi Miss,' said Asha, pulling her dupatta lower so Shashi could see the mangalsutra around her neck.

'Really? You didn't invite us? Where did you meet your husband? Where do you live now? Tell me everything,' said Shashi.

Asha looked at the storeowner and gestured with her eyebrows. Her smile took up almost all of her face. Shashi looked at the man, closely this time. He was haggling with a customer about change, scratching the back of his ear with his thumb. He was middle-aged and wearing a kurta with the MSS crest. As she watched, he tore open a sachet of Goumutra™ and poured it into his mouth. Shashi couldn't quite understand why Asha would be happy to be married to this man. Perhaps he was very good-natured. Young Asha, with her glitter hair extensions, who used to say she wanted a boyfriend like the movie star Salman Khan. Shashi looked for the shining strands in her hair. They were gone. Her hair was oiled and neatly braided back.

'Come and meet us at Yuva Vikas when you can,' said Shashi. 'Your friends will be happy to see you. And Sunita Miss too.'

'My husband doesn't like me going to that part of town any more. He's very protective,' Asha said, smiling coyly. Then she added, 'And about Robi sir. It is such a bad thing to happen to you, Shashi Miss. I cried and cried when I heard. I'm so sorry, Miss.'

Asha took Shashi's palms and held them between hers. It was not something she had done before. She went back inside the store and emerged with a packet of almonds and insisted that Shashi take it as a gift.

'Why don't you come home sometime?' said Shashi.

'To your house? Will Tara didi be there? You gave me so many of her clothes. I would love to meet her,' said Asha, adding, 'now I don't wear those kinds of clothes any more.'

'Tara is out of Delhi for some important work,' said Shashi. 'She will be home soon. You can meet her when you come next time.'

Shashi bought strips of antacids from the store and wrote down her address on the bill. Asha said she would visit her that week. Shashi had a headache as she slipped into the car. Poornima said it was because of the smells from the fish market and proceeded to fight with Jose all the way back home about driving too slowly.

A few days later, early in the evening, Asha arrived in an autorickshaw. She was wearing a bright red saree this time. It looked new, with many tiny sequins stitched into the fabric. Her husband dropped her off and said he would come to pick her up in an hour.

Shashi and Asha sat beside each other on the sofa. Poornima

brought them tea and samosas and tried not to stare at Asha's shiny red saree, her long eyelashes clumped with mascara, the frosted lipstick, the thick bangles of gold—Poornima was worried she might burst into a laugh and then Shashi didi would lecture her later to be kinder about the sartorial enthusiasm of newly married girls.

Asha told Shashi that after she left Yuva Vikas, she had worked in Sir ji's workshop for some time, sealing pouches of Goumutra™, stitching jholas and making floor purifiers with cow urine, camphor and neem, which they had a contract to supply to government offices. It was meant to be a temporary job. She had met many others from the shelter there. Then, under the Lakshman Rekha scheme, she had been placed with a man who needed a shop assistant. It turned out he was also looking for a wife and was of the same caste. The day the marriage had been registered in court she had worn a red and gold salwar-kameez with golden tassels hanging from her dupatta. She showed Shashi and Poornima a photo on her phone.

Asha told Shashi how lucky she was. She had married this man in whose house there was fruit for breakfast every day. And he also allowed her to work in the shop. They lived with his mother, who helped with the cooking. 'I'm so lucky, Shashi Miss. I never wanted to be stuck in the kitchen making rotis,' she said. They went for movies once a month, not to the single-screen theatres but to the multiplex where they bought flavoured popcorn in large tubs. At night, he gave her Ayurvedic tea that relaxed her.

Shashi thought about Sir ji and his oversized pouch. Sir ji, the social worker. As Asha ate her samosa, her happiness was palpable. She kept saying how lucky she was. Soon she was sobbing and talking about two of her friends from Yuva Vikas who had not been picked up by Sir ji because of their poor record—they were both at the shelter after having eloped as minors. Sir ji only took on girls of good character at the workshop, Asha explained.

Her friends had wound up in brothels on JB Road. One of them had texted her a month after their separation, when she had settled in and been given a phone. 'I'm so blessed, Shashi Miss. I'm so lucky to have found a husband,' said Asha.

In an hour, Ramcharan rang on the intercom to say that Asha's husband was back to pick her up. He waited at the gate. Asha left without the new saree that Shashi had gifted her; her husband had told her not to accept anything from a widow. Shashi and Poornima stood in the doorway and watched her as she walked away. Poornima agreed that the bright red saree looked less crude in the fading light.

Health Problems of Impure Children

Children born of mixed religion and intercaste marriage suffer from physical and neurological diseases. Help the innocent next generation born from illicit lust avoid these sufferings:

ASTHMA ✦ EPILEPSY ✦ ECZEMA ✦ PSORIASIS
✦ ATTENTION DEFICIT HYPERACTIVITY DISORDER (ADHD)
✦ PANIC ATTACKS ✦ LEFT-HANDEDNESS ✦ WEAK VISION
✦ COLOUR BLINDNESS ✦ EXCESSIVE TASTE FOR MEAT
AND OFFAL ✦ ADDICTIONS LIKE CIGARETTE, ALCOHOL AND
MANY FOREIGN DRUGS ✦ ADDICTIONS LIKE PORNOGRAPHY
AND VIOLENT VIDEO GAMES

WANT TO PROTECT YOUR SISTERS AND DAUGHTERS FROM
THE DANGERS OF IMPURE RELATIONS?
BECOME A LAKSHMAN REKHA SCHEME SOLDIER.
VISIT LAKSHMANREKHAFORALL.COM TO SHARE VIDEOS
AND SHAME VIOLATORS.

Call your
local
**Mahalaxmi
Seva Sangh
(MSS)**
chapter for
guidance.

MSS, HERE TO SERVE.

After Asha left, Shashi called Sunita.

'Kaisi hai tu?' said Sunita. 'How are you?'

'What do you know about Sir ji?' said Shashi.

'Social worker, no? He employs Yuva Vikas graduates in his workshops. Pays them fairly I've heard. Why?'

'I ran into Asha in a shop near the fish market a few days ago. She came to the house today.'

'Our beauty queen! How is she? I thought she'd be in the film industry by now.'

'Sir ji arranged her marriage to a sevak. Some shopkeeper, one of those…'

'She's married? What did she say? Such a bright girl.'

'She seems happy, Sunita. Too happy. Kept saying how lucky she was. She seems to believe her only other option was to be a house maid or a prostitute. What are we educating them for? Why do we organize vocational training?'

Sunita was quiet. Then Shashi heard a small storm, the sound of Sunita letting the air out of her lungs.

Shashi continued, 'There has to be a better plan in place for the girls. Internships, better vocational training, placement in companies. What about the police force? Will you talk to Surinder about placements?'

'Shashi, both you and I can make a lot of calls but we can't force people to hire Yuva Vikas girls,' said Sunita.

'We have to speak to the administrator,' said Shashi.

'And tell him what? You said Asha is happy.'

'How can she be? And what about the others?' said Shashi. She had never argued with Sunita before. She couldn't work out why her friend was being difficult about something so plain.

'Shashi, what are you really upset about? We both know Asha. No one can get her to do something she doesn't want to do. Are you sure she needs our help?' said Sunita.

Shashi had to end the call abruptly because the pressure cooker had whistled several times. If she didn't get up to attend to it, it would be one of those times the dal splattered all over the kitchen ceiling. Where was Poornima? She went to the kitchen and took the cooker off the stove. She wiped up the water, stained with turmeric, which had dripped down the sides of it. She immediately washed the kitchen towel and put it out to dry. Turmeric stains were unforgiving.

When she returned to the living room, she found Poornima crouched on one side of the sofa, her eyes fixed on the TV. Shashi turned to look at the screen. It had flashing text: 'Fisherwoman KC Meenakshi becomes chief minister of new state of Meenakshi, south of Mumbai.'

Shashi sat down on the sofa, one hand on Poornima's shoulder. The news made her stomach stiff, her breath short and her eyes wide. The body language of a football fan.

'It's happened! It's happened!' a news anchor with short hair was screaming on the screen.

Unexpected things were happening in the country these days. After Bibek had pointed out the news of the possibility of the Lakshman Rekha proposal becoming a bill, Shashi had started reading beyond the Arts & Books section in the newspaper.

Among other things, news of MSS protests and campaigns to protect Indian women appeared with alarming frequency on the Nation pages. It was also not uncommon to see headlines like 'Korea becomes no.1 importer of Indian cow urine' on page 1.

Apparently, Korean beauticians were now convinced that bathing in Indian cow urine was the latest skincare trend for glowing skin and purified pores. Its pH balance was different from that of the urine from Jersey and Holstein cows. Ayurveda was becoming such big business that legacy cement and steel companies were having public feuds about GI tags for traditional medicinal herbs like neem and giloy. Schools across urban districts were shutting down because parents were distraught about changes in curricula and withdrawing their children from formal education.

The news today was also unexpected. Demands for separate statehood had historically taken decades of agitation, riots and curfews but this had happened seemingly overnight. The new chief minister wasn't the scion of an old political family but a lower-caste fisherwoman.

On the TV screen, there were shots of women entering a compound. There were women walking with babies strapped to their backs, toddlers holding on to their fingers. The women carried laptops and files, and wore determined looks. Some were pushing elderly people in wheelchairs. This was one of the many unique features of the way the state government would work, the TV anchor explained. The government office building would have a day care centre for infants and one for the elderly. The TV anchor was now interviewing an international expert on women's labour force participation who said this was 'exemplary' and 'set a global precedent'.

Shashi then realized it wasn't just the formation of a new state and the chief minister's appointment that was making news. KC Meenakshi had said that she was looking at forming an all-woman cabinet. This felt far-fetched even for the TV serials they watched every evening.

'Women are running their country, Didi?' said Poornima.

'It's still our country,' said Shashi.

'Yes, it is a coup. It is absolutely what we call a coup. But it's been a long time in the planning. KC Meenakshi has been working behind the scenes for years,' the short-haired news anchor screamed again.

The news bulletin branched into a feature segment with a political analyst explaining the genesis of the state of Meenakshi.

It had started with business and commerce. For centuries, only the men from the fishing community went out to sea early in the morning. When women started going out to sea following KC Meenakshi's example half a decade ago, they realized they were very good at it. Their fingers, used to sorting coriander and peeling garlic in dimly lit kitchens, were better at untangling nets. They could wake up early; they had been doing so for years to fetch water and get their children ready for school. And their minds were sharp for navigation in the early hours unlike the men who would be drinking late into the night and were always groggy. They also had better intuition for approaching winds or waves. Besides, the boats were lighter than before and had power steering. They no longer needed brute force to manoeuvre them.

The political analyst explained that the fisherfolk had always worn their savings as thick gold chains and bangles around their neck and wrists. But it was KC Meenakshi who had encouraged women to pool money to form community banks that would give out loans to buy equipment and send their children to college. They had even set up alcohol de-addiction centres for their husbands and teenage sons, and counsellors to help intervene in cases of domestic violence.

With these measures, the local industry had turned around. The fishing lobby had become so powerful that a political wave had begun to form around it. Various local political parties had tried to appropriate KC Meenakshi's goodwill, gifting her land or a flat in exchange for a single appearance in a rally. She had attended a few, been disillusioned by their promises, and finally decided to contest as an independent candidate.

KC Meenakshi had won the local elections by such an overwhelming majority that other political candidates had all but withdrawn. Demanding a separate state had come next. States had been formed on far lesser grounds lately: language, disputes over a public monument, type of meat consumption. KC Meenakshi's union had gone on indefinite strike, blocking the country's fresh seafood supply, of which she controlled almost 70 per cent. The Union government had had to give in. It had all happened so quickly that organizations like Shudhh Manch—The Pure Platform and the MSS had not had time to organize protests. Perhaps that was part of the plan, the political analyst surmised. The Union government had a strategic push and pull with the MSS and this was not the first time that they had made a move that was a direct affront to the volunteer organization, which was growing in strength every day.

The MSS considered KC Meenakshi a dangerous ideological rival—a leader who was driving women to abandon their natural roles. On their social media networks, they called her a bloodthirsty rakshasi, an anti-national activist and a leftist lesbian whore.

In the newly formed state, women and transpersons would hold chief administrative roles. No special reservations or regulations were needed because the men from the fishing community, seeing merit in the plan, had agreed to refrain from participating. The country had a long and complex history of matrilineal societies in some pockets but nothing had ever translated to the sphere of contemporary politics. No one had seen anything like this before, the political analyst explained.

The TV anchor came back on screen to announce that the new chief minister's plans for her first term included giving every fishing family new boats with double outboard engines. Pictures of her campaign slogan flashed on the screen behind the anchor. The campaign posters said 'Lay the net for a better future'.

There was more to KC Meenakshi's political victory than sheer commercial might. She was beloved by the fishing community in the way only a woman can be. They called her Meenakshi Ai, their mother. They abided by her rules because they trusted her. She would always look out for them.

KC Meenakshi was now being interviewed on the TV screen. Her hair was in its usual tight knot, while the reporter's hair blew in the seaside wind. Besides KC Meenakshi stood a woman in a fitted black-and-white checked dress who the reporter introduced as a lawyer. Behind them there were people celebrating, dancing in a circle chanting 'Meenakshi Ai', wearing facemasks that looked like a flat rendition of her face.

When Bibek entered the living room, he found Shashi and Poornima completely enthralled. For Poornima, this was with both hands on her cheeks. For Shashi, it was by covering her mouth with her fingers.

It was past the time they usually had dinner. Poornima gestured to Bibek that she couldn't move while KC Meenakshi was on TV but hurriedly ran to the kitchen to bring a banana for him.

'Aren't you worried the men will fight you?' the TV reporter asked KC Meenakshi, holding the mic at a respectful distance from the new chief minister's face.

'They have a good life, our goddess Mumbadevi blesses them. We have chosen to do all the work... we did most of it anyway. They just have to stay sober, help with the children and housework and support us. We are keeping troublemongers like MSS sevaks out of our state. That will be better for their daughters and sisters too, won't it? They are thankful for that. This MSS, they talk about a Lakshman Rekha to protect women? I have drawn a Lakshman Rekha around our state and it's not to keep women in, it's to keep these people out...'

KC Meenakshi threw her head back and laughed. The sound of a woman's laughter took up a whole minute on primetime news. That was unprecedented too.

The reporter, visibly nervous, interrupted with her next question.

'So would men have to leave Meenakshi?'

'Ai ai, no no! We love our men. We might soon consider a 30 per cent quota for men in the state government, once things settle down.'

'There are talks of changing the calendar. How will that affect trade with outside parties?'

'See, the fishing community has always followed the lunar calendar. It guides us on tides, when to go out, how the catch will be. We've always had to adapt in order to sell, but it's a seller's market now. They will have to adapt to our calendar, our holidays and working hours now. Where will the country get fish otherwise? Everywhere else they have almost fished their waters to extinction with their aggressive practices.'

'Is it not against Indian culture for women to rule over men?'

The lawyer moved her face towards the mic. She wanted to take that one. KC Meenakshi put her arm around her shoulder.

'One needs to get out of these ruts. These notions of superiority, inferiority and equality must be discarded in order to start anew. Real change can only be achieved through a radical re-ordering of society. Throughout history there are examples of a certain group dominating a minority group for a period of time. But women are not a minority group. The problem is that women have never been organized as a unit. In Meenakshi we are giving all those who identify as women the solidarity of labour interests,' said the lawyer.

'Why was the agitation for a separate state necessary?'

'Until we are able to change the language of power completely, we have to speak in a language that is understood. Meenakshi is not an art project, it is a political endeavour. We want to ultimately reject paradigms of dominance but without autonomy, without statehood, without administrative rights, it was turning out to be difficult to realize our vision. Meenakshi is an intentional community, a living experiment. We will question ourselves every day on how to create a better future. We invite women from across the country to examine these questions with us with their own project proposals,' said the lawyer.

The reporter looked terrified. KC Meenakshi took the mic again as she held on to the lawyer's shoulder.

'Sisters, come to Meenakshi. You can bring your boys and men with you. We have provisions for them. We will help them reconnect with their true nature, allow them to be who they want to be.'

The TV screen switched to visuals of young men learning

pottery and making dried fish pickles. Some wore the traditional checked waistcloths, some wore shorts. Their bare chests gleamed in the sun, golden chains of various lengths hung around their necks. Something unidentifiable in them made them look ethereally beautiful. Poornima said all of them looked like her childhood playmate Noki, who had taught her how to curl into a ball when they jumped from the high branches of the sundari trees into the river.

To Shashi, one of the girls on screen now, learning how to steer a boat, the light catching her hair, looked like Asha. Another girl, carrying a load of blue nets, laughing, looked like Tara.

That night in bed, Shashi lay awake. In her dreams, KC Meenakshi appeared as many women. Here she was talking to the TV reporter as Sunita. Here she was inspecting the kitchen at the alcohol de-addiction centre as Poornima. Here she was, eating dinner with her husband... as Shashi.

EARLY IN the morning, Shashi walked out to the front garden. She stood near the Bankura horses, touching their cool terracotta faces with her palms. When Robi walked around them in the morning, barefoot, she would watch him through the window. There was always so much to do in the mornings: plan everybody's breakfasts, push the children to pack their bags for school, ensure Robi's black shirt for the day was ironed, wash Mishti's paws after her walk, instruct Poornima and Jose on the day's shopping.

She took off her slippers. Her feet only got damp, her cheeks became wet. She walked around the house and found Poornima in the back garden, pulling weeds from the jasmine.

'Poornima?' said Shashi. This was early even for Poornima.

'I like seeing the moon in the morning.'

'In the morning?' said Shashi.

'If you're lucky, and if you're nearing the full moon, you can see it in the morning, Didi.'

Shashi looked at the sky. The rising sun cast a golden halo behind the treetops. It was warm light, the colour of fire. It was too late. Or she was not lucky.

'Chand bibi has gone for her bath now,' said Poornima, and went back to her weeds.

Poornima used to tell Tara the story of Chand bibi, how the moon came to be, when she was small, as she ate her banana and milk. Poornima was a gifted storyteller. Her eyes danced, her fingers weaved the air. Shashi sat on one of the bamboo chairs in the garden, to see what she remembered.

When the earth was being sculpted and the sun had to pick a moon for it, the celestial bodies dressed in their brightest clothes to please him, so they would be the chosen one. But when they appeared before the sun, their clothes got scorched, and smelled like burnt tobacco. One celestial body, Chand bibi, hatched a plan. She made the stars her emissaries; together they planned a meeting with the sun on a cloudy day. She wore a robe made of fine wisps of cloud, that wouldn't get scorched or burnt. The sun was stunned by her beauty and ingenuity. He begged her to be the moon. The stars rejoiced. Not so quickly, said Chand bibi. She had conditions. The sun would have to be away when she came out to shine. The days are yours, and the nights are mine, she told him. 'So shall it be!' said the sun. And that's how Chand bibi became the mistress of her own sky.

Shashi looked at Poornima, who was waiting for the watering can to fill. When she was done filling it, she splashed her face with water, washed the soil off her fingers and hands.

At breakfast, the conversation turned to KC Meenakshi and the news from the night before. Bibek had spent the morning reading various analyses of the political development in the newspapers.

'The return of Romanticism,' said Bibek in an exaggerated voice to Shashi. 'Ei, is this taking you back to your Jadavpur days?'

'I don't think of Meenakshi as a romantic ideal. It's absolutely radical,' said Shashi.

'This is a fantasy, Shashi. And fantasies are never sustainable. This is going against the order of things,' said Bibek.

Shashi was about to peel an apple. She put her knife down.

'Godmen have tried all sorts of things over the centuries. No talking, no sex, no meat, no music... we didn't say they were going against the order of things,' said Shashi, pouring out their tea.

'Dividing men and women doesn't seem constructive to me. We are cut from the same cloth. We have to move together towards a higher purpose. These are worldly wars,' said Bibek.

'But this is the only world most of us will ever know. And we have a right to explore all its possibilities. Aren't you even a little bit curious?' said Shashi, as she sipped her tea. The plates in front of them were waiting to be filled with food.

Poornima brought round, fluffy white luchis to the table. She put the basket of deep-fried flatbread down on the table and served two each to Bibek and Shashi. Shashi placed her finger at the centre of the puffed-up luchis by habit, one after the other. She watched them deflate, and shook her head.

'Not hungry?' said Bibek. He wanted to tread carefully. Their exchanges had been stilted since he asked her to move to Kanyakumari.

In response, Shashi tore a large piece of her luchi, dipped it in the liquid jaggery that Poornima had served alongside, and folded it into her mouth.

'We have to have the courage to explore extremes. It's the only way to arrive at the centre,' said Shashi. 'Meenakshi is not a fantasy. There is a long history of communities around the world banding together for a purpose, exploring radical ways of living.'

'What has got into you? This is not who you are, Shashi,' said Bibek.

'That's why I would go there if I could,' said Shashi. 'To find out who I am.'

Poornima had been waiting for a pause in the exchange to make her announcement.

'I am going to Meenakshi,' she said.

'If you go, KC Meenakshi will make you chief architect,' said Bibek, laughing.

Poornima shot him a glance and looked at Shashi.

'They have called us there, Didi. They said it on TV last night. We have to go,' she said.

Shashi smiled. Poornima and her TV. Many years ago, she had got it into her head to become a detective and bought herself a magnifying glass and gloves, all because of a TV show.

'That is not for us, Poornima. We can't go like that,' she said, waving her greasy fingers in front of her face. She wished she had learnt from Robi how to make people change their minds and believe it was their own idea.

'Always can't. Can't. Can't. Why can't we go? You came from Kolkata to Delhi. I took two boats, one train and then sat on the floor of a bus to come to Kolkata,' said Poornima, now with her hands on her hips.

Shashi poured herself more tea. She folded and unfolded her napkin. Bibek was looking at Poornima. Poornima was looking at Shashi. And Shashi imagined she was surveying the scene herself from a distance. Effectively, there were three pairs of eyes on her. She was lost in constructing the visual details when Poornima spoke again, her voice softer this time.

'Didi, you know why Tara had so many questions about Chand bibi? It's because you city folk confuse children with your sun and moon stories,' said Poornima. 'Back home, we know it is Chand bibi who sends the sun away every night when she wants to play with the stars.'

Shashi reached out for Poornima's wrist.

'So when are we going to Meenakshi?' said Poornima.

TARA HAD still not responded to Shashi's phone calls. But Shashi had decided that she would drive down to Dharamsala with Bibek as soon as her students at Yuva Vikas were done with their exams. It was important not to spend any more days in this impasse with her daughter.

One evening, Sunita and Surinder came home with urgent news.

Surinder said he had something to share, information that

he was privy to, which would be public soon. He spoke with an apologetic face. His position in the police force made him feel responsible when it was something to do with the government. Shashi sat on the sofa with them, not knowing what to expect. It hadn't even been a week since the state of Meenakshi had been announced. What could it be now?

'Shashi, my colleagues and I are all very surprised but the MSS seems to have made a success of this one. The Lakshman Rekha proposal is going to be a bill to be discussed in parliament next month,' said Surinder. 'It's been drafted. We have reason to believe it will go through.'

'Tell her your plan now,' said Sunita to Surinder, making a rolling motion with her hands, urging him to speak faster.

'There's the issue of your needing a male guardian. Let's get you papers saying Surjo lives here or you could list Bibek as a family member—but he'll have to stay here then. You'll have to transfer the house and other assets into Surjo's name,' said Surinder. He paused to look at Shashi's face. He could not read it.

'Shashi, it's just paperwork. Many people are doing it. Your own neighbours are doing it. You have nothing to worry about. I'll manage it,' he added.

'What about Tara?' said Shashi.

'Surjo will probably have to be her guardian as well. Or your brothers? You'll have to think about how you want to do this,' said Surinder.

Shashi looked out through the window at the light fading on the frangipani trees.

'I don't want to think about it,' said Shashi. She held Sunita's gaze, then looked at Surinder.

'I won't be doing any of this. We are moving to Meenakshi. Poornima and I,' she said.

SURJO WAS troubled by what had come over his mother when they spoke on the phone that night.

'Moving? You've lived in that house all your life!'

'I have not lived here all my life,' Shashi said. She laughed, which troubled Surjo even more. 'I'm not sure I'm selling it. We are only packing it up for now.'

'The house needs to be lived in, it's our entire childhood, it's Baba's legacy, it's his...' said Surjo. Failing, he changed tack. 'That house has been featured in magazines, Ma. Who leaves a place like that? Surinder Uncle told me everything was under control. You don't have to move.'

'I have to, Surjo,' said Shashi.

'And what about Baba's memory?'

'I carry it with me,' said Shashi.

'I want to live in a house of my own,' she told a baffled Surjo over the phone a few days later.

'Ma, that is your house. We're not in one of your corny TV serials. Laura and I have no plans to displace you. Tara will settle in Europe, or someplace strange, you know her.'

'I want to build my house. Do you know Surjo, in Meenakshi there are incentives for women to build!' Shashi said in response.

HE OCCASIONALLY complained, but Bibek soon got swept up in the plans. Packers, movers, insurance papers, long calls with the liaison person in Meenakshi, a mission statement for her project proposal for a shelter home there.

Surjo tried appealing to Bibek. Meenakshi had made it to the inside pages of the *New York Times*. 'A Unique Social Experiment: A Threat to India's Rising Right', they had titled the story.

'I have nothing to do with this, Surjo, this is your mother and Poornima.'

'I'm sure Tara has something to do with this,' said Surjo.

'No, she still isn't talking to your mother.'

'What will Ma do there? Is it safe? What if it all fails? In the papers here they're calling it a living experiment. But experiments have a way of failing. The failed are punished. Who knows what these sevaks will do to the ones who return.'

'I'M PLANNING to build a shelter home for young people moving to Meenakshi,' Shashi told Surjo over another phone call. 'It will be a four-storeyed home in red laterite. There will be two badminton courts and maybe later, a pool.'

'A shelter home for girls?'

'For everyone.'

Surjo couldn't understand Ma at all these days. She was not herself any more. Since Laura was having a difficult pregnancy and he couldn't travel to Delhi, he left messages for Tara. But his sister didn't call back. She was being her usual stubborn self.

'DIDI, WHAT should I pack for the car ride?' Poornima asked the night before they were to leave for Dharamsala. There had been a lot of packing that week. It had all happened so fast. They were almost ready for the move to Meenakshi. Everything in the Delhi house had been packed, except the large furniture. The moving truck would have to be coordinated slyly, which Ramcharan, under the rule of Poornima, was capable of managing. If the MSS sevaks got wind, they could complicate matters. There had been parties interested in buying the house, but Shashi had decided against selling until Tara was in agreement. It was her home too. She had to speak to her daughter first.

Shashi and Bibek left Delhi at 6 a.m. with Jose, two small duffel bags and roti-rolls packed by Poornima that could feed a family. Shashi had left a message with Sonam at the language centre the day before to inform Tara of their arrival.

When they stopped for tea, the waiter asked Bibek what he and Mrs would like to have with tea. For a moment, Shashi felt time was moving backwards. Tara had told her there were languages in which it did. For that long moment, she rejoiced. Just the thought of it in someone else's mind, the thought that she was not a widow, not cleaved from life, was rain. It was easy.

When they got back in the car, Bibek sat up in the front with Jose. He wanted to roll down the windows and take in the world. Shashi slept the rest of the way. Jose had put up screens to block the sun but slivers of light hit her face.

That afternoon in the big house, when Robi had come home early from work, there had been so much light streaming into the room. She was polishing her nails wearing one of the satin petticoats her cousin had gifted her before the wedding. Robi had never seen her in them before. She had only undressed for him in the dark. Later, they had looked at each other for a long time as

279

they lay with their heads on the bolsters. When she thought about what love might be, this was what came to her. She knew love was her grandmother holding her face in her cool, wrinkled palms. And the first time her children took to her breast.

THE SAME morning that Poornima had proposed the move to Meenakshi, Noor was reading a poem aloud to Tara, sprawled on the mattress in the living room of Tara's flat:

When your father dies, say the Irish,
you lose your umbrella against bad weather.
May his sun be your light, say the Armenians.

When your father dies, say the Indians,
he comes back as the thunder.
May you inherit his light, say the Armenians.

When your father dies, say the Armenians,
your sun shifts forever.
And you walk in his light.

Some weeks ago, Tara might have cried. But now she felt a heaviness in her throat that she knew how to swallow. She leaned forward and put her arms around Noor; the asymmetrical embrace of close friends. Tara had come to understand that it was no longer about the extraordinary moments, the rollercoaster rides or the birthday presents. It was the everyday moments that floated before her when she thought of him. Her father slicing a boiled egg at the breakfast table, cracking open the newspaper, taking off his reading glasses to wipe them. These things would never occur again.

Somewhere over the months, despite her proclamation that there was not a creative hair on her body because of how normal her family was, Noor had begun to take an interest in poetry. Their mattress sessions were no longer restricted to the mornings or afternoons. A few days after the phone call from New Jersey, Noor moved into Tara's flat with a small bag. She suggested they rent a bigger place together but Tara was no longer sure how long she would stay in Dharamsala. Tashi came by almost every day with lunch. Tara had forgiven him. When your father dies, pride is a minor island in a sea of feeling.

Tara and Noor went for runs together. They bought dresses and scarves at the market stalls and shared them. Tashi had started calling them the Noras. 'The Begum of Lucknow and the Maharani of Delhi are now indistinguishable,' he joked. It was spring elsewhere, but here in the mountains, it was still cold. At night, they put one blanket on top of the other and shared them too. Noor made a hot breakfast most days: oatmeal, tofu omelettes, mushrooms on toast. Tara made vegan French toast one day but Noor said it tasted wrong. She liked it the way her mother made it, salty, with onions and 'all the pepper in Lucknow'. She seemed to miss home all the time but wouldn't visit, or even call. She said she loved her parents deeply but found it impossible to live with them, and both things were true. 'Sometimes you have to choose between love and your self,' she told Tara. As was her style, she made her point by citing Bikini Kill: *Sometimes being happy, baby, is what I'm most afraid of.*

'How can I blame my parents when even the great philosophers ultimately failed homosexuals,' she said.

On more than one morning, after breakfast, before they were about to start their studying for the day, Tara thought she would tell Noor in some detail about what had happened in Mysore. But Noor looked at her so warmly, told her so many times that she was 'hot stuff' and 'badass', that she felt something would change between them if she did. She didn't have the right words. All Noor knew, and occasionally teased her about, was that she was heartbroken over her 'silver-haired Sanskritist' and that they were playing some 'super kinky who-will-call-whom-first game'. She knew that the fellowship to Chicago hadn't worked out.

While in Dharamsala, Tara had kept her distance from *Chaurapanchasika* and the erotic verses of Bilhana and Bhartrihari. Jigme had asked her to attempt a translation of Sudraka's *Mricchakatika*, a fifth-century Sanskrit play that featured several Prakrita dialects. It was an important play in the category of prakarana or 'plays of invention', dealing with themes that were atypical for Sanskrit drama of the time. For one, its nayika, the intelligent and resourceful courtesan Vasantasena, has money and power. She is a woman of the world: she knows what to do, and when; whom to trust and whom to avoid. When she falls in love, it is Vasantasena who takes the initiative to meet her lover. In her, Tara was delighted to have found yet another Abhisarika nayika. Unlike other nayikas who express their love in a way that is inseparable from worship—Bhasa's Vasavadatta, Kalidasa's Shakuntala, Bhavabhuti's Sita—Sudraka's Vasantasena chooses her own way. Tara had never encountered her in her syllabus.

It was on one of these days, at the language centre, that Sonam told Tara that her mother had called to say she and Bibek would be arriving the next day. Did she want to use the phone to call her back, asked Sonam. Tara considered the question and then went back to her computer at the library. She could see Noor's head above a machine some rows ahead of her. She messaged her on the intranet.

My mother and Bibek are coming tomorrow, she wrote.

Ah, the princely family friend. Is there a scene there? Noor replied.

My mother's not into scenes.

Okay and you were gifted by the sun god.

My parents had an arranged marriage.

Mine too. So kinky, Noor responded.

Tara replied with five exclamation marks.

...And what about you and Bibek? Noor wrote.

Don't be gross, Noorie.

May I remind you that your smoking Sanskritist is past the half-century mark? Noor wrote.

Tara signed off the intranet. She raised her right hand, pointed her fingers like a gun, towards Noor.

Noor bent her head sideways from the screen and laughed.

THE NEXT afternoon, Tara heard a car pull up in front of her building. It was the cue for her to carry the morning's dirty cups to the sink. She had straightened up the living room, bought momos from Lung Ta and asked for extra Schezwan sauce. Noor had gone back to her own place for a few days to make room. Tara had bought milk from the grocery shop in her lane because she knew her mother would want to make tea as soon as she arrived.

With each flight of stairs that Shashi climbed, her vision

clouded. Bibek walked beside her, asking if she was all right every time she abruptly stopped. By the time they neared the third storey, Shashi was out of breath and her eyes were full. Tara opened the door and stood on the narrow balcony outside, holding on to the ledge. She tried to keep her face expressionless as she watched her mother struggle up the last flight of steps. But when she reached the balcony, Tara threw her arms around her. When she did that, she felt as if she had no bones holding her up any more. Bibek put down his bag and Tara smiled at him from over her mother's shoulder as they walked into the flat. She was supposed to be angry with her mother, and yet their bodies seemed fused. Bibek poured himself a glass of water and stepped out to the balcony again, shutting the door behind him.

Tara held her mother and cried. When they bent down to sit on the mattress on the floor, she didn't let go. Shashi cried for what she knew and what she didn't know. Tara cried because the soft gathers of cloth on her mother's shoulder invited her to.

'This is a nice place,' Shashi said, pulling away to look around at the walls, the arrangement of rugs and pottery. 'You have so much of your father in you.'

Tara dropped her head to her mother's lap. Shashi ran her fingers through her daughter's hair. She asked her about Dharamsala, about the friends she had mentioned: Noor and Tashi, how her thesis was shaping up, the Prakrit lessons, whether she was eating enough rice and wearing a sweater. At that, Tara groaned and sat up.

'Do you have a comb?' said Shashi.

Tara fetched a comb and sat with her back turned to her mother. As Shashi combed Tara's hair, she brought up what was weighing on her mind.

'I know you're cut off from everything here but do you know what's going on? Do you know about Meenakshi?' said Shashi.

'I do! I do because of Noor. You'll meet Noorie in a bit. She's obsessed,' said Tara.

'We are thinking of moving there.'

Tara turned to look at her.

'We?'

'Poornima and me. I'm thinking of setting up a shelter home in Meenakshi. They asked for project proposals and ours has been accepted.'

'Can you do that, Ma?' said Tara.

'Yes, I can,' said Shashi, though suddenly, under the scrutiny of her daughter, she didn't feel so sure. 'I'm also thinking of selling the house. I know Baba had promised you would always have that home. How do you feel about that?'

Tara's face was a picture of curiosity. And suddenly, fear.

'How can you give all of it up? What about my room, my things… Mishti's grave, Baba's garden…' said Tara. 'That house is everything. It's perfect.'

Shashi ran her palms over the handloom bedspread they were sitting on; its rough threads would create telltale textures on your cheek if you fell asleep while reading in the afternoon. But young people didn't fall asleep while reading.

'This flat, Tara, it's right for you,' Shashi said. 'I can see that you've grown here. I've lived in three homes. My father's home, my father-in-law's home, my husband's home. I want to live in one that is my own.

'When your Baba died, I realized I had given no thought to what I want to achieve while I'm alive. Each time I began to think

285

about it, I thought it was too late, but then I spent decades in that feeling.'

'I know that story. You wanted to be Dr Shashi Mallick and then I came in the way,' said Tara.

'You didn't come in the way. You could have been brought up by ayahs. Many children are. Most of your friends were. It was a choice I made,' said Shashi.

Tara frowned. She looked closely at her mother's face, which seemed changed. Perhaps it was the parting of her hair.

'Why a shelter home, Ma?' she said.

'It is something I want to do,' said Shashi.

Bibek came in at that moment, and the two stopped talking like they had been having an illicit conversation.

As they ate the momos, Bibek offered to find a guesthouse close by. But Tara said they would rent bedding from a shop at the market instead. 'I've been without my family for too long,' she said.

WHEN SHE went to sleep with her mother that night, squeezed against each other in the bedroom, Tara turned on to her side and held her knees. She turned her pillow upside down. She kicked the blanket a few times to straighten it. Finally, she turned to her mother, who was lying on her back with her arm folded above her head, her eyes fixed on the ceiling. She was awake as well.

'It wasn't right, Ma, what you people did. Daughters aren't needed for the last rites. But what about what I needed? What about what you needed? You didn't need me?' said Tara.

'It wasn't right, Tara,' said Shashi. 'We made a mistake.'

That her agony of several months could be settled so easily

disconcerted Tara. The moonlight from the open window hit light-coloured objects in the room, making them glow. Tara turned away from her mother again.

Shashi waited for a while, and then asked, 'Will you tell me what happened in Mysore?'

'Do you want tea?' Tara said, sitting up.

'Should I make it?'

'No, I want to make it,' said Tara.

Shashi walked with Tara to the kitchen. It was just past midnight. They moved quietly so as to not wake Bibek, a still figure buried under blankets on the mattress in the living room. Shashi watched her daughter measure out tea and sugar. She watched her wait patiently for the tea to colour the water.

When they went back to the bedroom with their cups, Tara told her what she knew now with the privilege of time that had passed.

'Ma, I'm not who I thought I was,' said Tara.

Shashi studied her daughter's face.

'People spend their whole lives trying to find out who they are. Most never even arrive at the question. One of the philosophers I studied said the main interest in life and work is to become someone that you were not in the beginning,' said Shashi.

'It's not that. I know who I am now. I am a person who is weak. I have no strength of my own, it is all borrowed.'

'You are not weak, Tara, you have never been weak. Perhaps you have only realized that you are not as different from other people as you thought you were?'

Tara told her about how her months in Dharamsala, and the death of her father, had pried open the knots in her chest. She was learning a new language, new utterances were coming to her, but

287

it was still all quite unintelligible. She told her mother what she had not told herself so far.

A man who she was deeply infatuated with had assaulted her in many ways. For reasons she could not understand, she had still developed a relationship with him. She had made herself believe that she was in love with him—a part of her still believed she was. She had trusted him, suffered minor humiliations for weeks. And then he had discarded her just like that. He had callously taken away from her something she had really wanted. Only that final crushing underfoot had made her see their relationship for what it was.

'It was wrong from the beginning, from the very first time,' said Tara. 'I keep asking myself why I didn't see it earlier. Why I tried to explain what was happening between us to myself in so many ways.'

What she knew now was that she might have wanted him, but nothing had happened on her terms. That first time she had gone to his room at the Mysore Palace Hotel, he had ambushed her. It was true that she had not asked him to stop. But he had never asked her if he could start. That was the truth. And later, she did want him. That was the truth, too. She was ashamed of herself. She was ashamed of the perversity of it all. Her body wasn't bruised. Something far inside her was deeply injured. How could something like this happen to someone like her? It happened to other girls, not Tara Mallick.

She felt weak when she thought about the way she had allowed her body to be moved here and there. How she had been unable to move her tongue, string words in her mouth. And worst of all, how she had laughed to absolve him, to absolve herself. The way she had welcomed sleep that night—the end to a rollercoaster ride. How she had rearranged her memory, told herself stories, transformed her rage to passion. How she had only been able to see her own degradation when it was in plain sight for others to see.

She couldn't speak to her mother about all of it. She couldn't tell her that she hadn't been able to stop thinking about why the apsaras in the epics were always victims of curses intended to lower their pride. She didn't need to. Her mother probably knew it all. Because when Tara cried, Shashi cried too.

The next morning, Tara told Bibek, who wore a pained look and kept saying that ideas of hierarchy had to be dismantled in the future we create. When Noor stopped by in the afternoon, Tara told her too. Repeating the story was giving it sharper edges. Tara thought Noor would be angry that she had not told her before. But she put her arm around Tara. She said she understood.

The three women sat beside each other on the mattress in the living room. Bibek sat on the floor facing them, running his hands over a broken stool. Shashi smoothed Tara's hair off her face.

'Have you thought about what you want to do?' said Noor.

'I've been thinking about it the whole time. But the more I think about it, the more knotty it becomes,' said Tara.

'Did you speak to anybody in your hostel or department about it?' said Noor.

'The other students? They never looked at me as someone who deserved their solidarity. That's on me,' said Tara. She was quiet for a moment.

'And if I confided in them, I was afraid I would have to do what they felt was the right thing to do.'

'What do you feel is the right thing to do?' said Shashi.

'What happened between us is not easy to explain, or even

understand. The way he treated me was bad. But the way everybody else treated me was worse. And there's surely no penal code for that.'

'While you think about all of this, could you seek redressal for the selection process for the Chicago fellowship? Tell them you believe it was compromised by a personal equation. That's well within your rights, isn't it?' said Noor.

'The idea of speaking to the dean about this disgusts me,' said Tara. 'But maybe I don't have to. Before I came to Dharamsala, the MSS sevaks had been coaxing me to write an official complaint letter about the selection process. They said they'd handle it. They sent me all these templates.'

The mention of the MSS alarmed Bibek. He looked up from the stool that had occupied his attention so far.

'Tara, the MSS are waging their own war. Don't fight somebody else's battle. They'll abandon you when they're through and you'll be the one left to drown,' he said. 'And even if they bring him down, will that get you what you want? What is it that you want?'

Tashi had joined the assembly by then. He believed social media was the way forward. 'All you have to do is write out exactly what happened,' he said. 'Use the right words, the correct terminology. These things are black and white now. We'll shame the miserable fucking bastard...' he said, before apologizing to Shashi and Bibek for swearing.

Tara said she was still searching for the right words. She had searched her emails and texts for clues but the conversation between the two of them largely consisted of bland logistical messages about when he would be back in the hotel and what time she would arrive. 'Everyone knew we were together. That's not what I need to establish. I feel what I have to say is not very believable. I come across as vindictive.'

'We believe you,' said Noor.

After lunch, once Tashi left for the café, Tara asked her mother if she'd make tea, and followed her to the kitchen. She watched as her mother measured out the tea leaves. She heard Noor and Bibek talking about the co-operative workshop in Kanyakumari. Knowing that they would be occupied for a while, Tara hoisted herself onto the kitchen counter. Shashi gave the pan a gentle shake. The tea leaves danced in the water, leaving brown swirls. Shashi leaned against the refrigerator.

'Ma, what terrifies me is knowing what would have happened if I had been picked for the Chicago fellowship. I would have never examined what had happened earlier. I would have coursed along, happy, blind. That's what took me a long time to understand,' said Tara. 'That's what makes me feel so uneasy. What else have I been blind to?'

Shashi poured out Tara's tea. She took a sip from it before handing her daughter the cup. They walked out to the living room, where Bibek and Noor were still engrossed in conversation. Shashi opened the door for them to step out onto the balcony. The balcony was narrow, just wide enough for a collapsible rack on one side to hang wet clothes. There was just enough room left over for two grown women to lean their elbows on the ledge and talk.

Shashi looked at Tara's face in the setting sun. Her nose was aquiline, like Robi's mother's. Her eyes were like Robi's, which Lata Jethi used to say were shaped like lotus petals. But her daughter was her own person.

'Tara, most times there is no one story, there are two, three, or more. You loved this man and he took advantage of you. One does not have to be false for the other to be true. Sometimes it's hard to see things as they are, so we teach ourselves not to see all of it, we keep some parts in the shadow,' said Shashi.

'The last few months have been hard for you. They have been hard for me too. I've come to understand that a single incident can make us see everything, maybe our whole lives, differently. The new way of seeing needs courage. You cannot blame yourself for what you did not see earlier, the important thing is that you see it now.

'As your mother I want to tell you that very rarely are we given this gift, this new way of seeing. The quality of light that we see things in matters. When the light shifts, we see the world differently.'

With the little sleep that Tara had had, Shashi's words were a balm. She held her mother as they walked back indoors. She went to the bedroom and put her head on her pillow.

She had a dream in which she entered a large house with many well-appointed rooms, all furnished well, all luxurious and sweet smelling, all filled with the sound of her father singing. But when she tried to switch the lights on, room after room remained plunged in darkness. In one of them, when she pressed the switch down, when she was least expecting it, everything became illuminated. She slept in that room. She slept for hours.

When Tara woke up and walked into the living room, Noor asked, 'Have you decided what you'd like to do?'

'First, I want to do something for myself,' said Tara.

*

TARA EMAILED Professor Amitabh Dhar on returning to Delhi. *'We need to have a meeting when you're back on campus. I've spoken to Professor Goyal and Thulasi, they will be in attendance too,'* she wrote.

She had travelled with Ma and Bibek to Benaras to immerse Baba's ashes in the Ganga. And now they were back in the house in Delhi for one last time. They had decided to go all in, to sell the house and move to Meenakshi.

She spoke to Noor every day, who promised to visit her in Meenakshi. Before writing to Amitabh, Tara had had a difficult phone call with Thulasi—she had told her that she was ready to have the conversation Thulasi had wanted to have with her, but that Thulasi would need to listen to her as well. She had written to Professor Goyal to say she would return to IILL next semester, and that she wanted to change the subject of her thesis from nayikas in Sanskrit erotic poetry to nayikas in Sanskrit prakarana, the plays of invention. She told him she had been reading one such play in Dharamsala, that her time away from campus had been fruitful. But there was more reading to do on that front. What texts would he recommend? It was Professor Goyal who had informed her that Amitabh was returning to the campus next semester as well, and he'd offered his advice on the matter when asked.

OVER THE next two months, setting up the shelter home in Meenakshi consumed all of them. They had moved all their furniture and boxes into a basic red laterite structure on the beachfront in Meenakshi, where everything belonged to a land trust. There was work to be done to make it a home. It would be the first stop for many young people moving to Meenakshi, and

Shashi was keen to make it a home, not a hostel or shelter. Beside it was Poornima's home. An independent structure with a storefront.

Trees could not be felled for construction work in Meenakshi and so Shashi's bedroom had the branch of a mango tree going through it. Shashi had the bedrooms painted red, the kitchen yellow. The study and work areas were large and open with hanging overhead tubelights. 'The girls will like their late-night reading,' Shashi told the contractor. She made her redo the shelves to fit wide magazines. 'Shelves are not just shelves, they are how we see ourselves,' she told the amused woman. The shelf in her bedroom had monographs by her beloved philosophers and old issues of *Starglow*. The house was airy. There was so much light.

Shashi wanted family there the day they boiled milk till it overflowed from the pan to bless the house. Tara, Poornima, Bibek, Noor, and Sunita and Surinder were there. Surjo and Laura joined on video call. KC Meenakshi came herself to inaugurate the shelter home. She stayed for a cup of tea. She had come with four others who all called themselves Meenakshi. Meenakshi, the one with eyes shaped like a fish, a name that belonged to rakshasis and goddesses alike.

'Every day I hear about your tea, Shashi tai. Good I tasted it today,' said KC Meenakshi, as she sipped from her cup.

When it was time for her to leave, Shashi and Tara walked her to the gate. As they stood there, watching KC Meenakshi and those who'd come with her cycle away, Shashi ran her fingers over the etching on the stone slab by the gate. It said 'Shashi'—though the shelter itself was pledged to the state of Meenakshi. It was the way KC Meenakshi ran things. You inhabited but didn't own.

Shashi looked at Tara. 'Your father promised you would always have a home. Have you forgiven me for taking that away from you?' she said.

'I have you,' said Tara.

They took a long walk along the beach. They took their time to walk back to the others. They took so long that the sky began to turn pink and purple. The Ladinos who believed that mother and daughter were like nail and flesh must never have seen a night sky like this one, where the moon and the stars rose together.

THE MORNING after, Tara was on the sunbed in front of the house in her white dress, reading. Mornings in Meenakshi were beautiful, fishing boats far at sea, boys mending nets, women chatting in groups, readying their baskets to take to the market. The elaborate dance of life. Poornima was returning with her morning shopping. At her food stall, she offered a hearty morning meal of rice and dal with dried fish and many kinds of pickles, which the fisherwomen ate on their return from sea. There were many such communal kitchens in Meenakshi.

The sun was just where it was every day when her mother called her in for tea—under the skin of the sky, eager to blush.

Tara looked down at the stainless steel bowl beside her on the sunbed. She peeled an orange. She took apart a segment and held it up to the light. It looked like congealed sunshine. She put it in her mouth and let the juices flood her mouth. Then she closed her eyes and swallowed it whole.

She heard her mother's voice calling her from behind. She turned to see her rise from her seat in the balcony. And she saw her glow.

POORNIMA
FULL MOON

*T*HIS IS NOT RAIN. THIS IS GOAT PISS.

Go to my home in the Sunderbans if you want to know what rain is. It rains six months in the year. Everything is always wet. The thatch of our homes, the skins of our goats, the skins of our bodies, the clothes we hang out to dry, they are still wet when we wear them again.

When I think of home, and the swaying sundari trees, I want to think of that afternoon when we fell asleep on the boat. When it floated away and got caught in the roots of the sundari. That's right, it was she who trapped us.

My brothers had just returned with a big catch of magur and we had been waiting hungry for two days, eating only rice and salt. As soon as they came all of us went about chopping chillies and onions, scaling and slicing the fish, rubbing it with turmeric and frying it in oil. We ate so much. We didn't know when such a catch would come again. Afterwards we had hooch, even Ma, and everybody fell asleep where they were. Polu didn't even wash her hands.

When I opened my eyes, I went to the pond to splash water on my face. The shaheb from the city was awake. He was taking photographs wearing a raincoat. His camera also had a raincoat. He turned the camera towards me and my heart stilled. Even when Brojo and I had seen a tigress at night, her green eyes glowing in the dark, I had not known fear. My heart had not stilled then. Once a crocodile had come very close to Polu when we were bathing in the river. Polu's feet had become white and Ma had rubbed them with mustard oil and slapped me for taking her to that part of the river. It must have been fear that made her feet white. But I had never felt it. Maybe this was fear—what else could it be? I could hear my heart when I walked towards the camera and the shaheb. I stopped and he took a photograph. Then he went away again to photograph the sundari and her hungry roots.

My brothers had brought this shaheb back home from one of their fishing trips. They said he was studying to help us but I don't know when he was going to start helping us. He had given my brothers shirts but apart from that for the last week we had only been helping him: feeding him the food we had, taking him here and there on boats, describing when the tiger comes, how we see his marks, how we collect honey and put it in bottles. He was a shaheb from a big college in Kolkata. He said he spoke Bangla but we couldn't understand anything he said. Only Brojo understood a little and he explained it to all of us and also explained what we were saying to him.

One day when the fish was less and my brothers caught a wild boar, the shaheb said he could not eat pig. After that day my brothers didn't talk to him so much. But they couldn't ask him to leave. Here in the Sundarbans, we never ask guests to leave. So he kept staying with us. He said he would go as soon as the flooding stopped. Nobody had boats to spare for him now.

I started going to the pond at the same time in the afternoon. I saw him another day and gestured to him to sit with me on a boat. It is the moment that changed my life but I don't remember it clearly. I remember the first time I ate a crab, I remember the games Polu and I played, I remember peeking into the shed on Brojo's wedding night, but I don't remember this moment. All I remember is that one night, while the others were sleeping, I put my hands on my hips and told him to follow me to the grove. I could hear my heart. I knew what to do because Noki had shown me once and at night we had all seen Brojo and his wife while they lay together just two cots away. The next morning the shaheb was gone, even though there was no boat still. We don't know how he left. My brothers said good riddance. Just because he has started wearing a gamcha around his head doesn't mean he is one of us, they said.

When my belly began to swell I tried to hide it for a while. My mother got afraid and gave me her large clothes to wear. When my brothers came to know they kicked me. On the day, they called the medicine woman who came with her needles and scissors and my son was born. They took him from me and gave him to Didi. I was very sick. For two moons I did not get up or move. Ma would feed me rice water and boiled fish so I would become strong again. They hadn't taken me to the hospital for the baby but they took me now to tie my tubes. Sometimes Didi would come to show him to me, always when my brothers were away. Every night, they locked me in the shed, where it was dark and there was no breeze, while the others slept under the open sky. I was missing it all. Everything important comes to us in the moonlight: dreams, babies, shiuli blooms. I know this. They call me Poornima because I was born when the moon was full.

Now, see, it was not such a big thing. We are not like you city folk. But my brothers were angry because the shaheb turned out to be moslem.

Even though we are Adivasis, my brothers have started to care about these things. And they were angry also because the shaheb was gone so suddenly. If this was anyone from the village we would have just got married and cut a goat for a feast. Nobody would be angry or kicking. They said he was dirty and I was dirty but they loved the child and they played with him and taught him things; he was one more hand to go fishing. I knew they would love him. In seven or eight years they would start teaching him to lay the nets. If it was a girl maybe they would have said it was dirty.

When I became better and started to walk a bit my brothers came and kicked me again, even Brojo, my eldest brother, who was a gentle one. When his wife told him not to, he pushed her to the floor and her coral bangles broke. My father woke up from his drunken sleep and slapped me. That was too much. Nobody had ever slapped me before, except my mother. That night I ate as much as I could before I went to sleep. I took some sarees and Brojo's silver watch, broke the window of the shed, and ran and ran. I would find Babloo da in Kolkata. Anyway the shaheb had said our homes were sinking. I wanted a different life. I wanted the moonlight again.

Acknowledgements

THANK YOU TO MY PARENTS FOR TEACHING ME THE VALUE OF perseverance, and to shine the light on what matters. To Didu, my first champion and last grandparent—I am so fortunate that you saw this book, and its dedication, a week before you left.

I owe a great debt to Hemali Sodhi of A Suitable Agency for believing in this book when it wasn't one. And to David Godwin, who stepped in to take *The Illuminated* out to the world.

I'm privileged to have the faith and expertise of my editor Maggie McKernan, Sophie Whitehead, Kate Appleton, Jessie Price and everyone at Head of Zeus who has played a role in the life of this book. And the team at HarperCollins India—Udayan Mitra, Ananth Padmanabhan, Bonita Vaz-Shimray and Shabnam Srivastava.

I'm thankful to the following writers for their extraordinary generosity or counsel, both direct and indirect: Akhil Sharma, William Dalrymple, Jonathan Franzen, Shanta Gokhale, André Aciman, Manu Joseph, Sarnath Banerjee and Shubhangi Swarup. Janice Pariat, for being there the day it started.

To the late Professor Judith Crist for giving me class honours at her writing workshop at Columbia University. Professor Biswamohan Pradhan from the University of Mumbai's linguistics department for being the best teacher I've had. My colleagues and editors at *Mint* and *Vogue*, you know who you are.

To my first writing cohort The Writers' Game and my most recent writing cohort, fellow writers at the Hawthornden Literary Retreat in September 2019—Mimi, Luis, Mary-Jane, Mackenzie—and the administrator Hamish Robinson, for avoiding talk of the day's progress at dinner.

As this is my first novel, I have the impossible task of acknowledging the writers and thinkers who have shaped me. That list is long but I must name the women whose words appear in these pages: Virginia Woolf, Simone de Beauvoir, Audre Lorde and Romila Thapar. I have benefited greatly from reading Thapar's *Sakuntala: Texts, Readings, Histories* (Women Unlimited, 2010). The Hegel by HyperText project by Andy Blunden was a most useful resource.

The translation of Bilhana's *Chaurapanchasika* I have used is *Black Marigolds* by E. Powys Mathers (B.H. Blackwell, Oxford, 1919). The *Meghaduta* translation is by Henry Aimé Ouvry (Williams and Norgate, London, 1868). The Sanskrit translation in the epigraph is from John Brough's *Poems from the Sanskrit* (Penguin Classics, 1968). Noor's poem is 'Shifting the Sun' by Diana Der Hovanessian from *About Time* (Ashod Press, New York, 1988).

Preparing for a debut publication comes with alternating waves of exhilaration and doubt. I must thank Diya Kar, Siddharth Dhanvant Shanghvi, Lisa Ray and Namita Gokhale for their big-heartedness at various stages. Prayaag Akbar and Avni Doshi for sharing their intelligence. Ambar Sahil Chatterjee for his perceptive editorial comments. Simran Lal and Suraj Yengde for specific insights that enriched both me and this book. Dipankar Sen, without whom the North Kolkata sections would have far less colour.

I'm grateful to my brother Abhishek for being an elder sibling with excellent reading taste. To the friends who broaden my horizon with their love and brilliance—Dharini Bhaskar, Shirin Johari, Natasha Ginwala, Neha Dighe, Arunima Sharma, Farah Khatri.

And to Raja, my first reader, for helping me make room for this book. Without you, *The Illuminated* would never have emerged.

About the Author

ANINDITA GHOSE is a writer and journalist based in Mumbai. She was previously the Editor of the Indian Saturday magazine *Mint Lounge* and the Features Director of *Vogue India*. She completed her MA in Linguistics and Semiotics from the University of Mumbai and has an MA in Arts & Culture Journalism from Columbia University's Graduate School of Journalism in New York. In 2019, she was a Hawthornden Writing Fellow. *The Illuminated* is her first novel.